ST. MARTIN'S

MINOTAUR

MYSTERIES

ALSO BY G. H. EPHRON

Addiction

Obsession

AVAILABLE FROM
ST. MARTIN'S/MINOTAUR PAPERBACKS

AMNESIA

G. H. EPHRON

St. Martin's Paperbacks

AMNESIA

Copyright © 2000 by G. H. Ephron.
Excerpt from *Addiction* copyright © 2001 by G. H. Ephron.

Cover photo © Ansgar/Zefa/Photonica

Library of Congress Catalog Card Number: 00-031730

ISBN: 0-312-98124-4

Printed in the United States of America

St. Martin's Press hardcover edition / September 2000
St. Martin's Paperbacks edition / September 2001

St. Martin's Paperbacks are published by St. Martin's Press, 175 Fifth Avenue, New York, NY 10010.

10 9 8 7 6 5 4 3 2

To Sue, Jerry, Naomi, and Molly

i closed my eyes and breathed, in through the nose, out

Acknowledgments

Special thanks to our agent, Louise Quayle; to Lorraine Bodger for editing and encouragement along the way; for their honest critique and suggestions, Alan Albert, Elenor Denker, Carolyn Ferrucci, Barbara Fournier, Michael Getz, Carolyn Heller, Joseph Kennedy, Patricia Kennedy, Rebecca Mayer, Josh Rosenthal, Donna Tramontozzi, and Lissa Weinstein; and to Delia Ephron for help finding the courage to get started and the backbone to stay with it.

Prologue

His hand rests gently on her thigh, warm through the thin cotton nightgown. His other hand, muscles and veins outlined in the moonlight, rides lightly on top of the steering wheel. She turns her head to study his calm profile. She wonders, why is he wearing combat fatigues? She shrugs and settles into the bucket seat, head back. The stars are bright in the clear, late winter sky, obscured now and then as trees fly past. She feels herself merging with the soft leather of the seat and melting through it.

From the backseat now, she sees the driver shrunken and hunched over the wheel, a glint of silver in one hand. The stars are gone, masked by trees and brush reaching for her, reaching for her car, scratching and scraping along the fenders and roof as the car slows and stops.

The driver turns, face in shadow. "Get out."

She doesn't want to get out.

The door beside her jerks open. The face is his, but not his. Angry. Younger. "Get out of the car."

She emerges into the cold. Her feet are bare. She wants to go home and get her boots and her down jacket.

"Open it," he says, pointing to the trunk.

Slowly the trunk lid swings up. She doesn't want to look but she can't look away. Inside, shadowy darkness. Empty. No, not completely empty. A crumpled pillowcase with an eyelet border. Her pillowcase. Streaked with red.

She looks up. He stands beside her, his hulking torso shrouded in the bloody pillowcase, a belt anchoring his arms to his sides.

Nausea and fear rise in her throat. "Who did this to you?" she cries.

"Come," he tells her. He walks toward a stone tower. As they reach its base, a massive wooden door swings open. Beyond, she sees her living room. She steps through. Shards of glass glitter on the floor. Pieces of the gold frame that once held the mirror lie scattered about. The blue-and-white sponge-printed walls are ruined, splattered and smeared with red.

Far away, she hears a dull thud followed by the rasping grunts of an animal caught in a trap. Again, a thud. Then pathetic whimpering sounds. And once again a thud, followed this time by sickening silence.

Terrified, she runs for the front door but trips over a body huddled on the floor, head covered with a bloody pillowcase, arms straining against their bonds. She tries to ask, "Who did this to you?" but the words stick in her throat.

Now a woman in white beckons to her from the staircase. She follows, longing for the safety of her bedroom. For her fleece bathrobe and fuzzy slippers. For him, warm and strong in bed. The woman is behind her now, the blade of a knife raised and gleaming. She scrabbles up the stairs to escape, stumbling in panic. The staircase turns and doubles back, again and again, soft carpeting giving way to cold, damp stone. The stairwell grows narrower and narrower, and at last she collapses, unable to push her way farther. She peers out through a slit in the wall.

Far below on a grassy hilltop, she sees herself. Her pale nightgown is luminous in the car's headlights Her long hair whips around her head, dark strands lashing at her cheeks. The ground is icy and her eye sockets throb with a dull pain. She kneels. Waits. And then, an explosion.

Calm now, she watches, floating above as her body falls to the ground and the earth around it grows red and warm and then cools and darkens.

From beyond the headlights' glare, a shadowy figure emerges from the darkness. He grows larger and larger, stepping into the light. He looks up toward her perch and she feels sadness.

A light touch on her shoulder. She turns. Beside her on the stairs, the woman is holding flowers. Paper flowers. But the smell is sweet, funereal. The flowers fall from her hands and turn into butterflies that float away down the steep stairwell.

"Who did this?" she cries out, over and over, pleading for an answer.

"Sylvia," the woman says gently.

Strong hands take hold of her shoulders and lift. She struggles against the pull. She wants to return to the slit in the wall. She wants to see, to be sure.

"Wake up, Syl. You're safe now," a woman in starched whiteness croons.

The stone stairway dissolves and in its place, the white and chrome of a hospital room.

"Did you have that dream again?"

Sylvia nods. "I'm afraid."

"I know. I know. Tell me about the dream."

"I keep seeing the same thing, over and over."

"And what do you see?"

"I see a man. He's driving my car. The man has a gun."

"Where are you?"

"In the back. He made me get into the backseat of the car."

"Where's Tony?"

She sobs. "In the trunk. The man made him get into the trunk."

"You say you keep seeing this?"

"Over and over. I don't want to believe."

"Why?"

"Because of who I'm seeing."

"Now do you know who did this to you?"

"Stuart."

The woman in white straightens and nods in the direction of the dark-suited official in the shadow behind her. She sniffs at the flowers on the bedside table with their little white card, its inscription. "Please get well. I miss you so. All my love, Stuart."

1

ANYONE WHO saw me that morning as I sprinted up the hill, hair longish and wet, coat frayed and flapping like the wings of a great bat, would have thought I was a patient. They would have been surprised when I hopped onto the porch, reached into my trousers, pulled out a key, and opened the back door of the Neuropsychiatric Unit.

I was late. That morning I'd pushed myself, slicing and pulling the oars through the quicksilver of the Charles, until there was only the physical pain—pain and peaceful oblivion. My racing shell was a sliver of white carbon fiber, the last gift from my wife, Kate.

The river had been exquisitely beautiful in the crisp fall stillness, free at last of the whining gnats and mosquitoes that torment rowers in the dead of summer. I knew it was getting late but I told myself just five minutes more, five more minutes of blessed mindlessness. Now I was paying. My muscles burned and I hoped no one would notice I wasn't wearing socks. In my rush to shower at the boathouse, get dressed, and get to morning meeting, I'd managed to misplace one of them.

My staff was waiting for me, packed in around a table in the narrow conference room.

"Don't ask." I raised my hand as if to ward off the onslaught and, in the process, to wave away their anxious concern that hung like ozone in the air.

Dr. Kwan Liu watched me with a bemused expression. We've been friends and colleagues since Kwan was chief resident and I was an intern at the Pearce. Now that he was approaching the big 4–0, he'd stopped reminding me that he's two years older and presumably wiser. He never tires of disparaging my psychologist's shingle, junk metal compared to his fourteen-karat M.D. As always, he was impeccably turned out in a dark suit that looked custom made. He finds my clothing an acute source of embarrassment while I find his indifference to the nuance of wine incomprehensible. Also, as always, he was going to be a pain in the ass.

"My dear sir," he intoned, "if we don't ask, then how will we unlock the secrets of the mind?"

I dropped my briefcase on the table. From the defunct hearth of an immense, ornately carved fireplace I hauled over a black Windsor chair whose chipped paint and missing spindles testified to years of abuse. The chair and the fireplace were remnants of bygone grandeur when this building and the others like it that stud the Olmsted-designed landscape of the Pearce Psychiatric Institute were a refuge for the very rich. Bloodied but not bowed before the steamroller of managed care, the place now had the air of an elegant hotel gone to seed.

"I'm late . . . again . . . sorry, everyone. I just lost track of time on the river this morning and now every muscle in my body feels like it's been mangled. . . ." I stopped when I caught Gloria Alspag, the nurse in charge of the ward, playing a phantom violin, her eyes sardonic behind the wire-rimmed glasses. She gave an imitation of Heifetz coaxing an *appassionata* from a Stradivarius. "Oh, give me a break," I said, sighing. It was almost like old times.

I rummaged in my briefcase until I found a pen and my notebook. Then I sat down, pushed my glasses to their proper place on the bridge of my nose, and cleared my throat. Suddenly, everyone was all business. All eyes were on the white board that listed our eighteen patients and gave us an at-a-glance feel for what we were up against. Despite the easygoing good humor of the group, none of us took this job lightly. We were camped out together on the borderlands of psychiatry, at the boundary between brain damage and emotional illness.

We had a new admission. "Jack O'Flanagan," Gloria said. "Seventy years old. The police found him wandering in the Forest Hills train yard. Told them he was an MBTA motorman. Couldn't produce an ID, so they arrested him. Turns out he *was* a motorman. Retired more than ten years ago."

"They brought him to the Carney," Kwan picked up the story. "They checked him out. There's nothing wrong with him, physically. But there are clear psychiatric problems. They called his family. Turns out his wife died suddenly a few weeks ago. His daughter was relieved that we'd Section-Twelved him. He's here for evaluation."

"He doesn't seem a bit bothered about being committed," Gloria commented.

A beeper went off. Like a synchronized swim team, all of us reached for our belts to see whose it was. It was mine. An unfamiliar number blinked on the readout. I let it wait because I knew our meeting wouldn't last long. The room's antiquated heating system had only two settings: hot and stifling. Soon the room would become unbearable and we'd break for walk rounds.

When we did, Kwan and I collided heading for the phone in the corner of the conference room. He pursed his lips and said sympathetically, "You've been having such a difficult day, Doctor. You go first."

"Thank you *so* much, Dr. Liu," I answered with a little bow.

I dialed. After one ring, someone picked up: "Massachusetts

Public Defender's Office." I froze and turned to face the wall. I felt as if I'd been punched in the gut. I could barely hear the voice on the other end of the line. "Massachusetts Public Defender's office . . . Hello? Is anyone there?"

"This is Dr. Peter Zak. Someone there just beeped me." The calm, professional voice turned out to be mine.

"Can you hold a minute?"

I stood there, paralyzed. In my head, I was banging down the receiver, slamming the door on the past. But a moment later, I was still holding when a familiar voice came on the line. "Peter? This is Chip."

I suppose I could have hung up then. But that would have taken action, and at the moment, anything resembling energy had been sucked out of me. I'd last seen Chip at my wife's funeral. I squeezed my eyes shut to blot out the memory, but it wouldn't go away. I could feel my clenched fist connect with Chip's jaw. I could see his shocked, hurt expression as he staggered backwards against the next person in the receiving line. Someone must have helped him up. All I remember is the silence that followed, the kind of big echoey silence you get when a throng of people suddenly turns still. And how after that, everyone acted as if nothing had happened.

"Hey, Chip. Long time no see," I managed to say. But it came out sounding like an accusation. And that wouldn't have been fair. After the funeral he'd called many times, tried to keep in touch. But I was avoiding all contact with humanity. I didn't return anyone's phone calls. I wanted to forget. After a few months, he must have stopped calling.

"I was thinking the same thing," he said. "Too long, in fact. How've you been?"

"Keeping busy, I guess. And you?"

"Same old same old," he said. There was an awkward pause. Once it had been easy to fill silences with empty words. "Actually, I've got a case I wanted to get your opinion about."

Was this how I'd gotten involved in the murder trial of Ralston Bridges? A beep? A phone call? I'd probably been intrigued, eager to help in the defense of an accused man whom I naively stereotyped as a poor schnook who deserved the same expert defense as the Von Bülows of the world. But all that had changed. Murder was no longer something that happened to strangers.

"You know I don't do that kind of work anymore," I told Chip.

"I know. But I was hoping—"

"Not a chance . . ."

"This one's right up your alley."

"That alley's been shut down."

"Just hear me out. All I'm asking for is a consult."

"I just don't think it's a good idea. You've been getting along without me. . . ."

"And it hasn't been easy. Usually we can find someone who can give us what we need. But this case—it needs your expertise. Tell you what, just give me an hour to get your take on this and then I'll leave you alone. An hour, that's all." When I didn't cut him off, he rushed on. "You see, this case turns on the memory of the surviving victim. She was shot in the head. Suffered severe brain trauma. Unresponsive for weeks in a coma. Now, she claims she remembers who did it." I couldn't stop myself. Already I was wondering, how many weeks in a coma? How did the bullet track? It would all depend on the extent of the damage the bullet left in its wake. Head wounds are quirky. Slight deviations, fractions of an inch one way or another can make a huge difference in their aftereffects. "We're defending the woman's ex-husband. He tried to commit suicide after he was arrested. They're holding him at Bridgewater for observation."

"Chip—" I protested. But even to me it sounded feeble.

"You're the expert in this area, Peter. There's no one better." Pause. "What do you say? Just an hour's meeting? It'll be painless, I promise. You won't even have to leave your office. Annie and I come by, we pick your brain. That's it. No muss, no fuss. No strings attached. Believe me, nothing like old times."

We'd been a team, defenders of the downtrodden—Chip Ferguson attorney, Annie Squires chief investigator, and Peter Zak expert witness. Was the funeral the last time I'd seen Annie Squires, too? I couldn't remember. "You and Annie still working together?"

"Annie's my right arm. When she packs it in, I'll have to pack it in, too. Annie's the one who urged me to call you."

"Just a consult."

"An hour. Nothing more. How's five o'clock?"

I mumbled something incoherent.

"Great! And Peter, thanks."

As I hung up the phone, I was already having second thoughts. How could I still be interested when I knew where this could lead? My shirt felt damp and sticky under my jacket. I caught my reflection in the mirror over the fireplace. I barely recognized the person who stared back, tired dark eyes beneath a tumult of black eyebrow hair flecked here and there with white. Lines etched my forehead. I straightened my tie. How long had that spot of grease just below the knot been there? It didn't occur to me to wonder when I'd last looked at myself in the mirror and noticed.

Kwan was watching from the doorway. His nonchalant pose, arms folded in front of him, didn't fool me a bit. "You okay?" he asked. I shrugged. Then he grinned, held his hand alongside his mouth, and stage-whispered, "Forget something?"

"Pray, enlighten me."

"You seem to have neglected to indulge in socks."

I looked down at my naked feet, very preppy, shoved in ox-blood penny loafers. I told him, "You couldn't just pretend not to notice, could you?" To everyone else I said, "How about we start walk rounds with Mr. O'Flanagan?"

I led the way down the hall, with its pink walls, tall windows, and gray industrial carpeting, past the brightly lit dining room where the patients took their meals.

From a doorway came a screechy voice, "Hello there!"

I turned to see a small, gray-haired woman in a blue night-gown and kneesocks, heaped into a large wheelchair. "Cataldo!" she sang out in a shrill soprano, waving an index finger in the air.

"Hello, Mrs. Blum," I called, resisting the impulse to bellow back something equally bizarre like "Geronimo!" We all waved and nodded.

"Who's Cataldo?" Suzanne Waters, our intern, asked. "Her doctor?"

"Not quite, but good guess. Cataldo is the name of an ambulance company," I said.

Gloria elaborated, "For Mrs. Blum, it's like standing on a street corner and yelling, *'Taxi!'* "

A few patients sat in the common area, a big living room with more pink walls, some plastic and metal chairs, and a pair of brown sofas. In a walkout bay surrounded by floor-to-ceiling windows stood a grand piano. An ugly fluorescent light fixture hung from the center of an elaborate plaster ceiling medallion. Jack O'Flanagan, thin and insubstantial, bald except for the puffs of gray down flanking his ears, sat hunched in a chair near the hall, his face a few inches from a dark television.

I walked over and put my hand on his shoulder. He didn't budge. I squatted so our faces were level. "Good morning," I said. He swam over to me through watery eyes. "What are you doing?"

"Doing?" he asked. He looked around and his attention snagged on the television. "Oh, I'm waiting for the damned TV to warm up."

"I'm Dr. Peter Zak," I offered my hand. Reluctantly he looked at the hand, and then shook it. "Do you mind if I sit with you and ask you a few questions?"

"Questions?" He shrugged. "Be my guest."

"What's your name?"

"John Patrick O'Flanagan. Same as my dad's."

I could feel myself relaxing as this familiar routine kicked in.

Work had become my salvation. "Do you know where you are right now?"

"Well, I'm . . . I'm . . ." he stammered, looking around as if seeing the place for the first time, "I'm in the Forest Hills ready room waiting for my train to be called."

"Do you know what day this is?"

"It's Tuesday," he said, sure of himself. Actually, it was Monday. He glanced outside. "April . . ." It wasn't a bad guess. April looks a lot like September in New England.

"And the year?"

"1963."

"And who's the president?"

He raised his eyebrows in surprise. "John Fitzgerald Kennedy, of course. I shouldn't have to tell you that, young man."

I nodded. "Mr. O'Flanagan, have you been having any problems with your memory lately?"

"Problems? None at all. My mind's right as rain," he said, rapping the top of his head with a knuckle.

"Do you mind if I give you a little test?"

"Suit yourself. But I may have to leave if they call me."

"I want you to remember three things. A bat, like a baseball bat. A table, like a dining-room table."

Mr. O'Flanagan nodded and repeated the words, "Bat, table . . ."

"And a bridge, like the Golden Gate Bridge."

". . . bridge."

"That's right. Have you got that? Bat, table, bridge."

He rolled his eyes at Kwan and Gloria and humored me with a response. "Bat, table, bridge."

"Okay. Now, remember those words because I'm going to ask you for them in just a few moments. I wonder if you've ever heard the expression, 'People who live in glass houses shouldn't throw stones'?"

"Sure, I've heard it."

"Can you explain to me what it means?"

"People who live in . . ." He thought for a few moments and started again. "It means . . ." He frowned. Then a lightbulb seemed to go off in his head. He formed a little tent out of his hands and intoned, "Judge not, that ye be not judged." He paused. "Matthew Seven." He winked at me.

"Right you are," I said. "You read the Bible often, Mr. O'Flanagan?"

"Me? Nah. The wife's the one. She's always quoting bits of it. That's one of her favorites."

"And how is your wife?"

"Right as rain," he said.

"Now, can you remember those three words we talked about?"

"What words?" he said.

"Baseball—" I prompted.

Reddening, he sputtered. "What are you talking about?"

"Golden Gate—"

"What kind of ridiculous nonsense? Why are you wasting my time when I have work to do?" He struggled to his feet. He looked around the room, baffled. "My train . . ." he said.

"You're absolutely right. Just a lot of nonsense. You can relax. We'll let you know when it's called."

The old man sank back down into his chair and dismissed me with a backhanded wave. Then he noticed the television, settled back, and stared placidly into it.

I stood and we left the room.

"Alzheimer's?" our intern, Suzanne, asked.

I shook my head. "Mr. O'Flanagan is your typical Korsakoff patient."

"I should have guessed from those spidery hemorrhages in his face. An alcoholic."

"Or what's left of one," I said. "Mr. O'Flanagan remembers how televisions worked forty years ago, when they took a few moments to warm up. But he doesn't remember that he hasn't turned it on. And he doesn't have any idea whether he's been waiting for a few minutes or a few hours."

As we continued down the hall, Gloria looked back and commented, "But he's a pretty contented guy. Nothing in this world worries him."

The mind can go bad in a lot of ways, and Mr. O'Flanagan's wasn't a bad way to go. His world was a benign twilight zone in which each moment that passed disappeared from his memory like a snowflake melting on a hot plate. There had been times when I gladly would have switched places. But I'd thought I was past that—until Chip called.

2

MY BEEPER went off at ten minutes to five. I hoped it was Chip calling to cancel. I blinked at the readout. My mother's number blinked back. I swallowed the panic that I knew was irrational. I ducked into the nurses' station and dialed the phone. I held my breath and counted rings. One . . . two . . . the phone picked up. "Ma?" I said.

There was my mother's reedy voice. "I'm fine," she said, getting that out of the way.

I breathed. "You beeped?"

"Petey, dear—" she started. I cringed. She's the only person in the world who calls me Petey and it's useless to protest. "Listen, about tonight."

"Tonight?" I'd forgotten. My mother had invited me to eat dinner with her. A nice break from the usual tuna on Styrofoam I'd get at the hospital cafeteria.

"You wouldn't mind, would you, if we make it tomorrow instead?"

My mother lives in the other half of the two-family side-by-side that Kate and I bought just after we were married. It's in the heart of one of the more blue-collar Cambridge neighborhoods. My parents moved in after my father got sick more than five years ago. So coming to dinner involves going out my door, standing briefly on our shared porch, and going in my mother's door.

"What, you got a better offer?"

"Actually," she hesitated, "actually, I have a ... date." Her voice cracked over the last word.

"A date?" My mother was sixty-eight years old, and since my father died four years ago, her weekly mah-jongg game and dinner with me had constituted her goings-out.

"And why shouldn't I have a date?"

"With a man?"

"No, dear, with a chimpanzee. Of course with a man."

"Anyone I know?" Here was a game we'd often played, but with the roles reversed.

"Mr. Kuppel," she said, "from the video store."

"Ah," I said. That explained how, as electronically challenged as she usually is, my mother had so quickly mastered the VCR I bought her a few months earlier. Mr. Kuppel was a round, avuncular fellow with a neatly clipped beard and mustache and a completely bald pate. He repaired VCRs and was a connoisseur of vintage films.

"You don't mind, do you, dear?"

Too bad I hadn't remembered earlier. It would have made the perfect excuse to give Chip.

My mother, attuned to every nuance, quickly turned the tables. "So what is it? You forgot? You're not feeling well? You have another engagement?" The last one was delivered with that hopeful, upward inflection at the end.

Multiple choice. I didn't rush to answer. I savored the moment. It felt good to slip back into our familiar roles, the thrust and parry of nagging mother, beleaguered son. Each answer had its downside. I forgot: I didn't care about her. I was sick: I'd need round-the-clock deliveries of chicken soup and ginger ale. I had a date: I'd be hounded for details.

None of the above. But telling her the truth was out of the question. If she knew I was even marginally involved in a homicide case, she'd freak and maybe even cancel her date. I sidestepped. "Actually, it's been so hectic and I've got tons of paperwork to finish up before I call it a day. Tomorrow is better for me, too." I glanced out the window. The sky was overcast, and in the early gloom Chip and Annie were walking up the hill toward the building entrance. I hit the button that sets off my own beeper. "Mom, my beeper just went off."

"You sure everything is all right?" She should be the psychologist, not me.

"Everything is fine, just fine. Gotta run."

"So run! Do what you have to do. Don't forget to turn on the outside light when you come in so I know you're safe." Click.

Safe. Would "safe" ever again be a word I'd use to describe myself?

When I looked out the window again, Annie and Chip had disappeared into the building. There wasn't time to meet them in the lobby so I headed for the stairs. I was in the middle of the second flight when I realized that what I wanted to do was turn around and run the other way. I slowed down, pushing myself to put one foot in front of the other. Was that an echo, or another set of footsteps just after mine? I paused. The stairwell descended into silence. When I finally reached the third floor, I leaned against the door to the hall and breathed evenly, trying to slow down my heart. With the back of my hand, I swiped away the perspiration that glazed my forehead. Then I entered the corridor. I had to walk to the end. My office was just around the bend. The hallway seemed to stretch out before me, the end getting farther away rather than closer with each step, until suddenly I had turned the corner and there they were.

"Peter!" Chip said and thumped me on the back. I tried to return the favor but stopped short after the first halfhearted thump. I backed off. He felt as if he'd forgotten to take the cardboard out of his shirt.

He reddened with embarrassment. "Sorry, I should have warned you. Bulletproof vest. I've been wearing it ever since . . ."

It made him look thicker, chunkier than usual in his dark, three-piece suit. "Not just in honor of a visit with me?"

"I wear it all the time," he admitted.

And does it make you feel safe? I wondered. Nice to know I wasn't the only one who felt as if my world had gone haywire.

"About what happened at the funeral," I said, wanting to get that out in the open. "I'm really sorry. You know I didn't mean anything by it. . . ." The words trailed off.

"I understood. We all did," Chip said, adjusting his tie and looking uncomfortable.

"Hey, Peter," Annie said, coming around from behind Chip, "we've missed you." She gave me a light kiss on the cheek.

Annie and Chip were a mismatched set. He oozed corporate conservatism and she was something else in sunglasses, jeans, boots, and a flannel shirt under a beat-up aviator's jacket, a leather backpack slung over her shoulder. Annie slipped off her shades and smiled the kind of smile that has pity lurking just behind its upturned edges.

I fumbled in my pocket for my keys and unlocked the office doors—there's an inner and an outer door with an air pocket in between for privacy. I followed them inside. I stooped as I walked around behind my desk to sit, avoiding the sloping ceiling punctuated by two little dormer windows.

Chip flipped opened his briefcase. Annie sat back in a chair and scanned the room. Her eyes flickered over the crayon drawing of the brain I'd produced at age eight—my mother framed it as a graduation present. She swallowed as she stared at the photograph of Kate hanging alongside. I'd taken the picture at a gallery in the Leather District where she'd had the first show of her ceramics.

Today, my office seemed dingier than I remembered. Even

the duct tape that held the gray carpet together here and there was frayed. Books seemed to tumble out of overloaded bookcases. The pinkish walls were badly in need of a fresh coat of paint. My *Wines of Provence* poster stood propped against the wall, a crack running through the glass. I couldn't remember how long ago it was that I'd brushed past and knocked it down.

In the past there would have been kidding, gossip to catch up on. Today, Chip cut to the chase. "This case, it's a murder that happened not too far from you. Six months ago. A man was killed and his girlfriend was shot and left for dead in Mount Auburn Cemetery. Maybe you read about it?"

"I did, actually," I admitted. I can't help myself. I read about every murder I can lay my hands on and this one stuck with me because the woman survived and because it happened so close to my home. She'd been found near the cemetery's seventy-foot Victorian stone tower. I used to climb that tower every spring to prepare for the crowded and raucous rowing race that Kwan and I dubbed the "Toe of the Charles," to distinguish it from its pedigreed namesake, the Head of the Charles. From the top, I could see most of the river's 2.5-mile course. We used to race the Toe, decked out in tuxes and top hats, arguing until the very last minute about who got to stroke.

"Annie, why don't you give Peter the details?" Chip said.

"Right," Annie began, her serious gray eyes trained on me. I leaned back, covered my mouth with my hand, and braced myself. "At dawn on March 9 of this year, a birder walking through the cemetery finds a woman's body. He thinks she's dead, runs out, calls 911, and when they get there, it turns out she isn't dead at all. This forty-year-old woman, Sylvia Jackson, an automobile insurance appraiser, has been shot in the head."

Annie waited a moment. I was processing what she said but I wasn't feeling squat. Good thing I'd been trained all those years to listen to the horror stories patients tell without getting emotionally sucked in. I nodded for her to continue.

"They race her to the hospital, and meanwhile, the police go to her house, which is about half a mile away. It's a mess." Annie paused again and pressed her lips together. I closed my eyes. She continued, "They found blood everywhere—inside, outside. Broken glass. The works. There, in the kitchen, they find the body of a man. He's not so lucky. Also apparently shot, though there are other injuries as well. Turns out the murder victim, Tony Ruggiero, is the woman's boyfriend."

Catching a breath, Annie hurried on. "Sylvia Jackson remains in a coma for weeks. When she comes out of it, she can't walk, has trouble talking, and doesn't remember a thing about the murder. They question her other boyfriends—this woman has lots of them. They question the ex-husband, Stuart Jackson. She was at his house the day before. Brought him an envelope full of paper butterflies she made for his birthday." I opened my eyes. I must have looked surprised because Annie explained, "Sylvia and Stuart Jackson were divorced, legally. But they were not your typical divorced couple. They continued to have what you might call a *close* relationship.

"None of the forensic evidence links any of the boyfriends or the ex to the murder. But the boyfriends have alibis. Jackson doesn't. Says he was home alone that night, sleeping off the flu. They search his apartment and come up empty."

Chip picked up the thread. "Then, a few months later, she's in the hospital and suddenly it comes back to her. 'Now I remember,' she tells the police. 'Stuart did it.' Based on her statement, they search Stuart Jackson's apartment . . . again. And lo and behold, this time they find a hat just like the one Sylvia Jackson claims her ex-husband wore when he shot her."

I couldn't keep myself from asking, "A hat?"

"Made of camouflage fatigue material," Annie explained. "Stuart claims he never saw it before."

"Bloodstained?" I was on a roll.

Annie shook her head. "Clean. It turns out some of the hairs found in the hat belong to Stuart. But oddly enough, some of the hairs belong to the murder victim. A blip that no one has yet been able to explain."

"That's when we get involved," Chip said. "Based on the evidence of the cap and Sylvia Jackson's memory, they lock up Stuart Jackson. He insists he's innocent. They still don't have the gun. Then, two days after his arrest, he tries to commit suicide. Nearly succeeds."

"So they move him to Bridgewater for evaluation?" I asked.

"Right."

I took off my glasses and rubbed the bridge of my nose. "So what you're telling me is that the only evidence they have is a hat found in the defendant's closet months after the murder, and the memory of a woman who was shot in the head? Nothing from the scene of the crime?"

"No bloody glove. But we've got a prosecutor who thinks he's got an airtight case."

"Who?" I asked.

"Monty Sherman." I didn't know the name. "He's the star D.A. and he's about to run for attorney general. And with this case, he'll be able to run his campaign from the front page of the paper. It's got all the makings of a showcase trial—distressed damsel, jealous husband who thought he could get away with murder. Enough clichés to give the press a field day. A win here and . . ." Chip stopped mid-thought. He licked his lips and looked away. He'd slipped so easily into the old patter in which murder trials are a game.

If I'd been my old self, I never would have asked the question I now asked. "You think he did it?" I looked back and forth from Annie to Chip. Even a consult was more than I was willing to give a murderer.

Chip looked at Annie. She leaned across the desk toward me. "I've talked to him at least a half dozen times. If he's a murderer, then I'm the Easter Bunny."

What was it she'd said two years ago about Ralston Bridges?

"He's a dangerous wacko." It summed him up nicely. If only I'd been paying attention.

"I'm telling you, Stuart Jackson is not a killer," she continued. "He's at the hospital every day while she's in a coma. She wakes up and the cops start to question her. They tell him he can't visit her anymore. He hangs around the lobby like a lost puppy. She accuses him of murder, they arrest him, and he tries to kill himself."

"Could be out of guilt and desperation. Prison's a depressing place."

"Maybe, but I don't think so."

Sending Stuart Jackson to Bridgewater would be Sherman's way of making sure he got well fast. After a week with the crazies, going back to county would seem like a day at the beach.

"And she was in a coma for how long?" I asked.

"More than six weeks."

I whistled. It's unusual for someone who's unconscious for that long to recover memories of events immediately preceding their injury. "They did an MRI?" I asked. Without being aware of it, I'd crossed the threshold. I was well on my way to being hooked.

"Several. I haven't had anyone analyze them yet," Chip said.

"He's competent to stand trial?" I asked. Chip shrugged his shoulders. I held up my hands. "Don't look at me . . ."

I hadn't been to Bridgewater since—well, since before. I couldn't have imagined myself even contemplating going back into a prison. And yet, that's what I found myself doing. I was imagining myself driving down there, going inside, talking to Stuart Jackson in a little examination room—me on one side of the table, him on the other, one of their panic button beepers attached to my belt. What if Stuart Jackson did kill his wife? What if he was just a very clever actor, playing a part? Ralston Bridges had been cunning enough to fool a jury. But I'd known. So had Annie.

Chip pulled a manila folder from his briefcase and took out

a pen. He started to jot a note. Annie rummaged in her pack for her daybook, opened it, and began flipping the pages. They were smart. They were waiting me out while the forces at war in my head took over. Suppose Stuart Jackson was an innocent man accused of killing his wife. Driven to attempt suicide. Left to rot in a hellhole worse than prison. It easily could have been me.

"So you're going to have someone evaluate him?" I asked.

"We've been trying to find the right person," Chip said, massaging his chin between thumb and forefinger, "someone who's got the expertise. Someone who'll understand what this guy is going through. Someone he'll trust."

I sighed. "I suppose I could . . ." Just one meeting, I told myself.

"I know, I know," Chip said. "If only things weren't the way they are. You'd be perfect."

"No, I mean it. I could see him." If a look of triumph flashed between Annie and Chip, I missed it. All I saw was Chip's dumbfounded look, his mouth hanging open. I swallowed it. "Just to give you a reading."

"You're sure about this?" he said, sounding genuinely astonished.

I nodded and pushed the phone toward him. A minute later, the wheels had been set in motion. I was to see Stuart Jackson the next morning.

Chip took a fat envelope from his briefcase and laid it on the desk. "Arrest report. Police interviews. You'll need to review them before you see the defendant."

I stared at the packet as if it were some kind of poisonous viper. You sneaky bastard, I thought. Just a consult, right? So why come armed with these records if you didn't think I'd be doing a competency evaluation?

Chip said apologetically, "We were hoping you'd do it." Then he looked at his watch. He wasn't going to give me time to back out. He closed his briefcase, snapped the latch shut, stood up, and shot out his hand. It was automatic. I wanted to get up and, just as automatically, shoot my hand out. But as the reality of what I'd committed to hit home, I couldn't find the strength to stand. His arm sagged. "We need you, Peter. Stuart Jackson needs you. You'll see, this is the right thing to do."

I let them see themselves out. I turned out the lights and sat in the shadowy office, staring out the window, still not believing that I'd agreed to evaluate another murderer. Hadn't I had enough excitement and fame for one lifetime? I opened the bottom drawer of my desk and pulled out the bottle of Jameson's. It was empty. I uncorked it and sniffed.

After an hour, I locked up and started home. I knew there wasn't much in the fridge. And I couldn't face the five or six hours alone in my house that it would take for me to feel exhausted enough to fall asleep. I found myself taking a detour to the Stavros Diner. Kate and I used to eat there at least once a week.

Jimmy had been running the Stavros since I'd started dropping by at daybreak ten years ago. Back then, I was another snot-nosed Pearce intern looking for a quick fix of salt and grease after night duty. Jimmy was working the grill when he saw me come in. He wiped his hands on the big white dish towel he had wrapped around his belly and nodded. I considered it an exquisite favor, his acting as if my arrival was no big deal.

I took a seat at the counter. Suddenly, I was ravenous. "Got any moussaka?" I asked.

He shook his head mournfully. "All out."

"All out?" I glanced around, noticing for the first time that the place was packed. "What's good, then?"

"How about some pastitsio?" he asked, putting a dish of his world-class olives under my nose. I nodded and put an olive in my mouth. It may as well have been sawdust for all I could taste.

"Pastitsio, then. And some stuffed grape leaves. A salad. And a Sam Adams."

Three hours later, I was still there. Jimmy had long since locked up and flipped the sign on the door. I was on my third beer. Just like old times, he was complaining about the twenty hours a day he worked his butt off for a brother-in-law who barely showed up to turn on the lights.

He turned his back to me to scrape the grill. "So, it's good you're here," he said.

I shrugged and swallowed the last of my beer.

"Really," he said, his back to me still. "You're alone. You're here. Not such an easy thing to do. It's old habits that are the hardest to get back to."

I mumbled something into my empty glass and got up to go home. Going home was the habit that was the hardest of all to get back to.

3

I'D SET my alarm for seven-thirty the next morning but woke up, as usual, long before six, finding myself, also as usual, sleeping on the left side of the bed leaving the right side looking untouched. I made a pot of coffee and poured myself a huge mug, intending to take it out to the garage where I'd been bringing my 1967 BMW back to life. For more than a year, the car had been my silent companion, the friend who got me out of the house, out of myself. Slowly it was turning into a swan. Under the hood it looked great. The trunk, the rear bumpers and fenders were waxed and pristine. I was just getting to the front fenders, which were dented from multiple encounters with hard objects. Formerly owned, no doubt, by a typical Boston driver.

I stopped halfway to the garage. Something wasn't right. I turned and stared at the house. The porch light was on, just the way I'd left it when I'd come home. My mother should have turned it off when she got in. She never forgets to turn out a light. It's part of her religion. I bounded up the steps and rang her bell. When I didn't hear her footsteps inside, I started banging on the front door. "Hey, Ma!" I called. "You in there?" I tried to ignore the strident note of panic in my voice. I was getting my keys out of my jeans pocket when the door jerked open.

My mother looked out, bleary-eyed, wisps of white hair escaping from the gauzy pink scarf she had tied around her head. She clutched the top of her pink bathrobe, the tendons standing out on the back of her hand. I stared down at her furry pink slippers, back up into her anxiety-filled eyes. "What is it? What's wrong?" she asked.

"You forgot to turn out the light," I accused her.

Relief flooded her face. She came out on the porch and stared at the light in disbelief. "My goodness, so I did." She looked at me. "Oh . . ." She reached up and put her cool hand on my cheek. "I'm so sorry, I didn't mean to worry you."

I closed my eyes, exhausted. Life had turned into a walk along a narrow precipice. It's so tiring, having to pay attention every instant so the people you love don't fall into the abyss. I knew I was being irrational. It had been understandable, predictable even. After all, last night was the first time in years that my mother had gotten home later than me and needed to be the one to turn off the porch light.

"So, how was your date?" I asked. She gave me a blank look. "Remember? Mr. Kuppel?"

"Oh, yes, Mr. Kuppel," she said and actually blushed. "We went to dinner, took in a movie."

"How was dinner?"

"Eh," she dismissed it.

"That memorable, huh? How about the movie?"

"Feh!" She screwed up her face as if she'd just taken a whiff of sour milk. "What language! And so much violence."

"And what about Mr. Kuppel? Was he eh or feh?"

She thought about that before she answered. Then she lowered her eyes and said, "Actually, he was good company." She smiled sheepishly. "I quite enjoyed myself." She looked as surprised as I felt. How could she be ready to move on when I wasn't ready yet myself?

I turned down my mother's offer of French toast and spent an hour working on the car. I deliberately left myself with barely enough time to shower and dress. If I was moving fast, I wouldn't think about where I was going. I decided to tempt fate and drive the BMW to Bridgewater. It was the longest I'd dared drive the car but I was feeling reckless. Maybe it wouldn't make it. Better yet, maybe it wouldn't start. But when I turned the key, the engine caught without a murmur, without a complaint.

Bridgewater State Hospital is about forty-five minutes south of Boston. To get there, I took the Pike inbound, poking along in traffic, wondering if I was going to overheat. The temperature gauge was dead so I turned on the heater for extra insurance and opened the windows so I wouldn't pass out. When I got on 93 South and headed away from the city with a trickle of other vehicles, I opened it up. At 60 miles an hour, it felt like a 2,000-pound stallion, cantering along at a comfortable pace.

I got off the highway, passed through the picture-perfect New England town of Bridgewater (complete with town green and steepled church, McDonald's, Wendy's, and Burger King), continued through housing developments, then corn fields. I turned left on a narrow wooded lane. About a mile farther on, the woods abruptly ended, giving way to a vast wasteland punctuated by five bleak cement warehouses, surrounded by metal fencing topped with razor wire.

I followed the HOSPITAL VISITORS sign and parked.

Then, I opened the car door and sat there, listening to my heart pound. This was where I'd met with Ralston Bridges. Nothing had changed. Chain-link fencing, expanses of graffiti-free concrete, not a tree in sight, utter silence — and that feeling that someone, somewhere is watching you.

Annie's words came back to me. "If he's a murderer, then I'm the Easter Bunny."

I closed my eyes and breathed, in through the nose, out through the mouth, concentrating on a point just between my eyes through which I imagined ribbons of air flowing. I counted backwards from fifty. I focused on releasing the tension from my neck, from my forehead, from around my mouth. I tried to find a completely peaceful, stress-free zone between my shoulder blades. When I got to zero, I took a deep breath and blew out hard. "Find automatic pilot," I ordered as I opened my eyes, grabbed my briefcase, got out of the car, and strode toward the entrance.

I pressed the button on the little box hanging alongside the prison hospital gate. "Dr. Peter Zak, here to see Stuart Jackson," I said and waved my driver's license and mentioned the official letter Chip's office should have faxed over. The little wall-mounted video camera swiveled toward me. A buzzer sounded and the gate silently slid aside. I stepped inside a wire cage and the gate closed behind me. I waited until a second gate opened. Once I was through and it had closed, a steel door just beyond clicked and an armed guard pulled it open from the other side. He checked my letter, pocketed my driver's license.

"You okay?" he asked.

It wasn't what I expected him to say and I didn't have an answer ready.

"We thought you might be sick, you sat there so long. One of the guards was about on his way over to check you out."

I glanced around the room and noticed two surveillance cameras tucked discreetly alongside fluorescent ceiling lights. "Just getting myself organized," I said.

"You're here to evaluate Stuart Jackson." He examined the paper attached to his clipboard and frowned, grunted, took a pen from behind his ear and delivered a big checkmark to the page. Then he steered me over to a metal detector.

This particular metal detector was a distinguished adversary that had once held me at bay for thirty minutes. It made the one at the entrance to the Cambridge courthouse seem like a wuss. While the guard checked through my briefcase for incendiary test materials, I shed my wallet, keys, change, jacket, belt, watch, and wedding ring. Finally, I took off my shoes and padded through in my stocking feet. I was rewarded by silence.

When I'd reassembled myself, the guard gave me a visitor's badge and an emergency beeper. I followed him to an examining room—a ten-foot cubicle painted brilliant yellow, barren inside except for a wooden table, two steel folding chairs, and an orange radiator.

He left me there. Alone, I paced the perimeter of the room and then pressed myself into a corner and stared at the small table, its top scratched with obscene graffiti. I'd evaluated Ralston Bridges over a table just like it. He'd been accused of stalking and killing a woman he'd met in a bar. She'd rebuffed him. According to the bartender, she'd walked away with a sniff and the words "What are you, some kind of a nut?" It was the one thing Bridges couldn't stand.

He was furious that I'd been sent to evaluate his competency to stand trial. He explained that he didn't need me to tell the court he wasn't competent because he was going to get off. "Look at me," he said, "who's going to believe this is the face of a fuckin' killer?" He had a point. He was Boy Scout cleancut and blond, handsome in a soft kind of way.

Wasn't it a shame, he said, about that woman he was accused of killing? Did I know that she had a five-year-old daughter, now left without a mother? It made him so sad to think about it. He had a little girl himself. He'd been there when she was born. It was the most incredible experience of his life. As he said this, as if on command, a single tear appeared at the corner of a dead, emotionless eye.

He was just as Annie described him—a dangerous wacko. But not the kind of wacko who gets declared mentally incompetent to stand trial. Intelligent, charming, hyperattuned to other people's expectations, he could morph, chameleonlike, to fit your expectations. He was a true psychopath.

Still, he might have had a shot at an insanity defense. When I suggested it, he bellowed, "I'M NOT CRAZY!" slamming each word down like a fist and coldly watching my reaction, as if his eyes were detached from his body.

"Do you understand what not guilty by reason of insanity means?" I'd asked, trying to engage him.

But he wouldn't engage. Instead, he shot back, "I keep a list, you know. A list of all the people who've ever called me that." I asked him where he kept this list and he tapped his forehead three times with an index finger. "I take care of them. Maybe not right away. But sooner or later, I take care of them. So you don't want to call me that." He smiled a nasty smile. By the end of my session with Ralston Bridges, he had added my name to his little list.

Bridges wouldn't allow Chip to call me to testify. And it turned out he was right—he didn't need me to tell the jury that he was insane, a psychopath with no capacity for feeling sympathy for his victims or their families, only a drive to satisfy his own cravings. He didn't need an insanity defense because the jury found him not guilty. Bridges, with his supreme self-confidence, his smug certainty that he could get away with murder, went free.

I stared up at the little window at ceiling level that let in a shaft of sunlight. This was the first time I'd allowed myself to remember Ralston Bridges, the interview, the calm empty watchfulness, the solitary tear that was more frightening than any wild-eyed rage. My memories of that interview, up to then, had come as involuntary warped nightmares in which I press and press the panic button, pound on the door, and watch myself through a glass panel making a cup of tea in my own kitchen.

I was startled when Stuart Jackson rushed into the cubicle like a burst of static. I peeled myself off the wall. "Mr. Jackson?" I said. "Dr. Peter Zak. I'm a psychologist working with your attorney. I'm here to interview you and assess your competency to stand trial."

He shook my extended hand and nailed me with intense, dark eyes. He was a wiry little man whose nondescript face was punctuated by a toothbrush mustache. "Are you here to screw me, too?" he asked, shifting from foot to foot, a scrawny bantam cock.

I sat down and waited. He backed into the empty chair and sat.

"What do you mean, screw you?" I asked.

"Please, Doctor. Don't patronize me," he said, clipping his words. His right knee jiggled. "I'm the only one without an alibi. Ergo, bingo. Prime suspect."

"Who do *you* think did it?"

Stuart Jackson looked down at his shoes, running sneakers without laces. One knee still jiggled up and down. "It could have been any one of them. Sylvia's like a cat in heat when it comes to attracting men. They cluster around her like bees to honey." He looked up at me. "Flies to puke."

He waited for a reaction. I blinked. "Tell me about your relationship."

"It's too corny."

"Tell me anyway."

"We were high school sweethearts." Jackson snorted a laugh. "We really were. I'd have done anything for her. Did anything for her. Oh, shit." Jackson stared up at the single lightbulb hanging from the ceiling. Then he looked at me hard, his eyes rimmed with red. "I could easily have killed any of them. But I never, ever would have laid a finger on my wife."

"So why did she accuse you?"

"Christ Almighty. Ask her."

"She's not here. You are."

Jackson grimaced and shook his head. "I guess I've always been there when she needed someone to fix her up. Right now, she needs an answer to the sixty-four-thousand-dollar question and, as usual, I'm it."

"But you're innocent?"

Jackson blinked at me. "You're a smart guy. Suppose your ex-wife is killed at home. You'd be the most likely suspect, wouldn't you? Your fingerprints on the fireplace poker, the kitchen knives. All the killer has to do is be careful and all the evidence points to you." His logic took my breath away. I wondered if he knew. But he wasn't looking for my reaction. He was wrapped in his own tale of woe. "And you know as well as I do she can't remember zilch with a traumatic fronto-temporal injury to the brain."

That was a mouthful for a layman. "You sound like an expert."

"I read up on it. Someone needed to keep an eye on her doctors. Keep them honest. So that was me. Old Faithful. There, like I always am whenever she needs to be burped."

"You knew the victim?"

"That asshole? So full of himself. To tell you the truth, I'm grateful to whoever killed him. Saved me the trouble."

"What made him an asshole?"

Jackson fixed me with his eyes for a moment and then looked away. He shrugged. "With him, it wasn't just sex. Said he was going to marry her. Kept putting it off. Said he was in the middle of some big business deal that was going to make a mint. As soon as his ship came in, they'd tie the knot. She swallowed it. Never did know what was good for her when it came to men."

I refrained from commenting on the irony of this. "How did that make you feel?"

"How do you think it made me feel, Doctor?" Jackson asked. "I wanted to take a fireplace poker and beat the shit out of him."

"And did you?"

"What do you think?"

This guy was wearing a hole in my patience. "Mr. Jackson, I'm not here to play games with you. I'm here to assess whether you're competent to stand trial. Are you feeling depressed right now?"

"Wouldn't you be?" He leaned across the table at me. "I'm depressed. I'm angry. And being in this hellhole sucks — it's worse than county."

"You were in county when you tried to kill yourself?"

He nodded and sank back into himself.

"Are you feeling suicidal now?"

"What's the right answer?"

"There is no right answer."

"Just help me understand this, Doc: You find me unfit for trial, they let me rot in here until I lose my mind completely. You find me competent, I get a lifelong vacation behind bars. Not much of a choice, is it?"

"Are those the only options?"

"You think a jury is going to find me innocent after sweet Syl points her pretty finger? I might as well commit suicide."

I contemplated Stuart Jackson. A smart man. A desperate man. Surely capable of passionate feelings, of violent anger. I admired his bravado in the face of a bleak future. I wondered, would a man this smart leave a piece of incriminating clothing as distinctive as a camouflage fatigue hat hanging around in a closet in his apartment? Maybe. If he were convinced that his victim couldn't remember.

"Mr. Jackson, has it occurred to you that if you succeed in taking your own life, everyone will assume that your ex-wife's attacker has given himself the death penalty? Case closed, end of investigation."

For the first time since the interview started, his knee stopped jiggling.

4

I LEFT Bridgewater and was halfway home, turning the interview with Stuart Jackson over and over in my head, when I realized I had the car pushed up to 85 and I was clenching and unclenching my jaw. I slowed, checked the rearview mirror, and thanked the patron saint of scofflaws that I hadn't been clocked. I didn't need another ticket.

Stuart Jackson hadn't been what I'd expected. It pained me to admit it, but I'd expected him to be me, accused of murder, waiting for me to save myself. Big surprise—Stuart Jackson was a whole other person with his own complicated set of issues. A mess emotionally, depressed. But after what had happened, who wouldn't be?

Why was Chip wasting my time talking to him? Clearly he was competent to stand trial. One, he had all his marbles. And two, he wasn't so guilt-ridden, confused, and depressed that he'd be out there helping the D.A. tie a noose around his own neck. Obviously the crux of the case, the proof of innocence or guilt, was in Sylvia Jackson's head. Could she remember what she claimed she did—that was the key.

That afternoon, I talked to Chip on the phone. He didn't

sound at all surprised when I told him Stuart Jackson was competent to stand trial. "And he's become quite an expert on his wife's condition," I told him. "He's right about one thing."

"What's that?"

"If Sylvia Jackson did suffer a traumatic fronto-temporal injury to the brain from the gunshot, then she shouldn't be remembering who shot her."

"Hmm," Chip said. "Very interesting."

I didn't smell a rat. I barreled on. "That's where you should be concentrating your efforts."

"On Sylvia Jackson?"

"On Sylvia Jackson."

"Assailing the credibility of the surviving victim? Very unorthodox, Peter. Could easily backfire."

He knows I find an argument irresistible. "Chip, you say there's no direct evidence."

"Right."

"No witnesses."

"None."

"So everything hangs on her testimony. Her memory."

"And you think we can establish reasonable doubt?"

"I think you've got a shot at it. Unless you have some other brilliant strategy up your sleeve."

"What do you need?"

"What do you mean, what do I need? I gave you your hour. I even evaluated your client. I'm finished."

"Tell me the truth. Do you really think he's guilty?"

"Well, I—" I stopped myself. I was trying not to get sucked in but I was already up to my knees in quicksand. I had to admit, Stuart Jackson didn't feel like a guilty man. He felt like a poor schnook.

"He's an innocent man who stands accused by the woman he loves." Chip was pulling out all the stops. "It's a double tragedy."

"She'll make a helluva witness," I commented.

"You're right about that. And you'd better believe, the prosecution's case depends on it because she's all they've got."

"Get the judge to let you examine her," I said before I could stop myself.

Chip choked and sputtered. "What judge is going to let us do that?"

The guy could have qualified for an Academy Award. If we'd been face-to-face, I'd have been up and pounding the table. "It's the only way."

"Can't we just get someone to give expert testimony on traumatic brain injury and memory, evaluate the medical reports and talk about how her injuries are so grave that she couldn't remember. . . . ?"

"Yeah, right," I scoffed. "Exciting stuff, memory theory. Guaranteed to anesthetize the jury. If you want a battle of the experts, then by all means get yourself a memory theorist. And don't blame me when you're disappointed because memory theory is full of qualifiers, maybes and buts standing in the way of the certainty you're looking for.

"But get an expert on brain trauma and memory in there to talk to her. Test her. See what's going on with her memory *now*, after the injury. Then you might uncover something that could save Stuart Jackson's skin."

"You know, there's no precedent for it."

"Then here's your chance. Create one." I was breathing hard. Exhilarated. Like I'd just rowed across the finish line first.

There was a pause. "I know of only one expert on brain trauma and memory who's good enough to walk a jury through test results and theory without making Sylvia Jackson into a martyr. I need you, Peter."

This was where Chip had been headed all along. The trap was sprung—second time. I'd make an exceptionally stupid maze rat.

"I'm not interested," I said, but by now, my heart wasn't in it. Chip didn't say anything. "Really, I'm not interested," I insisted, as if repetition could make a thing true.

"Peter, tomorrow I'm going to petition the judge to let us evaluate Sylvia Jackson. If I get him to agree, then will you do it?"

I swallowed. "We'll see."

"I'll take that as a maybe. I'll get back to you as soon as we have an answer."

5

I WAS at the nurses' station a couple of days later, getting ready for morning rounds when Kwan stopped to pour himself coffee. "You signing autographs?" he asked.

"Sure. Where do you want one?" I took a pen out of my pocket, uncapped it, and got ready to write on the sleeve of his Italian jacket.

He opened a newspaper to a small article tucked well into the first section. "Jackson Defense to Call on Memory Expert."

I took the paper from him and sat down heavily. "Just what I need," I muttered. Fortunately, the piece was short. Two inches of newsprint announced my being hired by the defense. By a small miracle, there was not one word in it about my wife's murder.

Until that moment, I'd been swept along in the good feeling of working again with Chip and Annie, distracted and energized by the intellectual challenge. Seeing it there in black and white made me queasy.

Chip hadn't actually come back to me and said, "So, what did you mean by 'maybe'? Is it a yes or a no?" Instead, like a good advocate, when the judge agreed to an evaluation of Sylvia

Jackson, Chip just kept moving forward as if I'd said I'd do it. And I hadn't contradicted him. In fact, I'd been grateful that he didn't put me on the spot—I might not have been able to wrap my mouth around an outright yes. Sending out a press release was his way of sealing the deal.

Surely I hadn't been naive enough to think I'd get through the investigation, the high-profile murder trial without finding my name in the press. Avoidance. Denial. Perfectly good coping mechanisms—perfect temporarily. Now I'd crashed head-on into reality. Time to face the consequences. If Kwan knew, so would anyone who read the *Boston Globe*. It was just a matter of time before my mother read it or one of her friends called her with the news. Better she heard it from me first.

I handed the paper back to Kwan. "Do me a favor, please don't post this one." A few years ago, they did a feature article on me in the Living section. He'd framed a copy and hung it in the conference room over a sign that said: "Our Fearless Leader."

"Peter, you're sure this is a smart thing? How'd they talk you into it?"

"Actually, they let me talk myself into it."

Kwan gave me a knowing look. "Smart. That and a little flattery—does it every time."

"Good morning, I suppose." It was Gloria. She yawned and sank heavily into the desk chair. "Could one of you take pity on me and pour me some coffee?"

Kwan folded the paper and tucked it under his arm. "Have trouble sleeping?" he asked.

"I slept like a stone, once I finally got home. I had to work a double." I poured Gloria a mug of coffee and handed it to her. She cupped her hands around it, closed her eyes, inhaled, and took a sip. "Ah, that's better." She looked at Kwan. "Did you tell him about last night's excitement?"

"I was getting to it," Kwan said.

Gloria frowned and looked from Kwan to me and back again.

Normally, we'd have discussed anything that went bump in the night first thing the next morning.

"Go ahead," Kwan suggested, "why don't you tell him."

Gloria started. "Kootz got into it with O'Flanagan and—"

Kwan jumped in, "and belted him upside the head, as they say."

"I thought you were going to let me tell this?" Gloria complained.

Kwan put up his hands in surrender and the newspaper fell to the floor. Gloria and I collided reaching for it but she got there first. She continued, holding the newspaper and waving it as she talked. "I didn't get in there until the fireworks were over. I think O'Flanagan was just in the wrong place at the wrong time. I know what that's like. . . ." She stopped. "What are you staring at?" She looked at the folded newspaper still in her hand, then back up at me, her head cocked to one side. "I may be tired but I'm not dead. Something's up." She opened the newspaper. "What is it?"

I pointed. She read the article. Then she took off her glasses and frowned. "Peter, you sure you're ready for this?"

I shrugged. I didn't know any such thing. "I got snookered. One minute I'm agreeing to an hour's consult and then, before I know it, I'm evaluating the surviving eyewitness."

Her look hardened. "Peter, if you get snookered, it's because you want to get snookered."

Gloria was right. I hadn't been snookered. I'd taken the bait, nibbled on it, liked the taste, then chewed and swallowed. Now I had heartburn.

I sighed. "I've got a phone call to make and then I think I'll check in on Mr. O'Flanagan."

I walked down to the conference room to use the phone. On the way, my beeper went off. I was relieved that it wasn't my mother. Whatever it was would hold until after I'd called her. She picked up on the first half-ring.

"Hello, dear," she chirped. She didn't know yet.

"Listen, I wanted you to hear it from me first—"

"What should I hear from you first?"

"I was thinking about working with the Public Defender's Office on a new case." It didn't sound so bad when I put it that way. Unfortunately, it was a lie. "Actually, I've already started working on it."

Silence.

"Mom?" More silence. "You still there?"

"Of course I am. And here's what I think of the idea. Bubkes. You don't make enough money there at that fancy hospital you work at?"

Nagging—it was a rare tactical error. For a moment, at least, I could feel put upon. "It's not the money," I said. My voice sounded brittle.

"So what is it then?"

That stopped me. Why *was* I getting involved in another murder case? Was my ego so big and my common sense so puny that I couldn't see where this could lead? I dusted off the answer I would have given anyone who asked me that question two years ago. "I guess because it's a mitzvah. Someone has to defend people who haven't got the wherewithal to defend themselves. And I'm pretty good at it."

"Pssh," my mother exhaled. She wasn't buying.

Now I had to defend myself. "You can say that all you like, but that's the truth. This guy, the defendant? He reminds me of Uncle Louie. You know, wiry and smart. But a sucker for a pretty face."

"If he's so smart . . ." she started, before amending it to, "so it's another murder case."

"He's innocent. I'm sure of it." I felt suddenly deflated. "Pretty sure of it."

She didn't say anything. I knew she'd be sitting there stone-faced. Silence had always been her greatest weapon. "Anyway—anyway, I wanted you to hear it from me. There's a little article about it in the morning paper." My mother groaned. "Page fourteen if you want to read about it."

"Please, please, please"—my mother sounded exhausted—"please, be careful."

I put down the phone feeling spent. I sat there breathing in and out, counting the breaths, and trying to collect enough energy to return the beep. I punched in the number. After one ring, an answering machine picked up. "You've reached Annie Squires. . . ."

"Annie? Peter Zak, returning your call. . . ."

There was a click, "Hey, Peter."

"Hey, yourself."

"I'm sitting here looking at a pile of Sylvia Jackson's medical records and police interviews with your name on them." I didn't say anything. I wasn't so sure that I was ready to start reading about bullet fragments lodged in the cerebral cortex. "I can drop them off later today."

I didn't say anything. *Bubkes*, I heard my mother's voice.

"Or do you want me to drop them off at your house? I'll be heading out that way late this afternoon. Either way—"

"Right. You know where I am," I muttered. Of course she did. The three of us had powwowed over cases in my living room many times. "Right. Sure, fine," I added, to no one in particular.

Annie ignored the awkwardness. "I don't know about you, but I was stunned when the judge agreed to let us evaluate Sylvia Jackson. I think the D.A. was completely blindsided when Chip made the request. He blinked and the judge ruled in our favor. Of course, the downside is that Sherman's been wounded where he hurts most—in his ego. This is not a guy who likes to be beaten."

I wasn't looking forward to meeting Monty Sherman. Generally speaking, D.A.'s are a prickly breed to begin with, and this one was already aggravated.

"Our office is setting up the dates and times for you to see her. Can you call in and tell them your schedule?"

"Will do," I said automatically.

"So I'll drop off the reports at your house?"

It was a good thing I'd called my mother. With her built-in sonar for detecting movement around the house, she wasn't likely to miss Annie Squires dropping off trial-related documents.

"You okay with this, Peter?" Annie asked. "You don't sound like yourself."

Of course I didn't sound like myself. Should I suddenly start to sound like my old self, now that I was doing something that I'd done regularly before everything fell apart? If I'd been my own patient, I'd have observed that it was a first step.

I hung up the phone and headed to the other end of the unit to visit Mr. O'Flanagan. I found myself wondering whether those reports would be there for me by the time I got home. Curiosity and interest were nestled in the anxiety lodged like a hairball in the pit of my stomach. Like many times over the last four days, I was actually thinking about something other than my patients or the past, and it felt good.

I ran into our intern on my way to the common area to find Mr. O'Flanagan. Suzanne had been evaluating him, so I invited her to join me. We found him sitting placidly, staring off into space. I stooped and brought my face close to his. I could just make out a dark smudge under his bruised eye.

"Mr. O'Flanagan, I heard you had a little problem last night." O'Flanagan frowned. "Do you remember what happened?"

"Happened?" He shook his head. "Nothing happened."

"Don't you remember how you got this bruise under your eye?"

"Oh, that," he said with a shrug. "It's nothing. You know, you have to watch out for walking into doors around here."

Just then, Mr. Kootz got up from a sofa on the opposite wall. He was a short, solid man, built like a human fire hydrant. He had a baseball cap jammed on his head. O'Flanagan flinched and cowered as Kootz, mumbling animatedly to himself and punching the air with a clenched fist, stomped out of the room, untied sneaker laces flapping.

"You know, that's a very bad man," O'Flanagan said.

"What do you mean?"

"He's just a bad man. I don't like him."

"Why don't you like him?" I pressed.

"He's just a bad man," O'Flanagan repeated, rubbing distractedly at his bruised eye.

"Well, I guess you should avoid bad men if you can. Anything I can get for you? Do you need anything?"

He shook his head.

Down the hall, I asked Suzanne, "What did you notice?"

"The way he got so upset when Mr. Kootz walked by—at some level, he does remember."

"Good." I nodded. "You're right. It's an example of how there are different kinds of memory. We remember facts one way, but we remember emotions another way. It's the facts that O'Flanagan has lost. He genuinely has no memory of the fight, but he does have an emotional recall of the pain. And so he knows something happened, something that he associates with Mr. Kootz."

"I get that. But why does he say he walked into a door?"

"He's confabulating—backfilling. When you can't remember something, it leaves a hole in your past, and such holes are intolerable. We tend to want to plug them up. So we fill in with something that happened some other time. Or we make something up. Mr. O'Flanagan isn't lying. He isn't aware that he's doing it. And with his alcoholic past, no doubt he's walked into plenty of doors."

6

I GOT home after six to find Annie at my front door. The weather
had become clear, crisp, and fall-like. She turned as I pulled
the car into the driveway and watched me approach the house.
"For you," she said, holding aloft a fat brown envelope. It was
already getting dark and Annie's curly hair shone like a halo in
the glow of the porch light behind her.

As she handed me the envelope, her fingers brushed mine,
causing a loud snap of static electricity. Annie laughed. "That
was a test to see if you're alive or just faking it."

I knew this was banter but the observation hit home. "And?"

"You're alive. Definitely alive. Good thing, too, because otherwise I'd have to report you to the authorities."

"For what?"

"For dishonest living."

That's just what I'd been doing. Living under false pretenses.
As I came alongside, Annie turned and her face moved from
shadow to light. I hadn't noticed before the light sprinkling of
freckles on her nose. "Dishonest living, eh? Could I get arrested
for that?"

"If you're living dishonestly, no one has to arrest you because you already are, by definition . . . "

"Arrested," I finished the thought. "Hmm. I see." We hung there, suspended, white puffs of dragon's breath mingling in the air between us.

Just then, my mother's door opened and her little white head peered out. She squinted into the dark. "Petey?" The sound was like a fingernail on a chalkboard. "You with someone?"

"Am I with someone?" I repeated the question.

"Hello," Annie said, coming around so my mother could get a better look. Annie towered over her by nearly a foot.

My mother gazed up at Annie. "You look familiar."

"You have a good memory, Mrs. Zak."

"Pearl."

"I'm Annie Squires. I work with Peter from time to time. I came by the house two years ago and we met then."

"Two years ago," my mother said, her face clouding as she realized that was for the funeral. "You're from the hospital?"

"Peter and I do trial work together."

"I thought we'd met before," my mother murmured as she put two and two together. Then my mother did this thing where she makes herself smile. It's as if she sticks her hand inside her own head and turns up the corners of her mouth and eyes. "It's lovely to see you again." She stuck her head into her apartment and called out, "It's Petey!"

An assortment of voices chorused back. "Hi, Petey!" Mahjongg night. She slipped into her apartment and quietly shut the door behind her.

"Petey?" Annie said.

I shrugged. "According to my mother, that's my name." I weighed the envelope in my hand. "Should take a couple of hours to get through." I looked at the door to my house. I couldn't remember the last time I'd spent two hours reading in my living room, alone. After ten minutes, I usually found an excuse to go work on the car, walk to the store, or look in on my mother.

Annie checked her watch. "I should get going. I've got a meeting in Somerville in fifteen minutes." She started down the steps and hesitated. "I'm free later. We could talk when you're finished."

I was grateful for an excuse to get out of the house. "Meet you somewhere? Ten-ish?"

"I was going to Johnny D's after my meeting. You know the place?"

It wasn't exactly what I had in mind. I'd been thinking somewhere quiet, coffee. Johnny D's was a club—probably raucous and I'd be drinking beer. I nodded. At least it wasn't somewhere Kate and I had gone.

"Catch ya later," Annie said. Then she rubbed her hand on her pant leg, held up an index finger, and waited. I laughed. As I raised my finger to hers, an enormous spark snapped. "It's cool when you know it's coming," Annie commented. "That electrical thing usually happens so fast you don't get a chance to see the spark."

I left the reports in the living room and descended to the cellar where there's a small door that leads to a climate-controlled room. I had to heave my full weight against the door before it gave way with a sigh and a little exhale, like when you pop the seal on a can of peanuts. I turned on the light and breathed the damp cool air. I ducked inside. No one had set foot in here for months. The last time I'd tried to drink any wine, grief had so dulled my sense of taste that the rich red liquid may as well have been water mixed with the dust that now coated the bottles. It had seemed like a terrible waste to drink wine without tasting it. So beer and whiskey had become my beverages of choice. That night, for some reason, I felt ready to risk it. I chose a 1990 Simi Reserve Cabernet.

Back in the kitchen, I wiped the bottle carefully with a clean dishcloth, opened it, and let the wine breathe. Then I poured myself a glass. I closed my eyes and inhaled gingerly. I felt the sharp smell make its way up my nose and come to rest somewhere between my eyes. I took a sip. I felt the bite but not much more. I swirled the wine in the glass and took another sip. Better. Sharp in the front of the mouth, mellow at the back. But it still felt like seeing a color photograph in tints of sepia. No rich purples. No acetic greens. I knocked back the remaining wine, corked the bottle, and left it on the kitchen counter. Then I put up a pot of coffee and left it to drip.

I shuffled into the living room, collapsed into the chair, and shucked my shoes. I wiggled my toes and noticed my big toe poking through a hole that I was sure hadn't been there this morning.

Three hours later, I was still there, surrounded by police reports and hospital records.

The crime scene reports told me that Sylvia Jackson was found in the Mount Auburn Cemetery, facedown near the base of the stone tower. There were tire tracks beside her body. They found her car a few blocks away, halfway between the cemetery and her house. The red paint on the right front fender was scratched. The car had a single, unidentified thumbprint on the wheel.

After the EMTs took her to the hospital, the police went to her home. There they discovered Tony Ruggiero dead in the living room. The reports described him as six-foot-one, two hundred forty pounds. The file contained grim photographs of his body. In death, he was a large middle-aged man, running to paunch. His teeth were clenched, lips parted in a rictus of pain. He wasn't tied up but there were rope burns on his wrists. His body was severely bruised and small amounts of coagulated blood surrounded innocuous-looking slits in his upper back and chest. He must have bled profusely from a single gunshot wound to the stomach.

Two kitchen knives, fireplace tongs, and a brass bookend were identified as weapons. All had been wiped clean of prints. The police didn't find a gun.

The attack must have taken time. Time to tie him up, time to go into the kitchen for knives, time to get the fireplace tongs, time to beat him, stab him, then shoot him. I couldn't imagine a big guy like Tony Ruggiero rolling over and submitting to a beating, leaving his attacker unbruised, as Stuart had apparently been unbruised a day later.

Sylvia Jackson was admitted to the Mount Auburn Hospital on the morning of March 9. The admitting form listed her as Jane Doe, address unknown, date of birth unknown, everything unknown except the type of accident—gunshot wound. The description made me stop and ponder. "Twenty-five-year-old female with bullet wound to the head." Twenty-five? That didn't sound right.

The hospital records described her wound exactly as Stuart Jackson had described it to me: a fronto-temporal penetrating bullet wound. She'd been shot above the right temple. The report said they performed "a bilateral craniectomy with craniotomy with debridement of the wound." They opened up her head, sucked the blood from the bullet wound, and picked out the bullet fragments. The MRI didn't paint a pretty picture. The bullet had tracked across the brain and ended up somewhere near the top of her left ear. That meant it first hit the right frontal lobe, then it tracked across the midline and across her left motor strip, probably affecting movement on her right side. Memory would probably be affected as well.

She had surgery to remove bone fragments, but bits of bone remained in the areas of the brain that control executive functions—I wondered if she might be having difficulty controlling her emotions and impulses as a result.

Her recovery had been slow and painful.

The notes quoted her. "I want to spend fifteen hours a day in bed. But when I try to sleep, I wake up all the time. And the only time I feel calm is when Sergeant MacRae is around."

Who, I wondered, was Sergeant MacRae?

Daily police interviews began shortly after she regained consciousness. Her first recorded words to the detective were, "I just want to know what happened."

"Do you mean about Tony?"

"Did something happen to Tony?"

Her interrogator told her Tony had been killed. The transcript said simply that she wept upon hearing this.

When the questioning resumed, the detective said to her, "Tell me about Stuart."

She explained that Stuart was her husband. She didn't appear to realize that they were divorced. She wondered, "Why hasn't Stuart been to see me?" The detective didn't tell her that Stuart had been a nearly constant visitor during her first weeks in the hospital. But by the time Sylvia Jackson woke up, the police were keeping all potential suspects away, including Stuart.

The following day, the recorded questions began: "Do you own a gun?"

She admitted that she did. She couldn't remember what kind, but it was a little gun. Stuart had gotten it for her and taught her how to shoot.

"Where do you keep it?"

"In my bedroom. By the bed. In a drawer."

"On what side?"

"On his side."

"His side?"

"On my husband's side."

"Do you keep it loaded?"

"Yes."

Then the officer shifted his focus. "Do you want to know what happened to you?"

"Who shot me?" she asked.

"We're not sure."

Over the weeks that followed, Sylvia Jackson complained of recurring nightmares. And she started to reconstruct her past, the hole in her memory shrinking like any other wound. She realized that she and Stuart were divorced. She remembered her birthday party, a month earlier. Each day she remembered more, got closer and closer, until she started to recall the night of the murder.

"Tony and I went out to dinner. We ate in Chinatown. When we got home, I parked in the driveway and came in through the back door."

"Was the door locked?"

"I opened it with my key."

"Did you notice anything unusual about the house?"

"There weren't any lights on. It was dark."

"Was that unusual?"

"No, not especially."

"Where did you keep your keys?"

"In my purse."

"Were there any other keys? Did you have any hidden around the house?"

"There was one under a rock by the back door."

"Did Stuart have a key to your house?"

"No. He used the key under the rock when he had to get in."

I could only imagine the pause that occurred next as Sylvia Jackson wondered about the direction these questions were leading. She asked, "Are you insinuating that Stuart did this?" And although the detective denied it—he was just asking about her keys—from then on, the questions focused on Stuart.

In the middle of an interrogation two weeks later, Sylvia Jackson broke down in tears. The notes describe her staring out the window and weeping.

"Is something wrong?" the detective asked.

"I keep having these nightmares," she said. "I'm afraid of them."

"Can you tell me about them?"

"I keep seeing the same thing, over and over."

"What do you see?"

· 55 ·

"A man. He's driving my car. He has a gun."

"Are you afraid of the man?"

There was no record of an answer.

"Are you in the car?"

"In the back. He made me get into the backseat of the car. And Tony—Oh God—Tony . . ."

"Where's Tony?" the detective asked.

"He's in the trunk. The man made him get into the trunk."

"What happens in the nightmare?"

"It's very cold. I climb up into a tower and I look out from the stairs. I see myself down below, on the grass. There's someone, a man, in the shadows. He shoots me in the head."

"Can you see who the man is?"

"I don't want to believe. It just can't be."

"What can't be?"

"The person I keep seeing. It can't be him."

"Who is it?"

"I think it's Stuart."

In the days that followed, Sylvia Jackson filled in the details of what she now referred to as a vision. A month after she woke from her coma, she announced that she was sure. Stuart did it.

All of the police interview reports had the same signature. Detective J. MacRae.

Two things struck me. First, Sylvia Jackson had lived through the kind of traumatic head injury that would have killed most people. And second, given the extent of her injuries, I would never have expected her to be able to recall what happened to her an hour, a day, or even a week before she was struck down. I wondered, how disoriented was Sylvia Jackson when she came out of the coma? How susceptible to suggestion as a result? Had she imprinted herself on her daily interrogator like a baby duck on its mama?

I surveyed the wreckage in my study. Papers and manila folders were strewn everywhere. An empty coffee mug rested on the wide, flat arm of my leather-cushioned Morris chair. I leaned back, marveling as I always did at how perfectly the chair suited my oversized body. I'd acquired the chair years ago at a yard sale, before people knew what Mission furniture was and before furnituremakers started knocking off reproduction pieces like parts of a Model T. Then, when it became an in thing, I haunted furniture auctions. That's where I met Kate. She was looking at pieces of art pottery that were being made at the same time the Stickley brothers were inventing the Mission style. She showed me a vase at that auction that she didn't have the money to buy. She thought it was exquisite. I thought it was squat and plain. Over the years, she taught me how to see texture, subtle nuance of color, sinuous curve. I taught her to appreciate the straight, elegant lines of the furniture and how to spot an original.

As I reassembled the stacks of paper and tucked them back into the envelope Annie had brought them in, I realized how engrossed I'd become. I hadn't once thought about my own pain. The clinical detail and detached tone of the reports allowed me to intellectualize without having to connect emotionally with the horror of the crime. In fact, there was a weird pleasure to it, almost like running your tongue over and over an empty socket where there was once a tooth.

7

AT NINE-THIRTY, I was weaving my way into Somerville, dodging pedestrians and wondering what traffic planning genius had synchronized the lights so it was impossible to go more than three blocks without hitting a red.

I turned off the four-lane boulevard, zigged over one block, and ended up at a messy merge of competing streets. A little later, the road detoured left, then right, then narrowed. As I drove, I registered the changes that mark the transition from Cambridge to Somerville. Brew pubs became Irish bars. Gourmet food stores turned into meat markets and delis. It was possible, once again, to find a parking spot.

Somerville had been my home when I first moved to Boston. I could take the trolley to MIT and I could afford the one-room, third-floor walk-up that overlooked an alley behind a Portuguese restaurant. The apartment smelled perpetually of linguica, potatoes, and grease. I waxed nostalgic as I drove past the spot that had once been home to Steve's Ice Cream. I yearned for a scoop of their vanilla ice cream, smashed onto a marble board, then sprinkled with chocolate-covered toffee and kneaded with a metal paddle until the two became an entirely new thing, neither ice cream nor candy, but a comfort food in a league of its own. I'd tried to re-create the effect with Breyer's vanilla, a Heath Bar, an ice cream scoop, and a hammer. But I'd always returned to wait the forty minutes on line so I could fork over a buck fifty and pay homage to Steve's artistry.

Steve's was an addiction Kate and I shared. We went there after our first time together. Hot fudge and ice cream seemed the only appropriate final act of indulgence.

I parked my car on the street and locked up. I walked the two blocks to Johnny D's, checking every so often over my shoulder. It was a habit I couldn't shake. I couldn't forget that for weeks, Kate and I had been completely unaware of Ralston Bridges stalking us as he carefully planned his attack. Knowing that I could so easily be followed, watched, without feeling even the slightest unease, made me uneasy now.

There was no sign of Annie's Jeep. Feeling like a dark-suited alien, I threaded my way through the little crowd of smokers standing outside. In the half-light inside, the sound of recorded blues filled the space. On the right side of the club, tiny white lights twinkled above the bar. A luminous television screen at the far end of the bar seemed to hover in a cloud of cigarette smoke. On the smoke-free side of the club, separated by a shoulder-high wall, were tables, a postage-stamp-sized dance floor, and a small elevated stage.

The place was packed and customers from the bar area jockeyed for position in the opening between the two halves of the club. I followed a young man with a ring through his lower lip to a table for two at the back with a good view of the stage. A kid whose hair was buzz-cut on the sides and green Brillo on top was checking out speakers and a tangled mass of cables. The people at the table next to me were laughing and pouring beer from a pitcher. I didn't recognize most of the groups featured in the posters that lined the walls. I took off my jacket and loosened my tie. Then I unbuttoned my shirt collar and rolled the sleeves. I opened and closed the menu, checked my watch.

When I glanced toward the entrance, Annie was making her way over. She stopped to exchange long-lost-pal greetings and hugs with a variety of bar denizens—male, female, and indeterminate.

"Something to drink?" the young, spiky-haired waitress asked us when Annie settled beside me.

"Do you have Sam Adams Bock Beer?" Annie asked. The waitress nodded and I wondered what it took to get her hair to stand up on end the way it did. "Do you want one, too?" Annie was asking me.

"What's it like?"

"It's like . . . You've never had it?" I shook my head. "Well, it's a little unusual. You can only get it at this time of year. They brew it from the dregs at the bottom of the barrel. They take all this slop and it comes out a dark, sweetish-tasting beer. I like it."

It sounded awful to me. "Sounds good. Make that two," I found myself saying.

Annie said, "Can I get an order of conch fritters, sweet potato fries, and crab cakes?"

The waitress looked expectantly at me. "I'll have the same," I said.

"Come here a lot?" I asked, glancing at the bar and noticing that one of the men she'd greeted warmly on arrival was staring at us.

Annie grinned. "Some. You know who else hangs out here . . . or at least used to?"

"Who?"

"Sylvia Jackson. She used to come in here all the time. Sometimes alone, sometimes not. But she rarely left alone."

"She had lots of boyfriends, I gather?" I asked.

"She certainly did. All the same type. Italian hairdressers and stunt doubles for Arnold Schwarzenegger. And then, we have

Stuart Jackson—a hundred twenty pounds dripping wet. Given her taste in men, I can't figure out what she sees in him. He's such a dweeb."

"A dweeb."

"To use the technical term."

"On the other hand, he adores her. And he's very smart," I said as our beer arrived.

Annie dipped her index finger into the creamy foam, put the finger into her mouth, and drew it out slowly. "I guess for some women, that's a turn-on," she said. I found myself wondering what it was that turned on Annie Squires. She gestured to my beer, which was sweating into a puddle. "See what you think."

I sniffed. Fermented molasses. The taste was better. Not subtle. But dark and rich, almost creamy. "Very nice," I conceded. "Interesting."

"Interesting?"

I took another drink and wiped the foam from my lip. "A little more of this and I'll be ready for a snooze," I commented, yawning.

Annie stared into her beer before saying, "I know you don't want to talk about it. I just want you to know that I . . . we all feel the work has changed since what happened."

Why couldn't people just leave well enough alone? What was the point? "Really, you don't have to—" I started.

But Annie was determined to finish. "So you're not coming back to the same place, really. It's a helluva way to learn about murder. But once you've seen it from the inside, you can't treat it quite the same." It was just a statement of fact. Annie's direct look didn't feel like pity.

"So how do you keep doing it?" I asked.

"It's still a job. It's how the system works. Don't think I haven't considered going over to the other side. I have. But that would be even harder. My heart wouldn't be in it. And leave the work completely?" She shook her head. "I could never do that."

"So you can still do this work, defending people you know in your heart of hearts are guilty?"

"When you put it that way . . ." She looked directly at me with those clear gray eyes. "Maybe you'd understand if you knew how I got into this work in the first place. I've never told you, have I?" She rested her chin in her hand and gave a wry smile. "I know it sounds corny, but I always wanted to be a cop. That's what the men in my family did. I was always pestering my uncles to let me sit in their patrol cars, or put on their caps, or wear their badges. My dad wasn't a cop, but that's only because he had this heart condition. Couldn't pass the physical. He became a printer. You know, a linotype operator. He worked six days a week and late on Saturday, sitting at this enormous keyboard— like one of those big old movie theater organs. Whenever I visited him at work, he'd make me a lead slug with my name in it. He'd hand it to me, still hot. I've got a whole collection of them. He'd always say the same corny thing, 'See, you're already making headlines.'

"Anyway, his employers were so grateful for all his hard work that when the linotype machine went extinct, they tried to fire my dad and all the people he worked with. Dad was a fighter. He'd take just so much abuse, and then, watch out. He walked picket lines. He'd lie down in front of the trucks trying to deliver newsprint. Quite a few times he got arrested. One time, when he was in jail waiting for the judge to set bail, he got beat up pretty badly. They didn't even call a doctor. When he got out, he looked like a human punching bag. His kidneys were damaged and he had a detached retina. He never did say who did it and I didn't ask. But I think it was cops who worked him over. Up until then, cops were family. That's what broke his spirit. By the time I was in eighth grade, he'd retired without a fuss and turned into a TV junky."

"So you didn't want to be a cop after that?"

"No way. Arresting people and putting them in jail lost its

allure. Working for the public defender seemed like a logical choice. So you can see why going over to the other side, working for the D.A., could never happen."

"Has it been a disappointment, not getting that badge?"

"I was going to find out cops are human sooner or later. Good thing I found out before I turned into one."

"Hey, being human isn't a bad thing."

"No, it isn't, Peter." She raised her beer and put it down again without drinking any. "So when are you going to let yourself be one?"

"Is it that obvious?"

"That you're not really here? That a piece of you is in some shadowy place? That you can't really connect? No, it's not obvious." Annie looked at me, leading with her jaw, lips pursed, challenging. She was right. A shadowy place was a good description of where I was much of the time when I wasn't working. To connect, I'd have to risk loss. And I wasn't ready for that.

I took a sip of beer. "I got through all the reports."

Annie sighed. "And?"

"And I think she survived one hell of an ordeal. By the way, did you notice the ER report describes her as twenty-five years old?"

"No, I didn't. But I can't say I'm surprised. She has this quality about her. Even now, damaged as she is. You'll see what I mean the minute you meet her."

"What?"

"Mmm," Annie inhaled deeply, "being around her reminds me of the atmosphere just before a hurricane. Humid. Close." Annie tilted her head and stared at me thoughtfully. "She attracts men."

"Like bees to honey?"

"Just like."

"That's what Stuart Jackson told me, along with another more colorful simile that I won't burden you with. You think all men are susceptible?"

"Well, most of them."

Present company excluded? I changed the subject. "Anyway, it's clear that she suffered massive head trauma. Her brains got pretty well shaken up. According to all the literature and my experience, she shouldn't be able to recall what happened to her."

"Shouldn't?" Annie asked.

"Right. Nothing about brain injury is one hundred percent predictable. Every brain injury is unique. But any time anybody suffers head trauma that results in unconsciousness, we know that at the very least, there's a correlation between length of coma and the amount of retrograde amnesia."

The waitress brought our food. To the waitress, Annie said, "Thanks." To me she said, "In English, please."

I tend to retreat into psychobabble when I'm nervous and I didn't like to admit that I was feeling a bit off center. I chewed on a conch fritter. "Right," I said. "Retrograde amnesia means you forget things that happened before the trauma. The longer you're out cold, the more you forget.

"What you have to understand is the massive amount of trauma this kind of wound causes. See, the brain itself is this mass of Jell-O surrounded by fluid, inside a hard bony shell. First of all, there's the actual damage caused by the bullet zipping through. Then think about what it takes, in terms of shock, to break open the skull. The pressure on the skull alone is going to cause brain damage. And any time you have an injury that causes unconsciousness, you become concerned about loss of memory for events immediately preceding it. And Sylvia Jackson was in a coma for six weeks."

There was a pause that neither of us rushed to fill.

"There was something about a Sergeant MacRae in one of the reports," I said. "Something she said—that he makes her feel safe."

"Sounds like she was referring to Detective Sergeant Joseph MacRae. Mac's the one who interviewed her. He's been hanging around the hospital from the minute she woke up."

"You know him?" I asked.

"I know a lot of cops," she said, avoiding my eyes. "Mac and I went to high school together. Somerville High. Class of '82. His dad was a cop. Dark blue blood—runs in families."

"Your families knew each other?"

"We were pretty close to the MacRaes. Once."

I had the distinct impression that there was more Annie wasn't saying. "Run into him much lately?" I asked.

"Now that you mention it, I saw him the other day when I went to pick up her medical records. I thought he was there on official business—" Annie paused. I knew we were both wondering why Detective Sergeant Joseph MacRae was still hanging around Sylvia Jackson. The usual police investigation would have been wrapped long ago. "Sylvia Jackson does have that thing about her."

"Hurricane?" I asked.

"Tropical storm," Annie whispered. Then, seriously, "How do you work with someone like that?"

"Like what?"

"Someone who's so . . . sexually charged. It's just there. All the time. You know, like an elephant in the living room that no one talks about. How do you keep yourself from being drawn in?"

I smiled. It was just the kind of question people are curious about but very few will come right out and ask. But then, asking questions was what Annie did. "I guess I compartmentalize. You can't ignore it. It's there. You recognize it's there. If you're attracted, then that's something to pull out and dissect. You say, okay, here's this emotional dialogue going on at the same time that there's a verbal and physical exchange. Part of it's coming from the patient, but part of it is coming from inside you. It's not that you shut down. You become hypersensitive. But instead of reacting, you start processing your own reactions."

"Compartmentalize."

"Right. I'm an expert at it."

Annie was staring at me. Appraising. "Sounds like a good skill."

Right, I thought. As long as it doesn't become a habit.

There was applause as a guy about my age strode up onto the stage. I wondered if I could get away with tight, low-slung blue jeans, a threadbare T-shirt, and that fringed leather vest. He conferred briefly with the lead guitar, blew tentatively into the mouthpiece of a harmonica, beat the air one, two, three, and the place started to rock.

We didn't talk again until the break between sets.

"So, was there anything in the police reports that struck you?" I asked.

"Just that the beating was long and especially brutal," Annie answered.

"Suggests the killer knew Tony and didn't like him. But why kill him in the house and then drive her to the cemetery before shooting her? Makes you wonder if it was planned out in advance."

"All of the weapons were right there in the house, waiting to be grabbed."

"The police didn't find the gun. Do you think they used Sylvia Jackson's gun?"

"They?" Annie looked at me, surprised. "What makes you say 'they'?"

I'd said it without even being aware that I was thinking it. "I guess it's a lot easier to imagine what might have happened if you conjure up an accomplice."

"Why would Sylvia Jackson accuse Stuart Jackson if he didn't do it?"

"Put yourself in her position. You wake up in the hospital. You're grievously injured, emotionally a mess, and you can't remember what happened to you. These caretakers and authority figures, these policemen, your anchors in a sea of confusion—they want you to remember. They make a suggestion here, another one there. Was this what happened? Maybe it was like that? Well, it's only natural to start borrowing their suggestions, building on that until you have a whole, plausible explanation. Not deliberately, but unconsciously you start stitching bits and pieces to the ragged edges of the hole in your brain. Or perhaps not." I shrugged. "That's the thing about memory. It's such an individual thing. You can't know what really happened."

As we were leaving. I paused at the door to watch a dozen couples swaying to a slow, soulful blues. "Peter," Annie whispered. She stood facing me, her back to the club. "See the guy standing near the end of the bar? The redhead wearing a Rangers sweatshirt."

I looked over her shoulder. "I see him," I said. The redhead she was referring to looked like a Marine. Medium height, solid and broad-shouldered, buzz-cut, he was shaped like a triangle. He stood ramrod straight. He and his buddies were watching a Bruins game. A tall blonde in jeans was attached to him at the hip and his hand rested casually on her bottom.

Annie reached for the finger I was unconsciously pointing. But it was too late. One of his friends had seen me, and now he was whispering and gesturing in my direction.

"Shit," I said as the redhead swiveled to gawk at me. "Uh-oh. I think he may have spotted me."

I swapped positions with Annie and sidled onto the dance floor, keeping my back to the bar. "Who is he, anyway?"

"That's the cop who's still at the hospital, sniffing around Sylvia Jackson."

I tried not to look around at the owner of the signature, J. MacRae, Sylvia Jackson's handler. The other couples on the dance floor were draped all over one another. Holding Annie at arm's length and shuffling to the music wasn't going to make me inconspicuous. I pulled her close.

It had been a long time since I'd held a woman, since I'd danced with anyone. Dancing with Kate had been so easy. We

· 68 ·

knew each other's bodies, our rhythms. Our contours fit like puzzle pieces. I closed my eyes and tried to remember, but the memory remained elusive. Annie was taller and she moved with her own sense of the music. She seemed to find an extra beat, a hidden syncopation, and she drew me into it. In spite of myself, I relaxed and let the rhythm of that syncopated bass line insinuate itself into my hips, make its way up into my spine, work its way up on through my shoulders and neck. Annie rested her head against me and I inhaled. She smelled like a fresh-cut melon.

On the drive home, the semi-deserted streets seemed to fly by. I let myself into the house and turned off the porch light. A few moments later, there was my mother's shave-and-a-haircut knock at the door. I opened it.

She stood on the darkened porch in her pink bathrobe and looked up at me defiantly. "I don't want to come in, but I can't sleep until I say something."

"Hi, Mom. Sure you don't want to come in for some decaf? Tea? I've got some of those cookies you like from Carberry's."

"The little Napoleon hats?" my mother said, leaning forward as if drawn inside by some magnetic pull.

"Come?" I stepped to one side.

She shook her head firmly. "No. I just wanted to say I'm glad you told me you were working on a case. And that whatever you do, I have no business saying yes or no. You've been doing what you thought was right since you were a little boy. It's what I brought you up to do."

"Maybe if I explain . . ."

"No need to explain. I'm your mother. Not your keeper. So you don't apologize and I won't complain." She bounced up on the balls of her feet. "Deal?"

How could I turn down such an offer? "Deal." I gave her a hug and felt as if I'd been given absolution.

She held me at arm's length. "Cigarette smoke." She sniffed. "Beer." Then she leaned in close for another sniff. "Watermelon?" She shook her head and yawned. "Now I can sleep."

8

A WEEK later, I was on my way to evaluate Sylvia Jackson. My appointment was scheduled for ten. At nine I was circling the hospital complex, an enormous, three-winged granite building tucked in the crook of an elbow where two highways meet. The Big Dig — Boston's massive, federally funded attempt to straighten the cow paths they call streets — had turned the hospital into a moat-surrounded fortress. The normal access road was now one-way, and the surrounding blocks had become staging arenas for earth-moving equipment.

Cursing the always courteous Boston drivers who cut me off, I hunkered down over the wheel and peered out through a rain-spattered windshield as I tried to figure out where the powers that be had hidden the temporary entrance to the parking garage. Boston has a strange philosophy about signage: If you don't know where you are, you don't belong here.

The garage was, of course, packed. My tires squealed each time I had to double back and climb to the next level of wall-to-wall vehicles. I passed up sliver after sliver of semi-spot left over after one of suburbia's answers to that pressing question, what to drive on a safari into the veldt, plumps itself into a space and a half. In an act of desperation, I left my classic Beemer in a space on the roof marked "Maintenance/Reserved." It was either there or squeeze onto the end of a row where I was afraid I'd get clipped.

By nine-thirty, I was staggering across a rickety wooden walkway that connected to the building entrance. I must have looked like a refuge, laden with bundles—two leather portfolios of testing materials, an enormous cloth shopping bag stuffed with binders and boxes, and a white Dunkin' Donuts bag that was slowly turning wet and brown as the coffee sloshed around inside. By the time I reached the building, my arms ached. As I entered the revolving door, the bag gave way and the coffee plopped down on the floor, splashing my pant leg and mingling with the mud on my shoes.

"Figures," I grumbled to no one in particular.

I entered the cavernous lobby, looking back to watch the empty cup roll around as the revolving door swept it inside, then outside, then inside again. I sighed and approached the circular granite reception desk. The brunette roosting there was on the phone. I dropped my burdens, cleared my throat loudly, and waited, counting the hoops that pierced her left ear. I reached twelve before she swiveled around to me.

"I'm here to see a patient, Sylvia Jackson," I told her. "Can you tell me what room she's in?"

With the phone still attached to one ear, she squawked, "It's not visiting hours. You'll have to come back at eleven."

I interrupted her mid-swivel. "I'm Dr. Peter Zak and I have an appointment to see her."

Without acknowledging what I'd said, she tap-tapped at her computer, paused, and then conceded, "Seven-Twelve West."

I stopped in the men's room to wipe the mud and coffee from my shoes and pants. Then I continued to the elevator. I got off at the seventh floor, headed down the west wing corridor, and stopped at the nurses' station.

Two nurses were standing behind the counter, watching me

approach. I smiled, hoping for but not getting a smile in return. It was going to be one of those days.

"I'm Dr. Peter Zak. I have a ten o'clock appointment to evaluate Sylvia Jackson. I'd like to check her chart before I begin." I let my voice rise to a question mark at the end.

The taller one, with the unlikely name LOVELY pinned to her starched white chest, shifted her position to block the gap between the counter and the wall. A tornado wouldn't have mussed her blond helmet.

"I assume you have a release?" she asked, planting her hands on her hips.

I dropped my bags on the floor, wiped my forehead, and groaned. Nothing was going to be easy today. I took off my coat and folded it deliberately over the back of a chair, straightened my tie, and approached her.

"My understanding is that the lawyers have arranged for that." She looked unmoved. "I'll need a release."

"Look. I have an appointment with Ms. Jackson. The court arranged it. Believe me, I wouldn't be here dragging all this stuff with me if it hadn't been set up properly."

"I need to see authorization. I'm not the one in charge around here, you know. I don't make the rules."

"Well, why don't you check with whoever does?" I paused and counted the holes in a ceiling tile. "My time is being paid for by the Commonwealth. I can wait."

I sat down with what I hoped was a look of infinite patience.

Reluctantly, Nurse Lovely went over to the desk and looked at the telephone. I could tell she was trying to decide on her next move. After a few beats, she sat down, flipped through a Rolodex on the desk, and punched in four numbers. She waited, frowning.

I watched the clock on the wall as the minute and hour hands met at ten minutes to ten. I looked longingly at a coffeepot, just visible through a glass door at the back of the nurses' station. When I glanced back toward the desk, Nurse Lovely was glaring at me. She quickly looked away, checked the Rolodex again, and punched in a bunch more numbers. Someone must have answered because she cupped her hand over the mouthpiece as she spoke. Apparently, the answer she got didn't please her. She shot the receiver back into its cradle.

I wondered about the animosity that radiated from Nurse Lovely. Nurses are often protective of their patients, especially when a patient needs the kind of long-term care Sylvia Jackson had required. Still, it seemed a bit excessive. Maybe I could kill her with kindness.

I approached the counter, smiling one of my most cheerful. "All set?" I chirped.

She muttered, "Help yourself."

"Thanks."

First I went over to the medication Kardex. I flipped through the cards on the metal rack until I found Sylvia Jackson's. I needed to know if she was taking anything that could affect her test results. She was on low doses of an antidepressant and something for seizures. No problem there. If she'd been sedated, that could have thrown off the cognitive tests.

As I leaned over to read, I could feel Nurse Lovely's eyes drilling holes in the top of my head. She stepped back when I passed in front of her to reach the metal chart rack.

"Okay if I sit here for a few minutes?" I asked, carrying the chart over to one of the desks.

Nurse Lovely gave me a tight little nod.

I hunched over the chart, checking the most recent entries in each section. Sylvia Jackson was making progress with her walking. Her speech was improving. Several times her therapists had noted "episodic dyscontrol." I could understand why she might be irritable and easily frustrated. She could probably remember precisely what it was like to be completely physically functional. Her injuries had left her far from that mark.

Lovely directed me to a conference room at the end of the hall. There, I unpacked my notebooks and test instruments.

While I waited for Sylvia Jackson to be brought in, I thought about the gradual progress she was making in her recovery. Superimposed on an upslope of slow, steady improvement were sine waves, blips of emotional upheaval. Brain trauma affecting her memory and executive functions could account for her slow progress and her lack of emotional control. Even a non-traumatized brain would be overwhelmed by her ordeal. I imagined a pathetic, wheelchair-bound invalid, racked by depression, torn by frustration.

I didn't hear the wheelchair rolling into the conference room. I didn't notice the little squeak as the brakes locked. I looked up sharply when a light, whispery voice broke the silence, first with a breathy exhale, followed by, "Hello, you must be Zap."

She extended her left hand as I reached across to shake her right.

"Dr. Zak. Pleased to meet you," I said.

Pathetic she was not. She had a short cap of well-cut, shiny black hair with a curtain of glossy bangs that hung down over dark eyes fringed with long lashes. She wore jeans and a fitted, long-sleeved western-style shirt that showed off the swell of her breasts and a slender waist. Her generous lips, the color of a ripe persimmon, parted to a toothy smile in a smooth face devoid of any age lines.

I squeezed her hand and then tried to let go. But she held on as she settled back in her chair studying me, her head tilted at an angle. There were dark smudges under her eyes, her skin pale and translucent.

She exhaled and whispered, "Doctor."

Finally, she dropped my hand. Annie's cryptic comment, "You'll see," came floating back to me on a wave of warm, tropical air.

"I'm sorry I'm late, Ms. Jackson," I said.

"Please, call me Syl," she said as she gazed at me speculatively.

Already, I felt a pang of conscience. She was a heartbreaking combination of ripe and vulnerable, without a clue as to what I was about. "Well, Syl, shall we get started?"

"Mmm," she purred, looking with interest at the test materials I'd arranged on the table.

"I brought a lot of tests. We probably won't get through them all today."

She gave me a slightly lopsided look. After an exhale and a pause, she said, "I was a little worried." She exhaled again before talking, as if she had to blow up her own voice balloons. "I do everything a little slower these days than I used to."

It occurred to me then that the tilt of her head, that angle of cool appraisal, probably wasn't intentional. The kind of brain damage she'd suffered would have caused everything on one side to droop. Likewise, the little breath that made me hang on the silence that preceded her words probably wasn't intentional. We take for granted that breathing and speaking are a single activity. But after brain damage, they can part company like a pair of gears that get wrenched apart. Anyone who is concentrating at every moment on the simple act of breathing will tire quickly. I made a mental note to keep that in mind.

I moved a chair away from the end of the table so she could pull her wheelchair in close. I rearranged my materials and riffled through the papers to find the first test protocol.

She locked her wheelchair in place and watched me expectantly. She leaned over, rested her hand on my thigh, and breathed, "Ready when you are." She squeezed my leg. "You are misleading." I felt a frisson of electricity and a tightening in my groin. Purely the autonomic nervous system kicking in, I told myself. "You don't look like a weight lifter, but you sure do feel like one."

I stood up to adjust a window shade that didn't need adjusting. Coming on to people wasn't something she could control. I sat again, this time beyond reaching distance.

"Do you?" she asked. "Do you lift weights?"

Normally, I would have discouraged this. Sharing personal

information cuts across exactly the kind of boundary that's essential to a therapeutic relationship. But Sylvia Jackson wasn't my patient and our relationship wasn't therapeutic. To do the job I'd come for, I'd need her cooperation. Testing could take four or five hours. I smiled and shook my head.

"Run marathons?"

"God forbid!"

"It's got to be something," she insisted. "Give me a clue."

"Actually, I row."

"I never thought shrinks were athletic. Now, rowing—isn't that something they do at Harvard?"

"And BU, MIT . . ."

"I used to date a guy who took me out on the river. We'd go out at sunset with a six-pack. Watch the students row." She arched her back and purred. "So romantic. Is that where you go? On the Charles?"

"I'm there every morning, six A.M., rain or shine."

"An obsession?"

Her remark left me momentarily speechless. It *had* turned into an obsession. I pride myself on being somewhat opaque, difficult to read when I need to be. She'd be easy to underestimate.

"It's just something I like to do," I said mildly, picking up my interview protocol and placing it between us. "Ready?" I asked.

"Shoot," she said.

The conference-room door opened and Nurse Lovely rattled into the room. She was pushing a metal cart loaded with cups of medication lined up in orderly rows and columns.

"What the—?" I started.

"Sorry to interrupt," Lovely cut in, "but it's time to take these." The cup that Lovely handed Syl was like a miniature Easter basket filled with multicolored eggs. She poured a cup of water and patted Sylvia gently on the back.

"Oh, Carolyn, already?" Syl groaned. "Seems like we just did this." She stared at the pills. She looked at me, then at Nurse Lovely. Then she gave a sly smile. "Did you meet Dr.—"

"Zak," I filled in the blank.

Nurse Lovely nodded.

"He's got the most amazing leg muscles."

"He does, does he?" Nurse Lovely raised an eyebrow in my direction and gave me a sour look. Was the lacquered hair real? A croquet mallet wouldn't dent its plastic perfection.

"You know those college guys who row on the Charles? That's what he does. Every morning. Crack of dawn."

"Remember?" Nurse Lovely tapped her clipboard. "Pills. Then you can get back to your tests. That is what you're up to here, isn't it, Doctor? Tests?"

Slowly and deliberately, Syl took three little whites. She gagged when she tried to swallow the big red, took an extra sip of water, and finally got it down. She took a deep breath and stared at the two green capsules, a yellow tablet, and the pink, torpedo-shaped pill that remained.

"You just take your time," Nurse Lovely said, waiting patiently.

The two greens went down. Then the yellow. When Syl had swallowed the last pill, Lovely delivered a final checkmark to the paper on the clipboard, turned, and exited with a clatter. But not before giving me a withering look.

I started with the standard questions of person, place, and time. Syl knew who she was, where she was, but she thought it was still August. Not surprising. Hospital routine doesn't change from one day to the next. People often lose track.

When I told her she was a month off, she shrugged. "I guess I don't pay much attention to the calendar. I stopped reading the paper and I can't stand to watch the news on television either."

Again, I wasn't surprised. People who have been through severe physical trauma try to keep their environments as neutral as possible. It's a healthy form of self-preservation, as long as it doesn't last too long. And for Syl, only six months after the nearly successful attempt on her life, it seemed entirely appropriate.

I expected the next question to be more stressful. "Can you tell me what you remember? What happened?"

There was a pause, then a little outrush of breath again preceded her words. "I can remember Stuart calling up that night . . . on the eighth. He wanted to come by but I said no."

She spoke slowly, one word smearing slightly up against the next. I wrote down her words and waited for her to continue.

". . . Mainly because I had someone else there." She paused and shifted slightly in her chair. "Then Stuart came . . . No, Stuart was in bed with me . . ." I continued writing. "No. Tony was in bed with me. The next thing I knew, I heard Stuart's car. Stuart's car makes this sound."

Syl paused. I looked up from my notes. She was gazing down at her hands lying loosely in her lap. Slowly, as if the words had multiple syllables, she said, "I was shot." I felt my heartbeat jump and anxiety, like dots of sweat, prickled at my hairline. I concentrated on breathing evenly, in and out. Compartmentalize, I told myself. ". . . He was dressed like a guerrilla, in a camouflage suit. He told Tony to put a pillowcase over his head. He belted it and told him to put his hands in front and belted them, too. Tony went down the stairway because Stuart told him to."

She paused. She was still looking into her lap. And though one fist was now clenched, her voice held little affect. She was telling a story she'd had to tell over and over and over again, and in the telling and retelling, it had lost its power.

She looked up slowly and held my eyes as she said quietly in her whispery voice, so I had to lean forward slightly to catch all the words, "Tony slipped at the bottom of the stairs. He . . . fell. Stuart gave him time to get up and ordered the two of us into the living room." There was a long pause before she continued. "Then he beat Tony with fireplace tongs. I guess I was too scared to do anything.

"Stuart ordered me out to the garage and into the car. I drove. Or . . . yes, he drove. We were going toward the cemetery. There was a tower in the cemetery. We went up into it. It was so cold there. Then he shot me."

"He shot you in the tower?"

"No." Syl looked confused. "On the grass. I was outside the car on the grass. That's where he shot me. I remember hearing the gun go off." She stopped and sighed, rubbed her forehead and gave me a questioning look. "Is that bad?" she breathed. "Does that put Stuart in a bad light?"

She made him sound like a swell guy—beat the shit out of her boyfriend, shot and left her for dead in the cemetery. Does that put him in a bad light? It certainly didn't put him in the running for the Nobel Peace Prize.

"What was the first thing you remember on awakening?" I asked

This answer, like her others, came slowly, after a pause and on the heels of a breath. "I was wondering why Stuart never showed up. And then I remembered why. It was like a dual memory."

I wondered about the differences between this story and the story Sergeant MacRae had recorded in his interview notes. What happened to the part where Stuart ordered Tony into the trunk? I made a mental note to check the police reports for other inconsistencies. And I reminded myself that if Sylvia Jackson's story had changed, it didn't necessarily mean she was lying. People with head injuries have malleable memories. Memories of the past get folded in with new information and fantasies. It becomes impossible to tell where truth ends and fabrication begins.

One thing was absolutely clear to me: Sylvia Jackson believed what she was saying. And it sounded plausible. After all, as Stuart Jackson had pointed out, everyone knows husbands kill wives. That was what Ralston Bridges had counted on. Had Sylvia Jackson's attacker done the same thing? Created a careful trail of evidence that pointed to a jealous, obsessive husband?

It would be so much better for Sylvia Jackson, so much easier all around, if a jury found Stuart Jackson guilty. There would be someone to blame, someone to lock up. Then, Syl's world could once again become benign. If I got him off, who would pay for this nightmare? If only Stuart Jackson had dropped by that night for one of his frequent visits. If only he'd walked in and been in time, maybe he could have saved her. At least he could have saved himself. But then, of course, he'd have had to go on living just as before. Only, as I knew too well, it would never again be just as before.

Don't go there, I told myself. I pulled over a large black binder from the materials I'd stacked on the table. I made myself focus on the question at hand: Could Sylvia Jackson remember what happened just before she was shot? Unlikely. But short of turning back the clock and becoming a fly on the wall, there was no way to tell for sure. The best I could do was to determine whether now, six months later, she could recall something that she'd just seen.

"I'm going to show you some pictures," I told her. "I want you to look at each one carefully for about five seconds. These pictures are very similar, one to the other. If you see a change from the one you've just been looking at, say 'stop' and tell me what change you see. Let's do a couple for practice."

I got my stopwatch out of my pocket. Syl pulled her wheelchair closer to the table. She was tense.

I opened the binder to a coloring book–style picture of a Christmas tree and pushed the start button. The second hand jerked forward. After five seconds, I turned the page. The angel at the top of the tree was gone. Syl said nothing.

I waited five more seconds and turned the page again. Now there was no change. I reminded her. "Say 'stop' if you see a change."

Five more seconds. Turn. The presents under the tree disappeared. I paused as the second hand continued to sweep the dial.

"You're going too fast," Syl complained.

"I know it may seem like I'm going too fast, but just try to keep focused on this and do the best you can."

Turn. This time there was no change.

"Stop," Syl murmured. I brought out a piece of white paper and covered the picture.

She looked at me, startled. "I need to—" she protested.

"Remember, we're just practicing to give you an idea how the test works," I explained. "You said 'stop.' Did you notice a change?"

She nodded slowly and in her breathy voice said, "There were gifts under the tree. Now they're gone."

"Very good. You see, that's how it goes," I said and put the practice cards aside.

Next, I showed her a series of line drawings of a house with a landscape around it. Over the course of fifty pictures, there are eighteen changes. The sun disappears. The front door. The chimney. The average person notices about fourteen changes. Syl caught three.

The second series of pictures was of a cowboy and an Indian fighting—not politically correct, but the test was developed back in the fifties. I repeated the directions and started my stopwatch. Syl glanced at me nervously and gripped the arms of her wheelchair with grim determination. Then she turned her attention to the first picture.

I turned the page. The cowboy's scarf disappeared. Syl just stared at the page.

Next page. No change. Syl remained still. Her frown deepened when I turned to the next page where, again, there was no change. I waited. Syl shifted nervously in her seat.

I turned the page. The Indian's headdress disappeared. Still she said nothing.

I turned the page again.

"Stop!" she cried out. I covered the picture. She squinted at the blank page and took a long breath before saying, "The Indian's feathers are gone." She looked at me anxiously and I nodded encouragement. She smiled brightly and ran her hand through her hair. Then she turned her attention back to the pictures on the table.

The next picture was identical to the previous one. Syl started to say something and ended up clearing her throat instead.

I turned the page. A knife on the ground disappeared. Syl stared at the picture.

I turned the page. No change. Pause.

I turned the page. No change. Pause.

I turned the page. The cowboy's upraised fists disappeared.

I continued, uncovering and covering each picture in turn. Syl flinched with each new page. She swore softly under her breath. She seemed to know that she should be seeing the details as they dropped out, but they were gone from her memory before she could grab hold.

I turned the page. The spurs on the cowboy's boots disappeared.

She whispered, "Stop!"

I waited as she sat there, her brow wrinkled, staring first at the white piece of paper I'd placed over the picture, then at my face as if looking for clues.

"The tree is gone," she said finally, sighing and releasing the tendons in her neck.

I recorded her response. There had been a tree in the house series, but none in the cowboy series.

Trying to keep my face neutral, I said, "You're doing just fine."

I turned the page. No change. Syl said nothing. She shifted in her seat.

I turned the page. A rifle leaning against a tree disappeared. She was holding the seat of her wheelchair as if it might take off at top speed at any moment. She said nothing.

Three pages later, after the fence posts disappeared, she said, "The barn."

"The barn," I repeated, to be sure I'd heard correctly.

She gave a staccato nod. "It's gone."

I made a note of her answer and wondered where it had come from. There was no barn in any of the pictures she'd been shown.

As she stared at the final picture—the cowboy and the Indian, now bareheaded, without weapons or upraised fists—there was a soft tap at the door behind me. Syl looked up. Her eyes widened, and her whole body seemed to reel back with terror. I jumped up, knocking over my chair, and positioned myself between Syl and whatever danger she saw. Then, just as quickly, the fear vanished and pleasure transformed her.

I turned around in time to see the door draw open. The face that had terrified Syl through the vertical strip of glass in the doorway reappeared through the widening gap.

"Angel!" Syl said, delighted to see him.

Olive-skinned, his dark hair slicked back from his face, Angel looked like he belonged in an Armani ad. His eyes had a hooded, sleepy look. He was big, though not especially tall. Massive shoulder muscles rippled under a yellow polo shirt.

"You okay, babe? Anything wrong?"

Syl touched her palm to her breast. "I was just surprised to see a face in the glass. You startled me is all." Syl stretched out a hand toward him. Angel came around behind and stood against her back, his big hands possessively on her shoulders, the fingers gently encircling her slim, pale neck.

She craned her head back to look up at him, pressing gently against the bulge in his pants. "Angel, this is Dr. Zip."

I was in a cold sweat, the aftermath of the adrenaline rush that had sent massive amounts of epinephrine cruising through my bloodstream. Definitely an overreaction. But it was nothing new — trauma creates a groove. Similar feelings can send you hurtling there without a moment's notice. Thinking consciously about it in the second person helped me hold it at arm's length.

I wiped my palms on my pants. "Dr. Peter Zak," I said.

He extended a beefy hand.

Syl gave me a coy smile. "Angelo is family."

"You're related to . . . ?" I asked

Angelo looked uncomfortable. Syl filled in the blank. "Tony was his uncle."

"I'm sorry," I said, not knowing what else to say. "I'm here to evaluate Ms. Jackson. I'm working for the public defender."

"Can't you people leave her alone?" He scowled. "First that cop, now you. What are you evaluating?"

"Ms. Jackson's memory."

He stared at me thoughtfully, his thumbs working at the back of Syl's neck. "You a friend of her ex?" he asked.

"No. I have to be impartial. Any connection with the defendant, the victim, the family, other than this professional one with Ms. Jackson, suggests a conflict of interest."

He looked intrigued and seemed to be about to ask another question when Syl stretched out her arms and yawned.

"Tired, babe?" Angelo asked.

She smiled weakly and shifted in her chair.

"I can come back tomorrow to finish up if you prefer," I offered.

Angelo came around and knelt in front of Syl. He took her face in his hands and kissed her gently on the forehead. "You look beat." She wearily lay her head against his palm and closed her eyes.

"No problem. Tomorrow, then." I was glad to have an excuse for bagging it early. I was suddenly overwhelmed by fatigue, left in the wake of those fight-or-flight hormones.

I gathered up my test materials and walked back to the nurses' station. A man in a baggy brown suit, his back to me, was leaning casually against the counter and chatting with Nurse Lovely. Lovely was perched on a stool, her chin resting flirtatiously on her palm, laughing at something he'd just said. When I got closer, I noticed his hand on the counter was covering hers. When she saw me, the pleasure melted from her face and she reddened. She yanked away her hand and drew herself up to a standing position. I pretended not to notice and reached past her to put away Sylvia Jackson's chart.

"Hey, Doc," Angelo called out as he came trotting down the hall. "Hang on a sec."

I turned and waited.

"So, how's she doing?"

"I really can't tell you how she's doing because I don't know. That's something you have to ask her doctor."

"But come on, Doc, how's her memory?"

I shrugged.

He continued, "Listen, she's going home in a couple of weeks. It would sure help me to know, you know, if there's anything I should set up to help her out."

"Really, I'm not the right person to ask."

"She remembers, Doc. She remembers everything that happened to her. You think so, too, don't you?"

Exasperated, I repeated myself, "I really wouldn't know. Head injury is very unpredictable. You never know what someone will remember." My voice echoed off the hospital walls. I turned around and realized both nurses and the brown-suited man were staring at me.

"What do you mean, unpredictable?" Angelo persisted.

He reminded me of a bulldog we had when I was a kid. Thick as a brick, physically and mentally. Couldn't let go once he'd latched onto something. I lowered my voice. "I once had a patient who ran his car into the back of a truck. He was ejected right through a closed sunroof. Didn't remember that he was in a car accident. Hadn't a clue where he was going. What does he remember? He remembers the license plate of the guy he hit. Head injury is a very unpredictable thing. I'm constantly surprised by it myself."

I left Angelo with his mouth hanging open, waggled my fingers at Lovely, and walked over to wait for the elevator.

The man in the brown suit must have followed me because a moment later, he'd inserted himself in the small space between me and the closed elevator doors, his face two inches from mine. This definitely wasn't my day. He hitched up his trousers, waved a gold badge at me, and boomed. "I understand you've been annoying Ms. Jackson."

Now I recognized him—the hair matched the blazing red ears. I wondered if Sergeant MacRae recognized me. It had been dark in Johnny D's and I'd kept my back to him.

"Annoying her? I could ask you the same thing. I'd have thought a legitimate police investigation would have been wrapped up by now."

MacRae glared at me, his eyes simmering. He poked a finger into my chest. "Why are they letting someone like you in here to mess with her recovery?"

"I'm neither messing with her recovery nor am I annoying her," I said, trying to resist the urge to poke back or pop him one. "And what the hell business is it of yours, anyway?"

"Just watch your step. She's already been through enough without quacks giving her more grief."

The elevator arrived. The doors slid open and the people waiting inside were baffled by the backside of a brown suit that filled the opening.

"Whatever you say, Mac."

He drew himself up. "Excuse me?" I enjoyed watching his reaction.

"That's what they call you, isn't it, Detective Sergeant MacRae?"

He stared at me, his eyes cold. "And I know what they call you, too, Dr. Zak."

Then slowly, deliberately, he started moving forward. I could stay where I was and get run over or shift aside. I shifted.

I got on the elevator and turned back. MacRae strode down the hall toward Sylvia Jackson's room. Nurse Lovely watched him moving off. Then her eyes locked briefly with mine, but not before she'd shut down an expression of anguish.

9

THE NEXT day started off auspiciously. I got to the boathouse before the crowd and was alone on the river as the sun was rising through a haze of pink and gold beyond the aquamarine glass Hancock Tower. The sun lit fires in the windows of one floor, then the next of MIT's Green Building, until all the windows were ablaze and I could imagine the weather dome on top taking off like a great flying saucer.

The water was flat as glass—the only sound the swooping of the oars, the only wake the ribbon of silver I was laying down behind me. Each dip of the oars left two indentations in the water, dots on either side of the silver line. I pulled harder until the stern cleared the puddles before the oars dipped again. Boat, body, mind became one as I pushed it, harder and harder, and the hull lifted, the water providing less and less resistance.

The Zen-like calmness, the exhilaration lingered long after I'd showered and dressed. I surfed my car through the morning traffic and there was no Lovely breathing fire at me from the nurses' station.

I found Sylvia Jackson in her room. She was in her wheel-chair, eating breakfast from a tray. She looked up at me without a flicker of recognition. She took a deep breath and pushed out the words. "You looking for someone?"

Detective MacRae was lounging in a plastic cushioned chair, his feet up on the bed. He'd traded the rumpled brown suit for a dark blue one. He took one look at me, scowled, picked up a newspaper from the bed, and put it in front of his face.

"Ms. Jackson? Dr. Zak. Back, as promised."

The light dawned. "Oh, gosh!" she said, smoothing her hair. "Of course."

"Hope I'm not interrupting," I said, checking my watch.

Syl said, "I was just finishing," as Mac growled something unintelligible.

She handed the tray to me and I set it down at the foot of the bed. "Can you just give me a minute?" she asked. "I need to use the little girls' room." She wheeled herself into the private bath and closed the door.

MacRae folded up the newspaper and slapped it down on the bed. He shook his head. "Next thing you know, they'll be fingerprinting people who get mugged."

"Listen, Sergeant. You have your job to do. I have mine. A man's life is at stake."

He stood up slowly, puffed out his chest so far his chin turned double. He hooked his thumbs over his belt. "Scumbag," he spat the word out. "Deserves everything that's coming to him. And more." He stomped out of the room.

Was this just a guy who'd seen too many creeps get away with murder? My own anger at the team who defended my wife's murderer came back to me. My fury at the supercilious psychologist whose evaluation traced Ralston Bridges's problems back to abuse he'd suffered as a child. Then I remembered the cop who had arrived that night to investigate. Like MacRae, he made no secret of what had probably been drilled into his head at the police academy and reinforced by experience — nine times out of ten, the husband did it.

Syl reappeared with a little pleated paper cup in her lap. "Sorry. I need another minute. Forgot to take my pills."

"Doesn't the nurse usually watch you take those?"

"I guess so." She looked momentarily perplexed, her eyebrows together. Then she brightened. "Oh, I know. I was on the phone so she left them for me. You know, Carolyn and I have a special relationship. I must have taken them into the bathroom and then forgotten all about them."

One by one, Syl placed each pill on the back of her tongue, took a drink of water, and swallowed deliberately. A verse from a folk song went through my head, "There's a green one, and a pink one, and a blue one, and a yellow one. . . ." Only instead of boxes made of ticky-tacky, these were a smorgasbord of the wonder drugs that have rendered straitjackets and talk therapy obsolete. There really did seem to be more of them today. I made a mental note to check Syl's chart to see whether they had her on any new meds.

On her way out of the room, the wheelchair got stuck on a large green gym bag that was half under the bed. She struggled, back and forth, to free herself. "He's always leaving his junk here."

"Sergeant MacRae?" I asked.

"No—Angelo. Says it's a Ruggiero family trait. Genetic. Tony's the same way . . ." Her voice broke. Then she cleared her throat, inhaled, and spoke carefully. "Was the same, that is. Always used to leave his things . . ." She left the sentence dangling, as if unsure where to go next.

"It's been hard, hasn't it?" I said.

Syl nodded as if she didn't trust herself to say the words. Then she stared at me. "You do understand, don't you?"

There was that uncanny intuition again. I tugged the gym bag from beneath the wheel. Then I pushed Syl down to the conference room. I was careful to sit at right angles and beyond arm's reach. Today we'd do the Rorschach Test, but I never start with it. It provides a peephole directly into the subject's emotional insides. I usually start with something much more neutral, as I did today with questions from an intelligence test.

Just as I'd expected, Syl scored well on the test of general knowledge. What direction does the sun set? On what continent is the Gobi Desert? If you went from New York to Rio de Janeiro, what direction would you be going? She knew the answers. Her recall of old stuff was largely intact. But after every question, there were long stretches of silence while Syl pondered, then picked her words, and finally tried to coordinate her breathing with her voice to get the words out. Occasionally she forgot the question before she could deliver her answer. And if I tried to move on to the next question while she was still thinking, she'd become upset and confused. The normally fifteen-minute test took nearly a half hour to complete.

When we finished, I pulled over the stack of inkblots I'd left facedown on the table. I'd learned to expect the unexpected with this test and I was interested to see how Syl would respond.

"Did you ever sit on a beach looking at clouds?" I asked her by way of preamble. Syl nodded. "Ever imagine that clouds look like something familiar?"

She shifted in her seat, like she was trying to get comfortable. I hadn't noticed how pale Syl was. The dark lines of her blood vessels, like long narrow bruises, ran down her neck and disappeared under the V-necked T-shirt. I tapped the stack of cards against the table edge to straighten them and flipped through quickly to be sure they were in the right order.

"Well, I'm going to show you some inkblots, and what I want you to do is tell me what they look like, what they could be. This is very much like looking at clouds. There are no right or wrong answers; different people see different things. Are you ready?" Syl was breathing rapidly. Her nod was little more than a shudder.

She grasped the arms of the chair. I took the first card, flipped it over, and held it out with one hand while starting the stopwatch with the other. I held it close to her so she could take it from me.

But she didn't. She brushed the back of her hand lightly across her forehead and looked distractedly around the room. "Doctor," she whispered. Then she reached out and clutched my hand instead of the card. Her fingers were icy cold. The skin of her face looked like parchment and her lips were bluish. She was breathing rapidly and pushing out the words, "I feel . . . funny . . . fuzzy . . . c-c-c-cold . . ."

She took a shallow breath and her head dropped. Then she lifted it and looked toward me with unfocused eyes. She shuddered violently just before her eyes slid up under her eyelids and she slumped over.

"Ms. Jackson?" I shouted, shaking her by the shoulder. "Help!" I shouted, even though no one could hear me through the closed door. I scanned the room. I hit the emergency call button. Then I yanked the door open and ran toward the nurses' station. "She's unconscious!" I yelled, hoping I was right.

Lovely appeared out of nowhere and charged past me with a what-have-you-done-to-her-now look on her face. The Code Blue announcement barely registered as a doctor and another nurse materialized, one from a stairwell and the other from a nearby room.

MacRae emerged from the men's room. The two of us watched from the hall, picking up little snatches of conversation from the group huddled over Syl, who was now stretched out on the conference table — "Blood pressure's falling," "When did she have her last meds?" and finally, "Lavage!"

"Shit, shit, shit," I hissed, under my breath. I couldn't stand that feeling of helplessness, of knowing something terrible was happening and being powerless to act, to help, to prevent.

"Worried this might throw off your schedule?" MacRae sneered.

I turned on him. "You stupid sonofabitch." I might have

taken a swing at him but just then, a nurse came out of the room and ran between us. She returned a moment later with rubber tubing and an oversized plastic syringe. The interruption gave me what I needed to regroup. I walked over to the window and stared out over the river. It was very quiet as they worked.

An orderly arrived with a gurney. A few moments later he departed, the gurney now bearing Syl's inert shape, one of the nurses trotting alongside holding aloft an IV bag.

MacRae turned to me and barked, "Don't leave the building." As he strode over to the nurses' station to grab the phone, I flipped him the bird.

All alone, I walked back into the now empty conference room. My notebooks and Rorschach cards were strewn on the floor. Syl's wheelchair looked forlorn, shunted off into a corner. I squatted to gather up my things. I gagged. The sweet smell of vomit permeated the room.

I left the room and walked down the hall. On the way, I stopped at a water cooler and helped myself to a drink. I steadied my hand to raise the little pleated paper cup to my mouth.

As I sat and waited in the solarium, I reviewed the symptoms: low blood pressure, pallor, low body temperature, rapid breathing. Any one of a million drugs could cause symptoms like that and she was probably taking some of them. But where had those pills come from? Were they really left by the nurse when Sylvia Jackson was on the phone? If so, when?

I didn't have to wait long before MacRae reappeared. "She's in the ICU. She's going to be okay." I didn't say anything. "It's a good thing someone was with her," he added grudgingly, "otherwise . . ." He took out a little pad and started to write. "Doctor, did you give her any medication?"

Now he wasn't being hostile. He needed something from me. I wanted to wrench the pad from him, tear off the pages, and shove them down his throat. Instead, I counted to five and said, "I'm not her doctor. It's not my job to prescribe or administer drugs. But I did see her take some." MacRae's pencil paused in midair. "When she came out of the bathroom, she had a little cup full of pills she said she'd forgotten to take."

"Pills? How many?"

"A lot. She usually takes a half dozen, give or take a few."

He scratched notes on his pad. "You say you watched her take them?"

"And I poured her some water." I could see Syl, rolling out of the bathroom, the little cup of brightly colored pills balanced in her lap. "I wonder what happened to the cup."

"Wait here," MacRae barked, and he was up and out the door. Maybe he wasn't so stupid after all. I tried to remember. Had she put it down on the bedside table? Did she throw it into the wastebasket?

He returned a minute later, empty-handed. "You sure about that cup?"

I nodded. "Definitely. A white pleated paper cup."

"Paper cup," he said, jotting the words into his notebook.

"White pleated paper cup," I said.

"Anyone else see her take those pills?"

I shook my head.

"Anyone else around at the time?"

"No one but you."

He ignored it. "Depending on what happens, we may need to call you in for questioning." He snapped his little notebook closed, fished a card from his pocket, and held it out to me. "Dr. Zak, if you remember anything, call me"—I looked at the card—"please." I took it and shoved it into my pocket.

When I got back to the Pearce, I called Chip. "Sylvia Jackson collapsed this morning while I was testing her. They rushed her to intensive care."

"The D.A.'s office called us. Already they're blaming us, though I'm not sure what for. Annie went over to the hospital to get it firsthand. So what do you think happened?"

"She'd just taken some pills she found in her bathroom."

"Found?"

"She said the nurse left them for her. Definitely not standard hospital procedure. But it can happen. It's also possible that they gave her the wrong meds. That happens sometimes. Especially with all the float nurses they're using these days who don't know one patient from another."

"Sounds suspicious."

"And there's something else fishy—when the detective went to Sylvia Jackson's room to look for the cup she'd taken the meds from, he couldn't find it." I wondered how hard he'd looked. "Of course, she might have thrown it away in the hall or in the conference room." Or he might have found it and tucked it into his pocket. "Or it might have been in her wheelchair. Didn't occur to me to check."

"Peter, could that many pills kill someone?"

"The pills that Sylvia Jackson takes regularly? Probably not. But a double dose could make you very sick. Have they analyzed stomach contents or done a toxic blood screen?"

"Annie's trying to find out. She said she'd stop by the Pearce early tomorrow morning at around eight and give you an update."

"Well, at least now we know one thing," I said.

"What's that?"

"If someone's still trying to kill Sylvia Jackson, it ain't Stuart."

10

My ALARM went off at six the next morning. Overnight, the air had developed a pre-winter chill and I awoke, cocooned in a double layer of blanket. It was dark, and I could tell that even after the sun came up, a damp overcast sky would make the day a perpetual twilight.

My mood matched the day. I wanted to sleep and go on sleeping. I must have dozed off because next thing I knew, it was after six-thirty. With a supreme act of will, I flung off the bedclothes and pulled on shorts and a T-shirt, shoved my feet into running shoes, grabbed a sweatshirt, and bolted out the door. I was halfway down the block when I realized I'd forgotten to bring a change of clothes. It was too late to turn back.

The jog to the river and a nasty wind whipping in from the north helped wake me up. The Charles was greasy gray, and choppy little whitecaps dotted its surface. I pushed open the door to the dark, fetid wooden boathouse. It was full of other equally unshaven, reluctant early risers who hadn't yet had their morning cups of coffee. Everyone there was intent on just one thing—getting a boat into the water. Civil greetings and conversation were for after.

I descended a flight of stairs, its ancient treads scooped out and worn smooth. At water level, I was surrounded by sleek white racing shells with an occasional red or blue one. They were perched in racks on either side of me and in slings overhead. A huge gray rectangle loomed ahead where the double doors were flung open to the river.

I pulled out my oars and put them outside on the edge of the dock. Then I went back and lowered my boat from its overhead sling and carried it out. I set it gently in the water, trying not to splash myself. I set the oars into the oarlocks, kicked off my sneakers, and got into the boat. I slid my bare feet into the shoes that were bolted to the cross-stretcher and pressed the Velcro fasteners into place. The boat was already rocking in the choppy water.

I pushed off from the dock, turned the boat, and started to row, the seat sliding with each pull of the oars. The ride was bumpy as little waves lapped up against the shell. The occasional splash of tepid riverwater quickly turned icy against my skin.

I started to get into a rhythm, my muscles warming, the tension in my back and shoulders easing. The boathouse grew smaller. The river widened. I passed the MIT boathouse on the opposite shore, a high-tech cube plunked down in the middle of the river, connected by a concrete gangway to the shore. I rowed on steadily, my senses coming to life. Mist wrapped me in a skin of moist coolness and the stench of the Charles—sea air and sewage—became pleasurable.

I pushed myself harder and was just starting to feel my mind disconnect from my body when a wave hit the boat from the Boston side, shattering my concentration. My entire left side—shirt, shorts, shoes—was soaked. Annoyed, I watched a white motorboat speed away. I tried to steady the shell, leaning away from the wake, raising the gunnel that separated me from the water. Like a roller coaster, the boat climbed and fell, the bow flipping back and forth.

I was cursing and telling myself to let it go, calm down, get back into a rhythm, when another motorboat appeared. This time, I watched as it sped toward me. The driver had on what looked like a dark sweatshirt with the hood pulled low over his face. I wanted to stand up and wave my arms but I knew the boat would capsize. More than that, I wanted to take a revolver out of my pocket and pop the jerk between the eyes. Instead, I steadied the oars across and waited in a cold fury. "Asshole!" I screamed as the motorboat roared past. All I could do was sit there as a second wake hit me. Now I was soaked on both sides.

I loosened my cramped hands and flexed my fingers. This was unheard of. Fucking unbelievable. There were never motorboats out this early, never mind two of them. I yearned to keep going, to get back to that place where I could zone out. But the water in the boat was nearly up to my ankles.

Angrily, I started to turn back. I was perpendicular to the river, rowing across to the other side, when an unpleasant thought occurred to me. Both times, it had been a small, white, nondescript speedboat. Suppose it was the same boat? Then I heard the sound. I hoped it was a plane making its approach to Logan. Or a motorcycle roaring down Memorial Drive. But I knew better. I turned and watched the boat speeding toward me. It skimmed along, slapping the surface, spray spewing behind. This time, the guy wasn't fooling around. He was aiming straight at me.

Quickly, I reversed the oars and backed the boat down, trying to avoid a direct hit. The drone turned edgy and sharp. I backed furiously, barely registering the panic and fear that had washed away my rage. It sounded as if a jet engine were bearing down on me. Push. Push. Push. And then the impact. The speedboat nipped a corner of the shell and flipped it.

My glasses flew off as I went over. The water was a warm soup compared to the chilly air. In the dark turbulence, I tried not to inhale. I thrashed around, losing all sense of direction, until my lungs felt as if they would burst. Then, from somewhere, a calmness grew out from the center of my chest. I relaxed, the dark behind my eyelids lifting like waves of heat lightning. I felt only weightlessness as I hung, suspended. I could just let go, inhale, and it would all be over. Then, as in a slow-motion ballet, my body curled fetal and righted itself, and my head emerged into the air pocket under the overturned shell. I gasped for air and reached out for the sides of the boat. I hung there, catching my breath, feeling the slimy water icing my head and shoulders. I listened to the wake lapping, lapping against the outside of the shell and my ragged breathing echoing inside.

I tried not to think about how deliberate it seemed. How the hooded figure seemed to draw a bead on me and then mow me down. I could see Ralston Bridges at the helm, laughing. But I knew it was a made-up memory, manufactured for this moment when all forms of danger and personal malice brought his face to mind.

I heard a distant buzzing. I froze. It was definitely growing louder. There wasn't time to check out what was coming or where it was coming from. In a blind panic, I took a gulp of air and dove down, swimming underwater as fast as I could in what I hoped was the direction of the Cambridge shore. By the time I surfaced, the drone of the motorboat was receding. A wave of relief washed over me. I took a few more strokes, reached a footing at the base of the Mass Ave Bridge, and climbed out, my arms and legs scraping against the rough stone. I huddled, clinging to the bridge abutment, shivering. Blood oozed from where my feet had been ripped loose from the shell. The acrid smell and the cooing that seemed to come from the bridge itself gave me a clue as to the origin of the white that coated the girders. Pigeon shit. I listened, straining to sort out the competing sounds. All I heard was the benign rumble of cars, the thump of an occasional bus crossing the bridge, and the rhythmic drone of what was probably a traffic helicopter checking out the morning rush on Storrow Drive.

I expected to see my boat bobbing in the ripples. But even without my glasses I could see it had vanished. A shard of white came floating over to me on the remains of the wake. I reached out and grabbed it. Barely five inches long, it was all I had left of my boat. I turned it over, my hands trembling. The boat had been a gift from Kate. "You bastard!" I screamed, my words carried away by the wind. "You shitty sonofabitch. What kind of dumb-ass would pull a stunt like—" And then I woke up to the certainty that this wasn't some idiot, some stunt. It had been quite deliberate, probably personal. The anger froze into fear. I steadied myself. I zipped the boat fragment into my shorts pocket and scanned up the river and down. Then I threw myself into the water and stroked as fast as I could to the river's edge. Winded, I clung to a steel ladder set into the stone wall. I hung there breathing heavily, my body feeling like dead weight, becoming colder by the second and nauseated by my own stench. I was so tired I couldn't twist around to see if anyone or anything was bearing down on me. Raw fear propelled me up the ladder, the metal rungs cutting into the bottoms of my bare feet. I grasped the top of the ancient cast-iron fence, the last obstacle between the river and the shore. I was hauling myself over when the top broke away and I came crashing down with it onto the grass. I struggled to my feet in a blind rage, wrenched the broken fencing free, and flung it as hard as I could toward the river. It hit the water with a satisfying splash.

I walked back, muttering to myself and ignoring the early morning dog walkers, joggers, and bicyclists who shared the pathway alongside the river. By the time I got to the boathouse, I had deluded myself into believing that I was completely rational and convinced myself that something serious was going on. I called the cops.

"Sorry, sir," a voice on the police emergency line whined, "did you say you had an accident with your boat along Memorial Drive? Is this a boat trailer?"

"No, I was rowing. Someone tried to run me over."

"Someone tried to run over your rowboat on Memorial Drive?"

By now I was steaming. "I was rowing on the Charles. You know, in the water. Someone tried to kill me."

"Someone . . . tried . . . to . . . kill . . . you," she repeated, I hoped she was writing it down. "And your name, sir?"

I wanted to scream, "Stop reading from that stupid script!" but instead I spelled my name.

She painstakingly repeated each letter. "And where are you now? And are you in any danger right now, sir? And sir, do you need medical attention?"

"No, I don't need medical attention."

"An officer will be with you shortly." Pause. "Sir, are you sure you don't need a doctor?"

"Not unless I have a stroke from talking to you!" I screamed. I slammed down the phone.

Next, I called the Pearce.

First thing Gloria says is, "Did you know you had an eight o'clock?"

Fireworks started going off again in my head. "Yes, I know I had an eight o'clock appointment. And guess what? I'm not there. Instead, I'm here at the boathouse trying to figure out who's trying to kill me."

"Whoa, calm down. Someone's trying to kill you?"

I recognized the tone. It's the one she uses with patients who think they're Jesus Christ.

"Gloria, it's not paranoia when you're surrounded by assassins," I said, exhausted.

"Peter, are you all right?"

I gave a weak laugh. "Right as rain."

"Hang on a sec, someone wants to talk to you."

Annie's voice came on, deadly serious. "Who's trying to kill you?"

The words rushed out. "Some asshole in a motorboat ran into

me. First he buzzes me from one side, then from the other. Then he runs me over. Then he comes back and smashes the boat to smithereens for good measure."

"Any witnesses?"

"I don't think so. I called the cops and they're sending someone over."

"Peter—" Annie started. I sneezed. "The nurse here says you're okay. Are you?"

I sneezed again.

"You don't sound okay. You sound miserable."

"I'm soaked to the bone, freezing cold. I smell like something that took a swim in a cesspool. And my foot looks like a chew toy. I desperately need a hot shower but I have to wait for the police to get here."

"Would coffee help?"

I felt a rush of gratitude. A cup of coffee at that very moment would have been a healing balm. The phantom aroma of French roast tickled the back of my nose. "It certainly would."

"It's on the way."

"You're an angel. Make it an extra large. Light, no sugar. And Annie, there's an old pair of sweats in my office. Would you mind bringing those over, too, with the pair of glasses that should be in my top desk drawer? Ask Gloria to let you in."

"You lost your glasses?"

I sneezed.

"Just sit tight. I'm on my way."

11

I DRAGGED a moldy blanket from a corner of the boathouse. With my teeth chattering, I shook it out and wrapped it around me. On my way out to the dock, the blanket caught on the doorjamb. I ripped a hole in it yanking it loose. Cursing, I stomped outside and got my sneakers.

By the time I got back up to street level, two cars had pulled up. One was a police cruiser, its lights flashing. The other was a dark sedan. A redhead in a rumpled suit jumped out of the sedan and sauntered over to the window of the cop car and chatted with the officer at the wheel. After a minute, the cruiser doused its lights and pulled away. I waited at the door to greet Detective Sergeant Joseph MacRae. He looked me up and down, took a whiff, and recoiled. I was not amused.

I took him down to the dock, and while I'm pointing out where I'd been run down and he's writing notes in his little book, he comments, "Yesterday, Sylvia Jackson OD's with you at her side. Today, some person wearing a hood over his face runs down your boat." He shook his head. "You accident-prone?"

The fury that I'd had more or less under control snapped at

the smart-ass bait. "Fuck you, too. I get run over and practically killed and you're playing the comic. And in answer to your question, no, I'm not accident-prone and I don't go in for recreational swimming in the Charles. What about you? You much of a boater?"

He stiffened and slapped his book down on a bench. "What's your point?" he said, poking an index finger into my chest.

I batted it away. "My point is that maybe I'm not the only one involved in two accidents in two days."

He stuck out his chin and drew himself up, the effort to stay calm turning him pink. "Why don't you just start over and tell me what happened."

"Why the hell should I trust you?"

"Because it's my job," he said, clenching his fists. "How about you let me do it?"

"Let you do your job?" I laughed and took a step toward him, closing the gap between us to inches. "Now where have I heard that before? How about you let me do my job?"

He was up on the balls of his feet. The top of his head barely reached the tip of my nose. "Your job?" he sneered. "Is that what they teach you at Harvard? How to intimidate defenseless women who . . ."

"So what are you saying? Huh? Has Sylvia Jackson complained that I intimidate her?"

"Sylvia Jackson is extremely vulnerable."

"And I suppose that's why you're hanging around all the time, to give her the protection she needs?"

He sputtered, reaching for a comeback. Then he narrowed his eyes and squinted up at me. "What I can't figure out is why you're involved in this case anyway, after what happened to you the last time—"

He didn't get a chance to finish. A red flash of anger grew out of my chest and I rammed my fist into his face. He staggered and slowly toppled over backwards into the water. Time seemed to stop as I stood there, stunned. It's out of character for me to get angry, never mind hit someone. My analytical side took over for an instant and I noted it felt damned good.

I didn't get to savor the moment. A minute later he came up thrashing, screaming profanities at the top of his lungs. He hauled himself up and came lunging back at me. His right to the jaw missed but the knee he brought up hard into my stomach didn't. I doubled over and he whacked his arm across my shoulder blades. I grunted and found myself spread-eagle on the dock. He yanked my arms back and handcuffed them together behind me.

"There, this is much better," he said as he ground his heel into my butt.

"You bastard," I wheezed, trying to catch my breath.

"Let's see, assaulting an officer, resisting arrest—"

I heard a yell, footsteps coming hard down the stairs and across the dock.

"Mac, what the hell are you doing?" It was Annie. "Peter, you all right?" Then, "What on earth—you're *both* soaked!"

"You know this bozo?" MacRae asked her.

"Yeah, I know him. He's a friend of mine."

"You've got strange taste in friends. Now I remember. You're working for the public defender. That explains it. Never did know what was good for you."

"And you did?" There was a long pause during which I assume Annie and MacRae engaged in a glaring contest while I tried to keep my face out of the duck shit that coated the dock. Annie finally broke the silence. "How's your mother these days? Last time I saw her was at the wake."

MacRae eased some of the pressure on my ass. "She's holding up. She's a strong woman. Misses my dad." The anger was gone from his voice.

"Yeah, I miss my dad, too," Annie said. "But then, we lost him long before his wake."

"Annie—" MacRae started.

He'd loosened up on me enough so that I scrambled free.

But I couldn't get far on my knees with my hands cuffed behind me.

"Time-out!" Annie cried and stepped between us. MacRae had his legs apart, knees flexed like he was ready to spring. "Just a darned minute here. What happened anyway?"

"He assaulted me," MacRae said, his voice petulant.

"And what are you doing here anyway?" Annie asked. "Since when have you taken up sculling?"

"Yeah, how come you sent that other cop away?" I threw in.

MacRae eased his stance. "I happened to hear the call so I came to investigate."

"Lucky me," I muttered, struggling to my feet, wondering if luck had anything to do with it.

"So how the hell did you two end up like this?" Annie pressed. "Come on, Mac, what's with the handcuffs? Put yourself in Peter's position. He's out on the river and someone tries to run him down. You'd be pretty ticked off, too."

MacRae mumbled something.

"Come on, Mac. Just pretend Peter's one of your buddies."

"Annie, that's not fair," MacRae protested.

"You cops always did have one set of rules for your friends, another for the rest of humanity." I had the distinct impression Annie was calling in some ancient chit.

Grudgingly, MacRae reached over and undid the cuffs, but not before yanking my arms back for good measure.

I sat on a wooden bench and rubbed my wrists. I coughed up some brackish water and grimaced. My ribs already ached and my back felt as if I'd been hit with a two-by-four. It was some consolation to see MacRae rubbing his jaw.

Annie passed me an extra large cup of Dunkin' Donuts coffee. I peeled back the lid and inhaled. I took a sip. It had been a long time since coffee tasted this good. "I'd have brought you a cup, too, if I'd known you were going to be here," she told MacRae.

He reached for a foot and was hopping around, struggling to

remove a shoe. I slid over to make room on the bench. He sat down and took off one shoe and then the other, draining each one onto the dock. Then he tilted his head one way, then the other, and banged on the opposite side to get the water out of his ears. He lifted an arm to his nose and sniffed. "And they say one day we're going to swim in this muck?"

He retrieved his pad, flipped it open, and started to write. "Okay," the word came out through gritted teeth, "so you went out rowing like you do every morning—"

"Yeah, like I do every morning, but you know that." I wondered what else Mac knew about my daily routine.

"And then what happened?" MacRae waited. He was trying to keep his teeth from chattering. I almost felt sorry for the guy.

I sighed and picked up the story where I'd left off earlier. He stopped writing when I got to the part where the motorboat came around one last time to smash my racing shell to smithereens.

"Did you notice anything in particular about the boat?"

"White. Small. About a twelve-footer."

"And the driver. Man or woman?"

I shrugged. "Beats me."

"And nobody saw this happen?"

"Hell, I don't know. It was still getting light. Between the traffic on Memorial Drive and the other rowers out on the river, somebody should have. But who, I don't know. Anyone report anything to the police?"

"Nada. So let me get this straight. You're telling me that someone in a motorboat takes a couple of practice runs and then mows you down and no one sees it. Then your boat gets blown away and there's nothing left of that either."

"Yeah, that's what I'm telling you. Do you have a problem with . . ." Just then I remembered. I unripped the pocket and pulled out my little keepsake.

"And this?"

"My boat."

"Get outta here," MacRae muttered, taking the shard of white and turning it over and looking up at me with what felt like newfound admiration.

"Listen, Doc, I'm going to write this up." MacRae flipped the notebook closed, started to shove it into a wet pocket, and thought better of it. "Can you come by headquarters later this afternoon? Make a formal statement. In the meanwhile, we'll see if we can find any witnesses."

He picked up his shoes and padded up the stairs. Annie and I watched as he made little toeprints on each step and disappeared into the boathouse.

Now I was starting to shiver. The blanket had ended up on the deck. I went over, picked it up, and wrapped it around my body.

"Peter," Annie asked, her voice serious, "do you think there's a connection?"

"Between what happened yesterday and this?"

"Well?"

"You know what Freud says about coincidences—there ain't no such animal."

"Who'd have known they could find you out on the river?"

I pulled the blanket closer around myself. "Just about anyone who knows me."

"Anyone connected with the Jackson case?"

I thought for a moment. "Shit. I mentioned it to Sylvia Jackson . . . and then she told Lovely. That's probably how MacRae knew."

"Lovely?"

"Great name for a nurse, don't you think? Particularly appropriate for this one. She's been less than helpful, to put it mildly."

"She probably realizes you're there to discredit her patient, even if Sylvia Jackson doesn't get it."

MacRae was right about one thing. Sylvia Jackson was very vulnerable. And she was doing a lousy job of picking whom to trust. But then, she didn't have a lot of options. "How's she doing?"

"Syl? She's recovering. But you won't be able to get back in there to finish testing for another week at least. She's telling everyone you're a hero. Saved her life."

"Yeah, right, big hero. And if I hadn't been there, she probably wouldn't have needed to have her life saved."

"What makes you think your being there had anything to do with what happened to her? I'd say it was just the opposite. If you hadn't been there, she might have died. She seems to have become quite attached to you. Could be, someone resents that attachment."

"And that's why they ran me down? Seems like a stretch. Was it a drug overdose?"

"Looks like it. They analyzed the food she had for breakfast. No poison. And they've ruled out the possibility that she got someone else's meds by mistake. So that leaves accidental—"

"—or deliberate overdose," I finished the thought. "It wouldn't be hard to engineer. All you'd have to do is leave pills lying around in her room. Eventually she'd notice and assume she'd forgotten to take them."

"So what do you make of her explanation that a nurse left the pills for her?"

"I'd take it with a grain of salt. She has a tendency to make up what she can't remember."

After Annie left, I walked back into the boathouse. I stared up at the sling where my boat should have been hanging. Why was this happening to me? My insides tightened with sadness. But then, just as quickly, the self-pity turned into rage and I yelled at the top of my lungs while the pigeons nesting in the eaves flew back and forth in confusion. When my voice gave out, I just sat there.

Later, while I was showering with my clothes on, lathering away the slime, I realized MacRae took with him all that was left of my boat. I wished I'd at least asked for a receipt.

12

THAT AFTERNOON, I drove over to the Cambridge police station and gave my statement. MacRae wasn't anywhere to be seen. An officious clerk promised that someone would call me if there were any developments.

Two days later, I hadn't heard a peep. The only reminder was my still tender rib cage. That and a deepening sense of loss. Gliding across the river at daybreak with only my racing shell and my own body had been like a purification ritual. If only for a short time, it cleared the miasma from my brain.

After a day's break, I was back rowing again. But in a borrowed shell and with the security of the crowd, it wasn't the same. Adding injury to insult, with every stroke, my muscles ached. The pain was like an annoying insect, constantly buzzing, keeping me from finding a comfortable rhythm.

Since my mind wouldn't let go, I chewed over the events of the past few days. Sylvia Jackson's overdose and the destruction of my boat had to be not only deliberate but connected. By the time I was showered, dressed, and back at work, my reluctance to get involved in this murder case had hardened into determination to see it through to the end.

As always, the routine at Pearce continued as if no outside world existed. Kwan gave me surprisingly little grief about my swim in the Charles. In fact, he was extremely solicitous. It was so out of character. So I decided to honor his birthday with a cake at staff meeting, reviving an old tradition. Traditions are good things—that's what I tell my patients. Patterns of behavior have a way of normalizing the extraordinary, of giving us the illusion that we're in control.

I drove over to Mike's in the North End to get a rum cake. I had them write, in turquoise letters across the top of the cake, *"40 and still kicking."* I had time to spare, or so I thought, until a truck driver who either couldn't read or couldn't measure got his truck wedged under a too low overpass. A trip that should have taken twenty minutes ended up taking an hour.

Kwan was ready for me. "Dr. Z! You're here! We're so glad you could find a moment in your busy schedule to grace us with your presence." He took off his jacket and laid it across the threshold. "Let me assist you. We wouldn't want you to get your feet dirty."

Kwan reached for my hand and finally noticed the box I was holding. "You come bearing gifts?"

"Beats the heck out of me," I said, looking at the box with surprise. "What could it be?" I pried open the cardboard and peeked inside. "Gadzooks! It is a cake. Now why do you suppose . . . ?"

As the light dawned, I had the pleasure of watching Kwan turn pink and then crimson as the color rose from the edge of his collar to his eyebrows, across his forehead to his hairline.

" 'Still kicking' Well, that's encouraging at least," he said.

"Now, don't you feel terrible?" Gloria asked him.

I couldn't resist adding, "This is what happens to you, my old friend. At forty, senility sets in and you forget your own birthday."

"I was trying to forget," he insisted. "It's a coping strategy, not a symptom."

"Yeah—and sometimes a cigar is just a cigar," I replied.

By the time we got around to business, only a ring of rum-flavored cream remained at the bottom of the box.

"A new patient, Maria Whitson," Gloria read the name from the board, "admitted last night. She tried to commit suicide. It's not the first time. Overdosed on an assortment of prescription drugs washed down with a pint of vodka. Her father brought her in after she called him on her cell phone."

"I saw her this morning after they pumped her stomach," Kwan said. "Kept asking if I was you."

"Me?" I asked, surprised. "She knows me?"

"Well, she must not. Or she'd have known that I'm not you, don't you think? After all, I am so much better-looking, not to mention the fact that I dress better."

I grinned. "Though you have to admit, after working together all these years, we have developed an uncanny resemblance."

Kwan continued, "She was definitely confused. Suffering from delirium. We'll have to wait till her system clears to tell what's going on. In the meantime, I've recommended suicide precautions."

Gloria jotted a note into her little book.

I reached for Maria Whitson's file from the nearby metal rack, opened it, and started to read: "Thirty-two years old. Divorced. No kids. Injured her head a few years ago when she got hit by a car. Since then she's been on the drug-du-jour program. They've got her taking a major tranquilizer, something for ulcers, lithium, Darvocet, an antidepressant, and, of course they've stuck her on two benzos at significant dosages." I shook my head but didn't hop on my usual soapbox about the dangerous, unpredictable long-term effects of these drugs. "A year ago she slit her wrists and climbed into a warm bath. Father found her that time, too. They treated her for severe depression and bulimia related to sexual abuse."

"Buh . . . lee . . . mee . . . ah." Gloria whispered, scratching more notes. Suicidal patients with eating disorders require special attention from the nursing staff.

"Jeez, Louise." I whistled. "This explains all the drugs. It looks like every time she got a new diagnosis, they added another drug. Listen to this: organic delusional disorder, bipolar illness, psychotic depression, post-traumatic stress disorder, multiple personality and borderline personality. Good grief. She was referred by Dr. Baldridge."

"Baldridge?" Gloria and Kwan echoed my surprise. Baldridge ran a little kingdom at the other end of the Pearce campus. I couldn't remember the last time we'd gotten a referral from him. Maybe the brain injury put her in a slightly different category from his average patient. Or maybe he'd just run out of wonder drugs.

I snapped the file shut and hung it back on the rack. "Gloria, how about we start walk rounds today by giving Ms. Whitson a mental status exam? Do you think she can tolerate the stimulation of having all the staff around her?"

"She's fragile but adjusting. I think she'll be all right with it."

Maria Whitson's room was the last one at the end of a corridor. The door was open. I knocked and entered, my colleagues close behind.

The corner room had two tall windows but the light that made it through the gray window shades did little to brighten the barren green walls and mud-colored linoleum tile floor. Invisible beneath the shades, metal screens were padlocked in place.

The mattress of the hospital bed had been stripped and the room smelled of disinfectant. In a corner, Maria's silent form looked like a pile of dirty laundry. She stared listlessly down into her lap. Her blond eyelashes were caked with white bits that stood out against the red outlines of her eyes. Her flesh was pale and doughy soft.

Kwan knelt beside Maria. "Hello," he said, "I'm Dr. Liu. I examined you earlier this morning."

Maria slowly raised her head to look at him. There was no recognition. Her eyes drifted about the room as he continued, "These are my colleagues." He introduced each of us in the courtly, respectful tone I've heard him, time and again, use so effectively with our patients.

He introduced me last. "And this is Dr. Peter Zak, the head of the unit here." As he said my name, she gave a slight start that dislodged a clump of stringy hair from behind her ear. "Dr. Zak would like to talk with you. Would that be all right?"

I held out my hand. Though she didn't grasp it in response, for an instant I had the sense that someone was peering over the barbed wire. Almost as quickly as I caught it, the look was gone.

"I would like to ask you a few questions," I said.

She looked at me blankly.

"Can you tell me who you are?" There was no response. "Your name?" I waited. "Your name is . . ."

Her mouth shaped the word, and in a little-girl voice she said, "Maria."

"Maria . . . ?"

"Whitson."

"Ms. Whitson, do you know where you are?"

No response.

I could feel Gloria's solid, reassuring figure moving to back me up. She came and squatted alongside me. I altered my position slightly as Gloria inched in closer. She took Maria Whitson's hand, the nails bitten down to the quick, a silver pinkie ring embedded in the flesh. "Maria?" she asked in a concerned, professional tone. "Do you remember me? I'm Gloria Alspag. I met you this morning. I'm the nurse in charge here. How are you doing? Is there anything we can get for you?"

We all waited. Maria opened her mouth but said nothing. She chewed on her lower lip. She began a low keening, rocking to and fro, hugging herself as if she were her own baby. The rocking slowed as she tilted her head to the side, allowing the clump of hair to shift away from her eyes.

Slowly and deliberately, she wiped her nose with the back of her hand. She asked, "Could I have a drink of water?"

Gloria started to get up but I placed my hand on her shoulder. I wanted Gloria to stay right where she was and hold the connection.

I stood. There was a little stack of paper cups on the bedside table, along with a telephone and an orange plastic pitcher. I took a cup and reached for the pitcher.

Maria started violently, and began to shake her head. "No, no, no, no. Poison," she whispered.

"How about some bottled water?" Gloria suggested.

She didn't say no, so I went out and filled the cup from the water dispenser in the nurses' station. I came back and handed the cup to Gloria.

"Thank you, Dr. Zak," Gloria said. Then she offered the cup to Maria. Open-mouthed, Maria stared. The four of us waited, held captive in that moment of indecision. Accepting the water would be an act of trust. Finally, Maria wrapped her fingers around the cup. A collective sigh released the tension in the room. She drank greedily, dribbling some water down her chin, her eyes darting back and forth.

When Maria finished, she held the empty cup in front of her. Gloria gently took it from her.

"Would you like to sit in a chair?" Gloria asked her.

Maria looked around as if realizing for the first time that she was on the floor. She struggled to get up. Gloria and I each took hold of an arm and hoisted her up and into a chair.

I pulled up another chair opposite her and looked for eye contact. "Ms. Whitson, do you know where you are?"

Maria's hands gripped the chair arms. She looked confused. She started, "I'm"—and then looked at each of us in turn— "where?" She shrank in her seat and whispered, "I'm scared." She paused, listening to the echoes of her own voice. "Where, scare," she repeated softly, "where, scare, scare, where . . ."

"Ms. Whitson, you're in a hospital. This is the Pearce Psychiatric Institute. We're the doctors and nurses who are here to take care of you. You're safe here."

She looked dazed, and again the keening sound began as she curled up in a ball, hugged her knees, and started to rock herself back and forth.

I asked her, "Ms. Whitson, do you know why you're here?" I paused, hoping she'd fill the void, but she said nothing. "You've been having some problems, and apparently they must be quite serious because you tried to commit suicide."

The rocking subsided as she uncurled.

"We're here to help you. What I need to do is get a sense of how you're doing, and one way we do that is by asking you some questions. I'd appreciate it if you could respond as best you can. Can you do that?"

This time there was a cautious but perceptible nod.

I took a pencil from my pocket and held it up. "Can you tell me what this is?"

I thought I saw a little smile start. Then her mouth worked as she struggled to shape the word. Finally, she whispered, "Pencil."

Encouraged, I continued, "That's fine. And what's this?" I asked, pointing to an empty chair. But her attention had already wandered and she was staring at the silver ring embedded in the flesh of her little finger. With little jerking motions she tried to twist it around.

"Ms. Whitson?" She stopped twisting for a moment and then started again. "Ms. Whitson? Could you put your right hand on top of your head?"

A hand floated upward and rested on top of her head. White lines scarred her wrist. Her head tilted sideways. She met my eyes. Then her gaze shifted to the faces of my colleagues and on to the flat, gray expanse of a window shade. The hand remained planted on top of her head.

"Ms. Whitson, could you wave your left hand and stick out your tongue?"

Now a definite smile appeared. Her lips parted and the tip of her tongue emerged. But the right hand on her head and the left one in her lap remained still.

I went through the other silly-sounding questions designed to take an instant picture of that mish-mash we refer to as mental status. Near the end, although I already knew the answer, I asked, "Have you ever thought about taking your own life?" This got her attention. She jerked slightly and then narrowed her eyes. I waited, wondering if she trusted me enough to answer.

Hesitantly, she nodded.

Encouraged, I continued, "Is that something you think about occasionally or a lot of the time?"

A tear spilled over and started down her cheek.

"I know this is difficult. Let me just ask you a few more questions. Do you ever see things that other people don't see? Or hear things that other people don't hear?"

This question seemed to confuse her. At first she shook her head, no, and then she stopped and looked at me, as if not sure what the answer was.

Finally, I asked her, "Do you feel safe here?"

Slowly and deliberately, she nodded. A smile tugged at the corners of her lips. It was an odd moment. I had the distinct impression that she was enjoying a little private joke.

13

CHIP HAD been calling me every other day since I'd started working on the case. Just checking in, he'd say, and then like a good coach who's afraid that his star player is getting cold feet, he'd start pumping me up. In the week since Sylvia Jackson's collapse, he'd been calling me daily. When he left only the brief message, "Let's huddle to talk about the case," I knew he was worried. We were experiencing more than the usual bumps in the road.

We met at the Stavros for a late lunch. I got there first and sat down at a table. Jimmy came over beaming. "Back so soon!"

"Hey, Jimmy. I'm meeting some people."

"Anything I can get for you while you..." He stopped, mouth open. I turned to see what he was gawking at. It was Annie, striding across the room, her hair frizzled in an aura of light and shadow around her face. I realized I wasn't used to noticing what women looked like. She slid into the chair opposite me.

"Jimmy, this is Annie Squires." She offered him her hand and he took it.

Annie ordered two Diet Cokes and two Greek salads—one

for herself and one for Chip. I ordered an iced tea along with a plate of fried calamari.

Annie gave me a concerned look. "You're looking tired." I didn't have a ready answer. "Sorry, I hate it when people say that to me."

"You're right. I haven't been sleeping. Losing my boat. And knowing that there's someone out there. It feels like it's starting all over again."

Annie was watching me intently, her mouth quivering. "Maybe it would be for the best if you stopped—"

"No," I said, surprised by the vehemence in my voice. "Before the boat accident, maybe. But not now. Now it's personal."

"Personal is not necessarily a good thing in this business."

"Look, I can either lie down and play dead or fight back. If I give up on this case, if I back out now, then whoever is doing this wins. I can't let that happen." Even to me, the words sounded like hollow bravado, but Annie let it pass. "And I think we have a case. I haven't finished testing Sylvia Jackson yet, but I can tell you this much: what you show her one minute she can't remember the next."

"Yeah, but being shot in the head isn't some test. You think she could forget that? And if she can't remember, then what *is* she remembering when she says Stuart shot her?"

"Someone can believe something happened because in some way, it solves a problem for them. Maybe it's just too painful for that thing *not* to have happened. People even turn other people's experiences into their own memories. You know, someone tells you a story about what happened to them, and later, you're telling it as if it happened to you. And you're not even aware that it happened to somebody else."

"Happened to somebody else," Annie whispered. Then, without any segue, she said, "Did you know that I have a sister?"

"No, I didn't." There was a lot about Annie that I didn't know.

"What you're saying reminds me of something that happened

once. My sister was asking me if I remembered a night when my parents were fighting, both of them smashed out of their gourds and my mother broke her arm. My sister had to drive her to the hospital. She could remember all of the details. How frightened she'd been that a cop would stop her and arrest her for driving without a license. How my mother lied to the people at the emergency room, saying she'd fallen down the cellar stairs. How my mother threw up when they gave her the codeine for the pain. But what my sister couldn't figure out was why I didn't drive my mother to the hospital. See, I'm two years older than her." Annie paused, looking at me intently. "The thing is, all that stuff about driving to the hospital, watching my mother throw up? It happened to me, not her. I was fifteen. I don't know where my sister was that night—maybe sleeping at a friends' house or staying over with a relative—but she wasn't even at home. I must have told her about it later. She's thirty-four now and she really thought it happened to her."

We sat in silence for a few moments. The memory had made Annie's eyes retreat behind a glaze of tears. I reached for her hand but she had jerked it from the table and straightened in her seat. "Chip, you made it," she said.

I turned. Chip was standing behind my right shoulder. He was rummaging in his briefcase, trying to look preoccupied. I wondered how long he'd been standing there. Annie took out a tissue and blew her nose. "I ordered you a salad," she told him.

Chip sat. Once again, we cut the small talk and got down to business. I described Sylvia Jackson's test results so far. "She was only able to identify a few of the items that disappeared. She confused the two sets of pictures. She scored off the scale, way down at the low end."

"Can we argue that Sylvia Jackson shouldn't be able to re-member the night of the murder?" Chip asked.

"Unfortunately, it's never that clear. But what we can say is that stuff just isn't getting into her short- or long-term memory. With her, we're dealing with a kind of double whammy. Head trauma that creates amnesia and also permanent damage to the structures that mediate memory. We can demonstrate that she's unable to take in new information and recall it, and we know she was unconscious for a long period of time. All the literature and all of our clinical knowledge suggests that it's unlikely that she's going to remember what happened immediately before she got shot."

"You can't find a stronger word than 'suggests'?" Chip asked.

"Sorry. Psychology is a soft science. What's intriguing is that she makes things up. She knows something is missing but she doesn't know what. So she invents a missing item that was never there. Psychologists call it confabulation. Unconsciously, someone like Syl is aware that she has holes in her memory. She fills those holes with other real experiences borrowed from earlier memories, or with made-up stuff that sounds real. Someone coming out of a coma, in an altered state of consciousness, is going to be very, very suggestible." It wasn't hard to imagine the relatives, friends, medical personnel, lawyer, and police who might, inadvertently or otherwise, have provided Syl with the stuffing for the holes in her memory.

"Catch-22," Annie commented. "Stuart Jackson could be found guilty because the jury believes Syl can remember when she really can't. Or he could be found innocent because the jury believes she can't remember when she really can."

I shifted uncomfortably. "I'm convinced she can't remember. Too bad we don't know what really happened."

"Peter, guilt is always a possibility," Chip said gently. "Our job is to defend the accused, guilt or innocence aside." That's your job. To me, it matters. "So here we have a woman whose brain is this leaky sieve. She loses a lot of what she takes in, and then distorts some of what remains. A credible witness?"

"From the jury's point of view? Definitely," I insisted. "She's sympathetic and vulnerable. And she believes every word she's saying."

"You have more tests?" Chip asked.

"I still need to finish up the personality tests."

"How are personality tests going to tell us anything about whether she can remember what happened to her?"

"If you want to know whether the brain injury has damaged the memory, you need to know what the memory was like before the damage occurred. A piece of that comes from understanding personality, because who you are affects the way you remember things."

Chip didn't look convinced.

I continued, "Suppose I give someone with a brain injury a picture to remember. She remembers the overall subject matter but not the details. To use the cliché, she sees the forest but not the trees. Now here's the problem: how can I tell if this is because of the brain damage, or because that's just who she is? That's what the personality tests tell me."

Chip still looked doubtful. He said, "Okay. So then we'll have the memory tests. And the personality tests."

"You're right. So what? I keep thinking about her description of the night of the murder. The version she told me was quite a bit different from the first version she gave to the police. For example, she told the police Tony was in the trunk."

"And now she knows he wasn't," Annie said.

"Right. She reads the newspaper. She talks to people. Little by little, she pieces together the story and lines up her memory with the evidence. So we need to focus on the details of her story that *aren't* corroborated by evidence."

"Then what?" Chip asked.

"Then try to figure out where those details come from. Look for earlier memories that could be getting pulled forward to fill in the details. Cast suspicion on some, and you cast suspicion on the lot.

"If you think about memory as a series of movies, some of which have to do with the past, some of which have to do with our fantasies and dreams, then what she's doing makes sense. It's like she has multiple movie tracks running in her head, and she's pulling a little from here, a little from there. She doesn't even know which tracks she's pulling from. To convince the jury, you need to make them doubt her ability to tell the difference."

"But what about the camouflage hat she says Stuart Jackson was wearing when he burst into her bedroom the night of the murder?" Annie asked.

That stopped me. "You're right. The camouflage hat is a problem."

"What kind of problem?" Chip asked.

Annie explained. "Well, she told the police about the hat *before* the police found one in Stuart's closet."

"Right," I agreed. "The evidence corroborated the memory rather than the other way round. So it couldn't have been a case of her molding her memory to incorporate new information."

"Stuart says that hat isn't his," Annie said. "Hasn't a clue where it came from. Seemed genuinely flabbergasted that they found it in his apartment."

"I need to talk to Stuart again," I said. "About that. And about other things. Maybe he can clue us into where some of the details in her story are coming from."

"I'll make arrangements," Chip said.

Then I flagged Jimmy. Chip picked up the tab.

We walked outside. Chip's car was parked at a meter right out front. Before he got in, he said, "I'll let you know as soon as we've made arrangements for you to interview Stuart Jackson again. In the meanwhile, please be careful."

"I promise to try," I said.

Annie and I watched Chip drive off. "Beautiful day," she said, the sun reflecting off her shades.

I felt the warmth on my back and closed my eyes. "Mmm. Feels good," I said. There was nothing pressing waiting for me back at the Pearce. I wanted to come up with an artful suggestion for prolonging lunchtime, but I was out of practice. The best I could do was, "Guess we should enjoy it while it lasts."

Annie must have been reading my mind. "I love this neighborhood," she said. She checked her watch. "There's a great bakery near here. I could use a little chocolate guilt to wash down that virtuous lunch. It's just a block that-a-way." She pointed down the street.

"I've got a little time before I have to get back," I said without even checking my watch. "I never pass up a good chocolate dessert." But it wasn't the chocolate that tempted me.

Annie hooked her arm in mine and we strolled down the block. We checked out the menu of a Turkish restaurant. The smell of sharp cheese and baking bread wafted out the door of an old-fashioned Italian deli. We admired the salamis and provolones hanging in the window. We continued on down the street, lingering in front of a store that had a ratty-looking sign in the window: ANTIQUES.

I shook my head. "Not bloody likely. That sign is probably the oldest thing they've . . ." The final word caught in my throat. Abandoning Annie, I hurried inside.

A small, round man sat cross-legged in the corner in a wing chair that had seen better days. He looked like a carved wooden Buddha I got when I was a kid. Someone told me rubbing the tummy brought good luck. He glanced at me as the bell over the door jangled. He nodded, then he went back to writing in a ledger.

Beside him, on a card table, was the thing that had stopped me in my tracks.

"Excuse me." I tried to sound nonchalant. "Could I see that?" I pointed.

He looked distractedly at the items on the table and held up a battered silver teapot. I shook my head. He put it back and lifted a green, gourd-shaped vase.

"Yeah. May I?"

He handed it to me.

I took the piece of pottery as he turned his attention back to his work. I closed my eyes and breathed deeply, opened them again, and the pot was still there. I turned it over. An unsigned Grueby. I wondered if the dealer knew what he had.

Annie had followed me in and was looking back and forth from my face to the pot, as if trying to solve a puzzle. She followed me to a more private corner of the store, out of the dealer's earshot. "You seem excited," she said.

"I hoped it wasn't that obvious. This is the kind of pot Kate collected. They've become so desirable, they're hard to find in places like this anymore." Annie looked at it doubtfully. "I know, I didn't appreciate them much at first, either." I handed Annie the pot and stood behind her as she held it under the light cast by a black panther lamp. Annie ran her long, slender fingers gently over its surface.

"Feel the shape," I told her, just as Kate had once instructed me to do. I touched Annie's fingers and guided them from the narrow opening and tapered neck across the swell of the center. Annie held her breath. "See how the designs, here, cut into the surface of the pot, are like scar tissue?" We traced one of the vertical grooves in the green surface. I whispered, "The glaze. It's the genius of the artist. See how the glaze makes it feel so organic? He does it with the textures. Here, how the green varies from a light feathery covering"—I moved Annie's hand gently from one part of its surface to another—"to this scaly, almost elephant skin texture."

"I see what you mean," Annie murmured. "It's . . . incredible."

"Anything I can help you with?" The spell was broken. It was the proprietor, now up and smiling benignly at us.

"Just curious, how much are you asking for this?" I asked with what I hoped was a disinterested tone.

"It's a very fine piece, don't you think?" he said, sizing me up as he rocked gently forward and back, his hands folded placidly across his rotund middle. "Just came in. Haven't even priced it yet. Let's see," he held out his hand and reluctantly I handed over the vase. He turned it over carefully. "Nice condition." He fished a small magnifying lens out of his pocket and examined the bottom. I knew there was nothing there to see, except the telltale marks of a hand-thrown pot. "I could let it go for a hundred"—I reached for my wallet—"and ninety-five dollars."

I quickly paid him in cash and tried not to gloat. He wrapped the pot in newspaper and put the bundle into a wrinkled plastic bag.

Annie was outside, waiting for me. "Well, you certainly look like the cat that ate the canary," she said.

"Tasty canary," I said, grinning.

When we reached the bakery, a half-block away, Annie's cell phone rang. I checked out the goodies in the window while she took the call. When she pocketed the phone, she looked pleased.

I brushed my fingers across my lips. "Canary feathers," I said. "Now you've got them."

"Just thought I'd check on whether anyone connected to the Jackson case owns a motorboat."

"And someone does?"

Was it going to be that simple? *Cherchez* the boat and we'd find the person who had, not to put too fine a point on it, tried to murder me? Syl had said an old boyfriend used to take her out on the river. I wondered, for the umpteenth time, if Sergeant MacRae had any relationship with Sylvia Jackson that we didn't know about.

"Someone did," Annie said.

"But doesn't own it anymore?"

"Can't own anything because he's deceased."

"No."

"Yes. Tony Ruggiero's motorboat fits the description of the one that hassled you." It and about half of the other boats owned by half of the other idiots who like to zoom up and down the Charles. "Kept it over in Marina Bay."

"Is that where it is now?" I asked.

"Nope. Now it's gone missing. Someone helped themselves to it in the last week and hasn't put it back."

"That's very interesting," I said. Just about anyone with access to Tony Ruggiero's belongings could have borrowed that boat. And where was it now?

"Food for thought," Annie said. Then she closed her eyes and sniffed. "Speaking of which, smell that chocolate." Annie looked at her watch. "Damn, no time to indulge. They've got this incredible brownie. It's called chocolate orgasm." Annie winked. "Check it out!"

I did. Then I bought a second one, intending to bring it to Kwan. But it didn't make it back to the hospital.

14

I WAS working on the unit that afternoon when Chip called. He'd arranged for me to see Stuart Jackson the next morning.

After I finished the call, I went to get myself a cup of coffee. The normally locked kitchen door was ajar. I groaned inwardly as I hurried forward. Inside, Maria Whitson was standing by the counter. She was wadding up piece after piece of bread and, without pausing to chew or swallow, cramming them into her mouth. An empty cookie bag sat on the counter. Four banana peels were all that remained of a bowl of fruit.

"Ms. Whitson," I called out. But she didn't react. She was like a machine, stuffing handful after handful of food into her mouth, her face expressionless concentration.

From behind me I heard a little gasp, "What the . . . ?" Gloria had come in. Ever practical, Gloria promptly put the bread out of reach. Then she took hold of Maria's hands. Maria, never taking her eyes off the bread, struggled to wiggle free.

I came around in front of her. "Ms. Whitson, can you tell me what you're doing?" A wave of rage washed over her face. Together, Gloria and I hustled her out into the dining room, making sure that this time the kitchen door was closed and locked. We sat her down at the table and I tried again.

"Ms. Whitson, can you stop and talk about what's happening here?" She wouldn't respond. She just glared at me. She was still chewing and soggy bits of bread dribbled from her mouth.

"Ms. Whitson," I said, and put my face close to hers. "Do you realize what you're doing?"

The rage drained from her face. Lines of tension around her mouth and eyes eased as her muscles went limp. She started to cry.

I repeated the question more gently. "Are you aware of what you were doing?"

She swallowed once, and again. Then she frowned. She looked at me, confused. "It's like I'm doing—and I'm watching at the same time," she said, her voice sounding far away and tremulous.

"You're aware and you're not aware."

"And the part of me that's watching isn't connected to the part that's doing."

I was encouraged. This was the longest, unbroken, meaningful conversation we'd had since she arrived. And she was demonstrating a surprising degree of self-awareness and intelligence, despite the depersonalization that she was describing.

"Doctor?" Gloria said.

I answered her unasked question. "Go ahead." Gloria left us alone.

"How long has this been going on for you?" I asked.

"Since the accident," she said, her voice turned flat, without emotion.

"The accident?"

She looked down into her lap and started to twist the silver pinkie ring. "Two years ago. My husband was driving my car and he hit me."

"It was an accident?" I asked.

"That's what he said," she mumbled, her mouth barely moving, her face without expression.

"Two years is a very long time to feel out of control. You've been seeing a doctor for this?"

She nodded again.

"Does this have anything to do with why you're here?"

I waited for affirmation. When none came, I pressed on. "I know this is hard for you, but I need to find out more about why you're here. I need to ask you some questions."

Maria stared vacantly at her hands. She seemed numb, unreadable.

I tried again. "Ms. Whitson, I know you're here because you tried to commit suicide. Why was that?"

Then her eyes flickered and she seemed to snap back into herself. She pushed her greasy hair back from her forehead. "Look at me," she spit out the words. "Just look at me. I'm a fat slob. I'm ugly. I'm stupid. No one can stand me. I'm too disgusting to even touch. I can't control my compulsion to eat."

Self-loathing feeds on itself and serves no useful purpose. I wanted to move her beyond it, get her to a place where she could use her intellect to get some perspective. "I see. Was there anything in particular that happened at the time that you tried to kill yourself?"

She started to answer and stopped. Started, and stopped again. At last, she folded her arms over her chest and narrowed her eyes at me. "They're all out to get me and I thought I would just save them the trouble."

"Everybody?" I asked, trying to keep my voice neutral.

Her lower lip quivered. "I have nobody in the world who cares about me," she declared. She hooked a piece of hair and started to twirl it, shifting her gaze to her lap.

"And you've been seeing a therapist to help you deal with these feelings?" I could have guessed the answer to this even if I hadn't seen Maria's file. Very few people use a term like "compulsion to eat" if they haven't been through talk therapy.

"Since the accident I've been seeing Dr. Baldridge. Right away, he suspected that I'd been sexually abused." It often took patients years of therapy, repeatedly describing the pain and humiliation of sexual abuse, before they could nonchalantly toss off the words. Only the hair, twirling now like a miniature propeller, gave any indication of the inner turmoil she must have felt.

I asked gently, "I'd like to call Dr. Baldridge and get his insights into your treatment. With your permission, of course."

She nodded.

"There's something else, too. We need to set up a meeting with the people who will be there to provide a support system for you when you leave us. Friends? Relatives?"

"There's no one," Maria said, her voice flat.

"Your father was the one who brought you in," I suggested.

The hair stopped and her hand hung in midair. "No. I don't want my father to come here."

"Perhaps your father and your mother both? You know they've been asking to see you."

"I don't want to see any of my family. Dr. Baldridge says it's because of them. Because of what they all did to me. He helped me remember."

I didn't say anything. We needed a plan for moving forward. But I had no intention of forcing a pain-filled family reunion. To the contrary, we might need a plan that protected her from her family.

"They're in denial." She'd gone back to the hair again, now spinning it quickly, around and around as her breath quickened and her eyes brightened. "Dr. Baldridge says that means they're dangerous."

"Are you still seeing Dr. Baldridge?"

Maria shook her head hard, once left and once right. The twirling slowed and she took in a huge breath of air, exhaling with a heavy sigh.

"Do you have a job?"

She dropped the hair. "Real estate. I sell houses."

"Do you enjoy that?"

"Yes," she said thoughtfully, "I really do. I like matching people up to the right house." She bit her lip, brought her pale eyebrows together, and concentrated on me. "Contemporary. I bet you go for real modern. Clean. Am I right?" She didn't wait for me to answer. She was stargazing at the ceiling. "You'd have loved this condo we had in . . . in . . ." Slowly her smile dissolved and her face collapsed. Two big tears oozed from her eyes. "Oh, God! I can't remember where it was."

Maria started to rock back and forth.

"Ms. Whitson, does the eating help?" I asked.

She stopped her rocking, apparently surprised by the question. "Uh—I guess it does." She paused and thought about that. "It helps me forget. When I'm eating, I'm not flooded with images."

Flooded with images. Sounded like Baldridge. "What kind of images?"

"Flashbacks. They're awful," Maria whispered. When she started talking again, the words came slowly. "When I eat, there's nothing. Nothing else but the eating. I eat—" Maria's mouth continued moving but there was no voice. She tried again. "I eat—" Again the voice faded. Her eyes became unfocused, the lids fluttering open and shut.

"Ms. Whitson? You eat and what happens?"

But it was no use. Maria's head wobbled forward, jerked back, then fell forward again. She was snoring gently.

I had to give up, but I felt satisfied. It was a good beginning.

Late that afternoon, I took refuge in the conference room to scribble the main points of my encounter with Maria Whitson into her chart while they were still fresh in my mind. I had nearly finished when I heard a light knock. I looked up. Gloria was standing in the doorway, resting heavily against the jamb.

"Long day?" I asked.

"Is there any other kind?" she groaned. She came in and collapsed in the chair next to me. She took off her glasses and ran her hands back and forth through her short hair until it stood straight up on its own. She'd probably been on her feet most of the day.

"I was just writing up my notes on Maria Whitson."

"How'd it go after I left?" Gloria asked as she massaged her temple.

"Reasonably well. She started out flat, depersonalized, and then she became surprisingly self-reflective about what's going on with her. In fact, we had quite a coherent conversation. She seemed to make a good connection until she fell asleep in the middle of a thought. Either she shut herself down because it was too much, or else she's still getting the meds out of her system. She's an odd one. Not quite the textbook case she appears to be at first glance."

Gloria stopped rubbing her head. "Which reminds me, something odd I didn't mention. When I looked in on her the day after we admitted her, she was still out of it, but somehow she'd managed to fold her underwear. And her own comb and toothbrush found their way into the bathroom."

"That is odd," I said. Maria Whitson's hair hadn't looked like she'd run a comb through it in days. "Habit?" Sometimes lifelong habits kick in, even through the most debilitating mental illness. "Or maybe she's having occasionally lucid moments, tucked in among the hours of delirium. She told me it all started with a car accident two years ago."

"Two years ago? I'd have thought it started before that."

"No doubt. But it wasn't until she hurt her head in a car accident two years ago that she realized she'd been sexually abused."

"Poor thing. Did she say who did it?"

I shook my head. "Blames her family. Refuses to see any of them."

We sat quietly for a few minutes. I finished my notes and Gloria rested her head back and shut her eyes.

"That's good," Gloria said. "She's following the protocol. Experts say it's best to cut off contact until you're strong enough to confront your abuser."

"So you assume it's a family member."

Gloria opened her eyes and sat forward. "Usually is. Someone close. But right now she's dealing with a lot more pressing business—delirium, depression."

"Possibly related to brain damage she sustained in the car accident, not to mention all the medication she's been on."

"I'm concerned she might try to harm herself again. I've got the other nurses on alert." Gloria stifled a yawn. "I know what she's going through."

I didn't say anything. I didn't want to pry. This wasn't something Gloria and I had ever talked about. Or if we had, it hadn't been quite so head-on and personal. I knew Gloria would tell me, if and when she felt like sharing whatever the bond was that she shared with Maria Whitson.

15

I'D HOPED to have an hour on the river before sunset, but by the time I got home, it was too late. The days were getting shorter and soon the river would ice up and put an end to the season. My mother was walking home when I pulled in.

"You're home kind of early," she said, eyeing me suspiciously.

I checked my watch. It wasn't quite six. "And you're home kind of late, aren't you?" I noticed the plastic bag she was carrying said VIDEOSMITH on it. "Aha! Movies?"

She turned a little pink. "Yes. Mr. Kuppel recommends," she said and drew a videotape from the bag and held it aloft, "Ta dah!"

She had *The Lady Vanishes*, a thriller in which Hitchcock takes the classic amnesia plot device and twists it. I looked at my mother suspiciously, wondering if this was a coincidence. Sheepishly, she admitted, "I showed him the article about the case you're working on."

"Well, he does have good taste — in movies." *The Lady Vanishes* is one of my all-time favorites, though I wondered what kind of message Mr. Kuppel was sending. Wasn't there a perfectly unctuous doctor in it? And doesn't he try to convince the sweet young heroine that she's only imagined the kindly old woman on the train who disappeared into thin air? His diagnosis, false memory caused by a bump on the head. The heroine, of course, spends the rest of the movie proving him wrong. Not only wrong—actually, I can't remember much else about the movie except no one on this whole entire train will admit to ever having seen the old woman whose name is Miss Froy. Such a wonderful name. Funny, isn't it, how little details get snagged in the brain, remaining crystal clear like sparkling bits of glass while the picture around it fades to black?

"And what have you got?" my mother asked, pointing to my bag.

"I bought a pot," I said, and left it at that. I fished out my keys and opened my front door.

I set the bag on the kitchen counter and took out a wineglass. I sniffed it, then rinsed to get rid of the cabinet smell. Then I uncorked the cabernet and poured myself a glass. I swirled the wine, inhaled, took a sip, and exhaled with pleasure. It had been an interesting day.

I carried the wine and my little bundle up to the second floor, crossed the landing, and stood looking up the stairway to the third floor. The door at the top led to Kate's studio. I hadn't been up there since the cleaners finished their grim work. I remembered the nauseating smell of cleaning fluid that permeated the house for weeks after, even though I'd closed the door. No amount of open windows, cigar smoke, and whiskey could make me stop smelling it. Even when I left the house, it seemed as if the stench clung to my clothes, to my skin, to my hair, so that for months it hung about me like a shroud wherever I went.

I trudged up the stairs, first one step, then the next, pausing midway, pushing myself up the rest of the way. A pink glow seemed to emanate from underneath the door. I took hold of the knob, twisted, and pushed. The door squeaked in protest before swinging open. The room, surrounded by windows on three sides, was flooded with rose-colored light from the setting sun. I stepped inside and inhaled cautiously. It smelled musty, close, but that was all. I crossed to one side and then to the other to open windows. A breeze immediately swept through the room, ruffling some papers Kate had left on her desk in the corner.

This was the room that had sold Kate on the house. Her studio. We thought the original owner must have been an artist—how else to explain the cement floor, paint-splattered even before Kate took it over? Kate called it her sanctuary. There would to be no distractions—no telephone, no radio, no TV. In a concession to the visitors, the writers and collectors who came and wanted to see where she worked, she'd bought a small settee and shoved it off into one corner.

I had thought coming up there would make me unbearably sad, but it didn't. The beauty of the room, the last of the late afternoon sun, the fresh breeze that pushed the stale air from the room gave me a sense of peace.

Silhouetted on glass shelves against the windows were Kate's pots. Some of them were her own, some of them the Arts and Crafts pottery she collected. In one of the spaces where there should have been a pot, there were the pieces of a broken one. I hadn't been able to throw them away.

Bridges must have watched, learned our schedule, known Kate would be alone in the studio at work. She wouldn't have heard him break the glass in the back door so he could reach around and let himself in. She'd have been unaware as he crept from the kitchen to the foot of the stairs. When they removed her body, they'd found this pot broken beneath her. She must have been holding it when he attacked her. I picked up one of the pottery shards and turned it over and over. It was as I'd remembered it, the glaze very much like the pot I'd just bought.

I took the new pot from the bag and unwrapped it. It was

perfect. No hairline cracks. No chips. No signature, but undoubtedly Grueby. Kate would have been dancing around, hugging me with glee.

I brushed the broken pieces from the shelf and caught them in the empty plastic bag. I got a rag from the sink, dampened it, and wiped down the spot on the shelf. Then I set the new pot in place.

I stood back to admire the effect, but I knew immediately that it was wrong. The new pot was nice, but not in that spot. I moved it to the end of one of the shelves. And then I poured the broken pieces from the bag back in their place on the shelf.

I walked slowly around the room, running my fingers lightly over each of Kate's own pots. On one she'd tooled a figure of a woman in outline, generous breasts, swollen belly. It was an early work, one she wouldn't sell. It was one of my favorites.

The earthy, slightly sour smell of clay hung in the air. Unfinished pieces still sat on her workbench, waiting to be glazed. Her kiln was cold and shut. The potter's wheel had bits of dried clay adhering to it. She'd never have left it that way. The cabinet door hung open and inside, glazes, tools, and supplies were stored neatly on shelves.

I crouched to touch the floor where I knew the reddish tint was not paint but the blood that had refused to come clean, where my Kate had died while I stood two floors down, oblivious. The cement was cold and hard. I squeezed my eyes shut, my mouth opened as a vise tightened around my chest. I gasped for breath. If only I'd come up sooner that day. We were so close, so connected, why didn't I know what was going on?

Later, I stood at the window and drank my wine as the clouds became edged with charcoal and cooled from pink to purple. The evening star had just appeared at the horizon when I closed the windows and left the room, this time leaving the door open behind me.

16

"THEY TOLD me you were coming back but I didn't believe it," Stuart Jackson told me two days later when he appeared in the vile yellow cubicle at Bridgewater. "You must bill by the hour."

I didn't respond. The words were offensive but the body language was not. Everything about him drooped. His shoulders sagged. Under bloodshot eyes, the flesh was pouched in flabby bags. The bantam rooster was now a shuffling old man.

"You doing okay?" I asked.

He gave a bitter laugh that sent a wave of mildewy odor in my direction. "You want the truth? I'm doing shitty. What's the use?"

"You getting any sleep?"

He shrugged. "How is she?"

"Syl? She's getting better. Day by day. By the way, did you know this guy, Angelo?"

"The Italian Ken doll?"

"That's the one."

"He showed up around the time she came out of the coma."

"Was that when they told you that you couldn't visit her anymore?"

"She traded one guardian angel for another."

"That's what she calls him, you know. Her guardian angel. Had you seen or heard of him before that?"

Stuart shook his head. "The day he shows up the first time, she acts like she's never seen him before. But then, that's how she reacted when she first saw me. He still hanging around?"

"Very much so."

"Sylvia," he said. "Think she'll ever be the same?"

"As you say yourself, in a lot of ways, she *is* the same."

"You know what I mean."

"Problem is, Mr. Jackson, I don't know exactly what she was like to start with. So it's hard for me to judge. In fact, that's one of the reasons I wanted to see you. You're probably the number one expert on the subject of Sylvia Jackson."

"She's not on trial for murder."

"No, she's not. You are." I waited. The second hand on the wall clock ticked. Far off, I could hear a muffled shout, a door slamming. "I came to talk to you about your ex-wife's account of what happened that night. What I want to get at is whether there's any detail, something that we might corroborate from another witness, that might actually have occurred in her past."

Stuart Jackson sat forward. "Detail? Like what?"

"Like, did she ever carry anything live, a person or an animal perhaps, in the trunk of her car?"

Jackson thought a moment and shook his head.

"Did she let other people drive her car?"

"Drive her car? You gotta be kidding. That car was her baby. No one, and I mean no one, could drive it but her."

"So if someone else drove it, that would have been unusual."

"Very. You'd have to hold a gun to her head." He stopped.

"Did you ever walk in on her when she was in bed with someone else?"

Stuart Jackson flinched and then steeled himself. "Shit. All the time." He reddened. "If only I'd walked in on her that night,

I wouldn't be here now." He stopped and looked at the palms of his hands, then turned the left hand over and fingered the gold band on his ring finger. "I still love her," he said, looking at me, his eyes glazing over. He sniffed and ran the back of his hand across his nose. "I never wanted to split up. Even when I walked in on her with her . . . *friends*," he spat the final word.

"Did that happen a lot?" I asked.

"She'd give the damned boyfriends house keys! When *he* walked in on *us*, that was the last straw."

"He?"

"Tony—Tony what's-his-name. The guy I'm supposed to have killed. Must have thought he was Rambo or something."

"Rambo?"

"We're in bed and he bursts in. And he's got on this getup. You know, like they wore in Vietnam. Like it was Halloween or something."

"Camouflage fatigues?"

"Yeah. Camouflage fatigues."

"Did he have a gun?"

"With that outfit, he needed an Uzi. No, he didn't have a gun."

"Did you have words?"

"No. I invited him in for a cup of tea. What do you think? Of course we had words!"

I laughed. Anger is a good antidote to depression. "Where were you when you had words?"

"Downstairs."

"She go down with you?"

"No, she didn't go down with us. I don't know what she did."

"Did you call the police?"

"And tell them what? She gave the guy the *key*, for God's sake."

"Have you told the police about this encounter?"

Jackson stared at the table and shook his head.

"Why the hell not?"

"It's too fucking humiliating," he whispered, "and besides . . ." His voice trailed off.

"Besides what?"

"She likes men in uniform."

It took a minute for the significance of this to sink in. "Some of the men you walked in on in bed with your wife were—"

"Cops."

"Lots of cops? Or one in particular?"

"More than one. A few. But those are only the ones I saw. Who knows what was going on that I didn't know about."

"Could you identify any of them?"

"It was awhile ago. I doubt it. Maybe if they got undressed."

I had a thought. "Any redheads?"

"None that I remember."

"The police found a camouflage hat in your closet," I said.

"Maybe the police put a camouflage hat in my closet so they could find it there." It didn't sound that far-fetched. "It's not mine. Honest to God. Do I look like the sort of person who'd own something like that?"

I had to admit, he had a point.

17

THE NEXT morning, I called Annie and told her about my conversation with Stuart Jackson.

"She brought cops home to her bed," Annie said thoughtfully. Then she asked the obvious question. "You think one of them could have been Mac?"

"Well, what do you think?"

"I'm not exactly unbiased, you know."

"I gathered as much. I thought you two had some unfinished business."

It sounded like Annie took a long drag on a cigarette, but I knew she didn't smoke. "Our families were real close, you know. His mom and mine, best friends when I was little. His dad was a police officer. But when my dad was beat up, his father kept his mouth shut, even though rumor was he knew who did it. Protecting other cops mattered more than bringing them to justice, even when one of his friends was the victim. After Dad recovered, they never came by the house again. I don't suppose it's fair to saddle the son with the sins of the father. Still, I've always kept my distance. Never did trust the guy."

"Even if he didn't know Sylvia Jackson before the murder,

he'd know if she had relationships with other police officers, wouldn't he?"

"Definitely," Annie agreed. "But that conspiracy of silence . . . I don't remember any police officer boyfriends being interviewed during the investigation."

"MacRae could be protecting someone."

"Or he could be protecting himself. Men." Annie gave a disgusted snort. "I'll ask around. It shouldn't be too hard to figure out which police officers were banging Sylvia Jackson. And whether Mac was one of them."

Then I told Annie about Stuart's account of Tony Ruggiero bursting in while Stuart and Syl were in bed together. "Trade the players," I said, "and the story's the same as Syl's version of what happened the night of the murder."

"Earlier memories," Annie murmured. "So you really think she could have taken the image of Tony walking in on her with Stuart. . . ."

"Switched the roles and now she remembers Stuart walking in on her in bed with Tony. It's a logical way to plug the hole in her memory for what happened the night Tony was killed," I said.

"Do you think the earlier incident really happened?"

"It could have happened just the way Stuart says it did. Or *he* could have made it up. Stuart Jackson's been reading up on brain damage. He knows the significance of an earlier incident like this one. He might invent a parallel scenario because he knows I'd buy it."

"If someone walked in on me like that, I might not report it to the police," Annie commented, "but you better believe I'd talk about it. Maybe Stuart or Sylvia Jackson told someone—a friend, a colleague, someone. And maybe that person remembers. I'll check it out."

After we hung up, I called Maria Whitson's therapist. Of course, the good Dr. Baldridge wasn't available. His secretary took down the times I suggested for a call-back. I'd hoped to be in my office when the call came but I was on the unit when my beeper went off. I called him from there.

"This is Peter Zak from the Neuropsychiatric Unit," I told him. "I wanted to talk to you about a patient you referred to us. Maria Whitson."

"Hello, Peter," he said congenially. "Yes, I thought you might be able to help her."

"Hmm, right," I said. "How long have you been treating her?"

"I'm not treating her right now."

"Yes, she mentioned that. But you were, weren't you?"

"Yes. For the last two years."

"What did you see as her problem?"

"She's an incest survivor."

"Actually, I meant what kind of symptoms were you treating her for."

He cleared his throat and I could hear some papers rattling. "She has an eating disorder. You know, Peter, eating disorders often indicate repressed memories of sexual abuse. In addition, she was anxious, depressed, had night terrors. Typical situation. Cold, distant mother. Abusive father and uncle. She adored them. Married a control freak hoping he'd be able to get a handle on what she couldn't."

As I listened, Mr. Kootz scuttled by, his shoelaces flapping, muttering to himself. He paused, mid-flap, to stare at an exit door on which a hand-lettered sign stated tersely, SPLIT RISK, a reminder to us all how quickly a patient like Mr. Kootz can slip out behind you through a locked door without even being noticed.

Then the elevator across from the nurses' station opened to reveal Mr. O'Flanagan standing inside. It closed again.

"Did you prescribe medication for her?" I asked.

"Medication?" he said vaguely. "Oh, yes. Of course."

"What did you prescribe?"

More papers shuffled. "Xanax for anxiety. Prozac for depression. Lithium to stabilize her moods. And some Halcion for sleep."

To name a few, I thought. "I understand you terminated her?"

"That's right. I'm no longer seeing her."

"I understand she was still symptomatic."

He cleared his throat. "When I discharged her, she was stable and in control. There was no reason to expect anything would happen. I gave her prescriptions to continue the medications and told her to check back with me in six months."

The elevator opened and an orderly stepped out pushing a metal cart filled with juice and crackers. I could just make out Mr. O'Flanagan lounging against the back wall of the elevator as the door slid shut.

"Peter," Dr. Baldridge said impatiently, "I've got a survivors group starting in a few minutes. Will there be much more?"

"No, I'm just about finished. I was wondering, why did you terminate her?"

"I didn't terminate her. Part of her therapeutic regimen is that she needs to find her own way in the world. I'd done as much insight work with her as possible. I'd helped her recover her memories, given her the understanding of what happened to her, helped her to confront her abusers. Now she needs to integrate that."

"And what was the insight you gave her?"

"That she'd been repeatedly raped by the uncle and by the father from the time she was three until the time she was twelve."

"She told you this?"

"I suspected as much when I first saw her. All the telltale signs. Of course, the memories were repressed."

"So you stopped treating Ms. Whitson and yet you continued to prescribe drugs for her?" I knew it was provocative but I couldn't help myself.

He didn't answer.

"You do know what you referred her to us for, don't you? She tried to kill herself with a self-administered overdose of prescription drugs. She mixed herself quite a lethal cocktail." He may as well have given her an artillery of loaded guns to choose from.

"Peter," Baldridge said, indulging me, "you don't work with many incest survivors, do you?"

"I don't make it my exclusive practice."

"Then you probably don't realize that I was following the regimen I outline in my book, *Surviving*."

I thought, too bad Ms. Whitson didn't read your book. But then, she probably had to as part of her "treatment." I wanted to ask if he had a stack of copies he sold to patients. But I didn't. We were on a lot of the same committees. It wouldn't pay to piss him off more than I already had.

"Will there be anything else, Peter?"

"Not right now. But I might need to contact you again."

"Any time at all," he said pleasantly. "And do let me know how she's getting on."

As I hung up the phone, the elevator door opened. This time, one of the neurology residents stepped out. Mr. O'Flanagan was still inside. I lunged at the open door. Mr. O'Flanagan looked startled. I led him out of the elevator and down the hall to the common room where the orderly was distributing an afternoon snack to all takers.

When I returned to the nurses' station, Gloria was there talking to Suzanne. "You don't know, by any chance, how Mr. O'Flanagan ended up stuck in the elevator?" I asked.

"The elevator got stuck? I didn't hear anything," Gloria said.

"No, it didn't get stuck. He did."

"Wasn't he upstairs with you?" Gloria asked Suzanne.

"He was with me earlier. I was finishing up my evaluation of him. But that was about forty minutes ago. Oh, Jeez! You found him in the elevator, didn't you?"

I nodded.

Suzanne hit herself in the head with the butt of her hand. "Dumb! And you know, that's just what I keep finding in all the test results—no short-term memory. None." She looked like she wanted to dig a hole in the floor and climb into it. "I'm so sorry."

"He's already forgotten all about it," I said.

"It's a good thing Peter noticed," Gloria added, "or Mr. O'Flanagan could have been riding around forever in the elevator, like Charlie on the MTA."

"It's a good lesson," I said. "There's nothing theoretical about test results. They can explain past behavior and predict what someone's likely to do."

"Right," Suzanne said. "If a patient's got no short-term memory, don't stick him in an elevator and expect him to get off when he reaches the first floor."

"And don't leave medication lying around his room," I added.

"What? Of course not," Gloria said indignantly. "That would be an accident waiting to happen, much worse than getting stuck in an elevator."

I knew Gloria expected all the nurses on the unit not only to watch each patient take their pills, but to check hands and mouths afterward. It was standard operating procedure. But then, our average patients don't know the time of day, never mind whether they've taken their meds. "Gloria, what about at other hospitals, say one that treats trauma victims, physical rehab? Would a nurse leave pills for a patient to take?"

"It's just not done," Gloria insisted. "Any nurse worth her salt isn't going to leave medication in a patient's room." Period. End of discussion.

So if Sylvia Jackson's goody basket of pills hadn't been left for her by a nurse, then how had those pills found their way to her bathroom?

18

A few days later, I returned to the hospital to finish testing
Sylvia Jackson. When I arrived, Angelo was shouting encouragement from one end of the hall while Syl struggled on
crutches, painstakingly inching her way along the corridor.
When she saw me, she flashed an enormous smile, obviously
well pleased with herself.

I went to stand alongside Angelo.

"She's determined to walk to the witness stand," he told me.

It was smart. The jury couldn't help but be moved, as I was
watching her.

"Come on, baby, I know you can do it," Angelo called out.

Just then, Sergeant MacRae appeared at the far end of the
corridor. He'd been barreling ahead, in a hurry to get somewhere, but when he saw us he screeched to a halt.

Syl struggled forward, her right leg dragging, gradually closing
the gap between us. Twenty feet. Ten feet. Five feet. Two feet.
As Syl lurched to one side and fell toward me, I found myself
reaching out to catch her. She dropped the crutches to the floor
and struggled to a standing position, rubbing up against me. I

adjusted my grip and held her at arm's length. How had I gotten myself into this position?

MacRae bumped my shoulder going past in high gear, scowling, but Syl didn't see him. She had reached for Angelo and shifted to where she could nestle up against him, oblivious to his stiff coldness. In sixty seconds, she'd managed to piss off two boyfriends. As Annie said, Sylvia Jackson did have that thing about her.

The wheelchair sat empty at the other end of the long corridor. I fetched it and pushed it back. Syl struggled to move closer, to position herself near the chair. Angelo gave her a rough push and she landed on the arm of the wheelchair, arched her back, and slid into the seat. "Angelo, what the—" Syl started to protest. But the words died when she saw his dark, angry face. There was an awkward silence. Then Angelo turned on his heel, stomped down the hall, and disappeared into Syl's room.

I pushed Syl quickly toward the conference room. She reached down and held the wheel of the chair as we were passing the open door of her room. The chair skidded to a stop. Inside, Angelo was shrugging on a windbreaker. "I'll meet you in a minute," she told me and rolled silently inside. I continued to the conference room.

I was still arranging the test materials on the table when Syl joined me. She pulled herself into position at the head of the table. "Men," she sighed. "Can't live with 'em. And I sure as hell can't live without them." She cupped her hand over her mouth and leaned toward me. "Tell you a secret. Today's my birthday."

"Well, Happy Birthday! Are you going to celebrate?"

"Carolyn is taking me out for drinks. Right after we're done, in fact. You know, I even had to get permission from the docs. Just like being a teenager again. Oh, God, I haven't been out for actual drinks for—not since . . ." She steadied herself. Then she gave a forced smile, lowered her eyelids, and asked, "So what do *you* think about a woman my age seeing a younger man?"

I didn't know what to say. I reminded myself—frontal lobe damage. She couldn't keep herself from breaching those unseen boundaries that keep inappropriate thoughts from popping out. She'd probably always been a sensual person, hyperattuned to body language and sexual nuance. But now, that aspect of her overpowered the rest.

Smiling brightly and tossing her head, she asked, "Can you tell? He's five years younger than I am. Of course, I haven't told him exactly how old I am." I didn't point out that any newspaper account of the crime would have tipped him off.

I looked at my watch and said, "We need to get started, Ms. Jackson. Taking tests isn't a very nice way to spend your birth-day—"

She continued as if I hadn't said anything. "And know what else? I'm going home! At the end of the week. I'm counting the days. Angel's been getting the house ready for me. Mowed my lawn. Built a ramp. When I try to thank him, he says it's the least he can do for Tony."

"He and his uncle must have been very close," I said.

"They were. Just like this." She held up two fingers, side by side.

"They were in business together, too?" I asked.

"Mmm," she said vaguely. "Tony and Angelo Ruggiero. People used to say they were like brothers. They really are a lot alike." Her lower lip trembled. Syl closed her eyes and bent her head. She unlocked the wheelchair's brakes and put her hands on the wheels, pushing and pulling the chair back and forth, rocking herself gently in place. Then she reset the brakes.

"Sorry," she said, fiercely wiping away the tears that were making their way down her face. "This happens all the time. Whenever I think . . ."

I'm right there with you, I thought. I handed her a tissue from the stash I always keep in my pocket. "Loss leaves your life pockmarked with holes that you're constantly falling into. You can't really forget because there's so much that reminds you."

"But then, would you really want to?" she said. "At least let them be remembered. Because after that, what is there?"

I didn't trust myself to look at her. Remembering was too painful. Keeping busy, that had been my salvation.

"You would have liked Tony," she said.

"I'm sure I would have."

"He was a sweetheart. I knew the first time I met him, he was something special. He brought in a car to be appraised. I wrote it up. Damaged front fender, dented hood, cracked windshield, a ding in the roof. See, my memory's not so bad."

It was true. Her memory for some events predating her injuries did seem to be intact, preserved like a fly in amber. It was the present that was drifting away like smoke.

"Tony was real anxious about that car. He was bringing it in for Angelo. Came on like a tough guy. Lots of attitude. People always assumed I'd be out to get them when I was just doing my job. But we hit it off anyway." She chewed on her lower lip. "I wish I could remember. Angel says the three of us spent lots of time together. And I can sort of remember, but it's like shadows dancing in the back of my brain. There's a lot I can't remember. Do you think it will ever come back to me?"

"Your doctors know how you're doing. You should ask them." I was grateful that it wasn't my job to tell her that six months after a brain injury, what you see is pretty much what you get.

She paused, appearing to size me up before continuing. "Carolyn doesn't like you very much."

"Nurse Lovely?"

"Of course she doesn't have any real reason not to like you. I mean, she hardly even knows you. She just thinks you're going to hurt me." She leaned forward in her chair, beseeching me. "But you're not out to get me, are you?"

Was I out to get her? In a sense, I was. And Sylvia Jackson didn't need another betrayal from someone she trusted. On the other hand, if Stuart Jackson was innocent, would I be "getting" Sylvia Jackson by testifying that the memories that condemned him might be less than genuine?

"No, Ms. Jackson, I'm not out to get you. And I have more good news for you—today's tests are the last. After this, we're finished."

"Yes, I guess that is good news." She didn't look convinced. "So, maybe I'll see you at the trial?" It felt like the end of a date when one person says, "So, you'll call?" and then waits for the answer to find out whether or not they're getting dumped. Wrong context, but still, that's how it felt. Sylvia Jackson lived in a world where everything had become personal.

"Actually, probably not. We're both witnesses. Neither of us can watch the trial. That's the key to being a good witness, expert or otherwise. You've got to remain unbiased."

She didn't look too disappointed. "I feel real bad about Stuart." She took a deep, shuddering breath.

"You were married for a long time."

"Ten years. And we've been friends—seems like forever and ever. He knew what I was thinking before I did. And I used to be able to finish his sentences. That pisses him off. See, he can't figure out how come I can finish his thoughts when he's so much smarter than me. And he is. But still, half the time, I know just what he's going to say."

I thought about how Syl was coming out of her ordeal incomplete in so many ways. And it would be my job to point out to the jury just how broken she was. I felt like a heel. I consoled myself by remembering the lack of physical evidence. Surely whoever shot Syl and Tony left behind or took with them some link to the crime.

I arranged my test materials and taped a TESTING, DO NOT DISTURB sign to the door. Then I gave Syl a piece of paper and a pencil and asked her to draw a person. She held the pencil, hesitated, then started to draw. She sketched out the figure of a woman that filled most of the page. The marks were hard and clean. The face was oval, with well-defined eyes, ears, and mouth. Shoulder-length hair. Then she drew shoes that looked like Mary Janes. But when she handed me the paper, the body was nothing but the outline of a dress. There was not a single detail—no buttons, no collar, no curves. Nothing but flat emptiness.

Then I gave her a second piece of paper and asked her to draw a man. She approached it in the same way—sketching the overall shape, starting with an oval face. She drew eyes, a nose, and a mouth, longish strands of hair on the head. She added shoelaces and heels to suggest oxfords on the feet. But after that, the difference between the two drawings was striking. The man had broad shoulders, narrow hips. He wore a suit. The jacket had carefully drawn buttons and lapels; the shirt had a collar, the corner of a breast pocket, and buttons; the pants had a belt, and even a line to suggest the fly on his pants.

"Thank you. Very nice work," I said as I tucked the drawings away. She beamed.

I reached for the stack of inkblots. Syl looked at them warily and swallowed. "Right," I said, "here's where all hell broke loose last time. You okay today? Need to take a break? After this, we're done."

"No, I'm okay." She took a breath. "Let's do it."

I went through my opening spiel and handed Syl the first card. She took it from me slowly and, as I timed her, she rotated it in a complete circle, coming back to what is considered the right-side-up position. It was a full two minutes before she said anything.

She exhaled and then filled the breath with sound. "It looks like a butterfly. With wings. Or . . . a bat. Here are its teeth," she said, indicating sharp little points along one edge of the inkblot—the teeth of a vampire bat silhouetted against the upper half of the bat's mouth.

She pivoted the card a quarter-turn and smiled. "It's a flower." She pouted, adding, "The flower doesn't have many leaves." Then she brightened again. "There's a butterfly, over here, coming to the flower."

She turned the card again and wrinkled her brow. "It's a face. With four eyes and a mouth. The mouth is down here." She pointed to the lower edge of the inkblot, which was shaped like an open half-circle. "Well, it would be a mouth, if it were all there. And the eyes are staring straight at me."

She put her hand over the inkblot before turning it again.

Staring thoughtfully, she smiled. "Now I see a bird. A bird flying."

I turned to the next card. Syl glanced at me anxiously. "I'm doing all right, aren't I?"

"Absolutely. It's like I said, there are no right and wrong answers." That's what psychologists always say, and strictly speaking, it's true. But responses can be very revealing, almost like looking at someone's emotional insides not quite head-on but through a periscope. Of course, there are plenty of folks who say Rorschach cards are a crock, and I guess some patients have seen them so many times their responses are tainted. But I find them illuminating in a way that other tests aren't.

This time, it took her less than a minute to come up with a response. "It's two people. Two women. They're dancing."

"What makes it look like women dancing?" I asked.

"Because of the breasts," she said. "They're touching . . . here . . . and dancing."

Then she turned the card upside down. "It looks a little different this way. This is an arm," she said, pointing to one section of the blot, "and here's a leg." She pointed to another section. "This looks like something you chop with."

Sure enough, in the upper corner she had isolated an image that resembled a meat cleaver.

The next words came in a rush. "This is the chopping block.

This is the leg on the right and the ax over here. They're going to hack the leg into pieces."

Syl was flushed and breathing faster. She looked at me and I nodded for her to continue. She gave the picture a quarter-turn to the right and sighed, suddenly relaxed. "Now it looks like a butterfly. A paper butterfly. But one of its wings is missing." She took a deep breath as her face and neck grew paler, revealing hot pink streaks running down her neck and chest.

I waited for her to continue. Instead, she said, "Do you mind if I take a break? I need to go to the little girls' room." The last card had struck a nerve.

When she returned, she rolled the wheelchair into the room slowly. She pulled herself into position. It seemed to take an effort for her to lift her arms and set them on the table. "How much more?" she asked. She looked as if someone had turned off the light behind her face.

"Hang in there. Just two more and we're done." I flipped the next card.

She stared for a few seconds. She stifled a yawn and started, "It looks like a big bear. You know, with a lot of muscle on his arms and legs. This part up here could be the head. He has a large penis." She pointed to a massive dark smudge between what could have been huge hairy legs.

As she rotated the card, there was a tap at the door and in came Nurse Lovely, preceded by a rattling cart of medications. Angry, I got up and stood in her way.

"You must have missed the sign on the door," I sputtered.

She looked at the door. "What sign?"

"We're testing."

"Ms. Jackson needs to take her medication." As she talked, I marveled at how she could speak so clearly without unclenching her teeth. A few choice words sprang to mind but I kept them to myself.

She poured Syl a cup of water and handed her a small plastic cup of pills. As Syl took each one, I stared at the rows of medication neatly lined up on the tray.

"Do you always use those cups for pills?" I asked.

"I guess they're not as nice as the silver cups you use over at the Pearce, but we get by."

I looked at her impassively. "What I meant was, you don't ever use white pleated cups to deliver pills, do you?"

She held up a white pleated cup from the stack on her tray like a teacher showing an exceptionally stupid child. Pointing, she announced, "Drinking cup." Then she held up one of the white plastic cups. "Medications cup. No, we don't ever use these," she said, toasting me with the little pleated cup, "for pills."

In my mind's eye, I juggled competing images — the pleated paper cup of pills Syl had found in her bathroom, the white plastic cups on Nurse Lovely's medications tray. I felt like Syl with multiple videotapes jockeying for position in my brain.

Lovely watched until the last pill went down. "Good girl. The emergency call button is just over there in case you need anything," she said, before clattering out of the room.

After Lovely left, I held out the final card. "This is it. End of test."

Syl stifled a yawn and reached for the card in slow motion. She turned it upside down. Then right side up. "This is pretty," she said, probably responding to the different colors. Then she traced her finger down the middle. "My mother used to tell me that if I was naughty, an evil spirit would take me away and leave behind a changeling."

"A changeling?"

"Yeah. Like a little dead baby. Only not dead. Just empty, you know, without a soul. Doesn't this look like one?"

Syl was pointing to a narrow, wormlike shape at the center of the card.

She turned the card upside down. "Now it's upside down. Only it hasn't got any hands or feet. And it's so small." She flipped it again. "There are wings growing where the hands and feet should be."

"What makes it look like a changeling?" I asked.

"She's so small. And transparent." Then, in her small, breathy voice she added, "She's a tiny, tiny little person trying to fly."

19

AFTER SYLVIA Jackson returned to her room, I remained alone in the conference room writing up my notes. I put her figure drawings side by side and considered the contrast. The well-formed male figure, the attention to detail, spoke to her interest in men and their power over her. The void of the female figure, no more than an outline sandwiched between head and feet, echoed her own feeling of emptiness and loss. These same themes rippled through her responses to the Rorschach cards.

It had been painful to watch her struggle. I was glad the testing was over. It wasn't my goal to be Syl's tormentor, but that's what I'd become. She reminded me of my father, when he still had enough of his mind intact to realize that he was losing it. I remembered one time I was in New York for a conference. I was going to my parents' apartment for lunch and then catching the shuttle back to Boston. I called that morning to ask if there was anything I could bring. My mother said they were all set. Dad was going to walk to the market to get coffee and milk. He liked the exercise.

When I arrived, their apartment door was ajar and I could hear my mother inside, talking on the phone. An open apartment door in Brooklyn is about as common as a hippopotamus on the subway. I knew something was wrong. My mother's voice was high and shrill. "But he's been gone for two hours. The market is only fifteen minutes from here!" When she saw me, she hung up in disgust. "Your father hasn't come back and the police are useless," she said, her voice tight.

I sprinted to the store where my mother thought he'd gone. I found him there, wandering down an aisle carrying a box of Brillo and a package of chicken cutlets. He didn't know where he was and he didn't know how he'd gotten there.

During the walk home, he brooded silently. At the first street corner, he hesitated, anxious, starting and stopping, like a kid trying to dart into a rapidly turning jump rope. I took his arm and he let me lead him across.

"I didn't want to worry you" was my mother's explanation for why she hadn't told me Dad was having problems. This came on top of a series of lesser incidents—forgetting phone numbers, burning pots on the stove, repeating things—that marked the boundary between benign everyday forgetfulness and a more pathological situation. He was still taking in information, still cataloguing every time he screwed up, comparing his screw-ups to how he used to function. He was becoming increasingly anxious and depressed, afraid he was losing his mind. And in fact, he was.

I remember his relief when I told him that I thought he was in the early stages of Alzheimer's. At least it was an illness, something organic with a name other than crazy. And I remember my own distress. Here was a disease about which I knew everything there was to know. I'd written papers, given talks. And I knew there was nothing I could do to make it go away.

It turned out that our tenant gave notice a few months later. I called my mother and asked if they would consider moving into the apartment.

The mercy of Alzheimer's is that as a patient becomes more

demented, the awareness of the dementia disappears. The opposite would probably turn out to be the case for Sylvia Jackson. As she continued to heal, she'd become more, not less, aware of her deficits.

By the time I'd packed up the test materials and headed to my car, it was after six. I took the elevator down and walked along the nearly deserted hallway, through the lobby, and out to the temporary bridge to the parking garage. Outside, it was gray and raining. A stream of water clattered from a disconnected downspout onto the corrugated sheet metal that did little to protect people crossing the wooden walkway.

I was relieved to get inside the glass vestibule of the garage where I pushed the elevator button and waited. Following a series of muffled creaks and groans, the elevator doors opened. The ride up three floors was slow and the elevator seemed to sway back and forth in the shaft. Its doors slid open to reveal a shadowy landing. I got out and squinted into the gloom. When the elevator doors shut, it became darker still.

Fortunately, I'd managed to find a spot just opposite the elevator. My footsteps echoed across the pavement. Although the level I'd parked on was half-empty, a Jeep and a Dodge Caravan hemmed me in on either side.

I slid sideways between my car and the Jeep, relieved to discover that, close as my neighbor was, he'd managed to get out of his car without damaging the recently painted green of my car door. I wedged my way inside. I turned the key in the ignition and the engine immediately caught. I exhaled and sat back. The warm smell of leather was comforting. I turned on my headlights and the concrete pillars I was parked up against lit up. I rolled down the window, adjusted the side mirror, and shifted the car into reverse. My backup lights brought the dark area behind me to life, light and shadows shifting slowly as I inched backwards. I jammed on the brakes as a car came whipping around the corner and past me. You took your life in your hands, backing out of a parking spot at the beginning of a row with assholes like that tearing down ramps as if they're practicing for the Indy 500.

I checked my rearview mirror again. The elevator doors were open. Someone in a dark coat was backing out of the elevator, turning around and pushing a wheelchair out into the garage. I could hear voices and laughter. Sylvia Jackson and Nurse Lovely were on their way to celebrate Syl's birthday.

Nurse Lovely eased the wheelchair down from the raised sidewalk and out onto the ramp. From far above us, I could hear the squeal of tires. Someone was starting his decent.

Nurse Lovely paused to rummage in her purse. Then she continued, pushing Syl past my car and on toward the remaining cars parked on the level.

Tires squealed, closer now. I could hear the roar of a car's engine. Oblivious as only pedestrians can be, Nurse Lovely was taking her time. With her dark coat, she'd be nearly impossible to see, even if the descending driver were observing the posted five-mile-an-hour speed limit.

I inched my car out, put it in neutral, and shouted, "Get out of the way!"

Nurse Lovely stopped. "Oh, cool your jets, asshole, we'll be out of your way in a minute."

Then she pushed the wheelchair steadily, deliberately, down the center of the ramp. The car I'd heard was now closing in. The tires squealed again, much closer. Headlights appeared and disappeared in the gaps between the concrete dividers that separated the level I was on from the adjacent ramp to the next level up. I leaned on the horn, filling the garage with a blast of noise, hoping it would slow down the oncoming car or at least motivate Nurse Lovely to step aside. She flipped me the bird.

The tires squealed for what I knew would be the last time and the engine roared as whoever was driving accelerated onto our level. I leaned on the horn again, slammed my car into reverse, and gunned it. I shot out into the middle of the ramp, my tires screeching in harmony with another set of tires.

A low red car swerved, clipped me, and jumped the curb by the elevator before caroming off the cinder block wall. The sound of metal against metal made me sick to my stomach. It figured—I'd just finished replacing the rear panels. I watched the taillights recede. The car's rear end sashaying as it roared into the turn and disappeared down the ramp. The driver never even slowed down to see if anyone was hurt.

I jumped out of the car. The wheelchair lay overturned near the bumper of a parked car. I ran over and righted it, expecting to find Sylvia Jackson lying crumpled beneath it. But she wasn't. I heard her labored breathing before I saw her, huddled between two nearby parked cars. She was standing, but barely. In two steps, I was beside her, holding her up.

"Are you hurt?" I asked.

She was trembling.

"Hey. Everything's going to be okay." I helped her back to the wheelchair and crouched in front of her. "Just some idiot driver." My voice sounded completely calm but I was feeling like I wanted to punch a hole in something or somebody.

"Goddammit . . . shit . . . where the hell!" Nurse Carolyn Lovely was furiously gathering up the belongings that must have spewed from her purse when it hit the ground. "You—you idiot!" she sputtered at me. She reached underneath a nearby car and scooped out an open cell phone, its aerial bent. "I might have guessed it would be you. Don't you look when you back up?"

"I *did* look. That's why I backed up! That guy could have killed you both."

"Don't you mean *you* could have killed us both?" she demanded.

Nurse Lovely shook the voluminous bag and peered inside. Then she stalked up and down the cars near her, checking underneath and in between.

I went to fetch Syl's purse, which was near where her wheel-

chair had upended. There, I found what Nurse Lovely was looking for.

"This yours?" I asked.

She came over and peered into my hand. She snatched the
small silver handgun from my open palm. Then she stared down
the ramp after the now vanished car. She looked back at me.
"It wasn't your fault? You didn't—?" she started to ask, but didn't
seem able to wrap words around what it was that I hadn't done.

"No, I didn't. I just tried to get in the way so you wouldn't
get hurt."

"Sylvia," Nurse Lovely said urgently, remembering her companion.

"I'm okay, Carolyn. Shaken. But I'm not hurt."

"Did you see the car?" Nurse Lovely asked, more urgently.

"It looked kind of like what I drive," Syl offered. "Red. Maybe
a Firebird or a Camaro."

"Is that what you were expecting?" I asked Nurse Lovely.

She glared at me. "What I was expecting is none of your
business," she snapped. The hand she lifted to brush away a
piece of hair was trembling.

A formidable presence in the hospital, here she seemed
smaller, younger, and far more vulnerable. I held out my hand
to her and she didn't resist. I helped her over to my open car
door, where she sat, her shoulders shuddering beneath the dark
wool of her coat. She was ashen and a film of perspiration
coated her forehead. When people feel threatened, first there's
anger, then shock. I knew I'd be there, too, when I let my guard
down.

She shook her head. "It's nothing. Really nothing. It's so fool-
ish of me. It's over. It's all over. And still, all it takes is something
like this to stir up the feelings again, to make me lose it."

Syl had wheeled herself silently over beside us. "Carolyn's ex-
husband. He's been harassing her for years."

"Do the police—?" I started to ask.

Nurse Lovely cut me off. "Restraining orders," she sneered,

"are a joke. You're the lucky one," she said to Syl. "At least your ex is in jail where he can't get at you."

We all jumped at the sound of screeching tires. A car pulled up behind mine and slowly eased its way around. A man leaned out the window. "That's a helluva place to leave your car," he called out before continuing on his way. The words of a rocket scientist.

Syl rolled over to examine the back of my car. She let out a breathy whistle. "Nice car," she said. "Vintage—'67 or '68. A 2000 TC. Pretty rare. And nicely restored." She sounded impressed. My glow of pride faded as she continued. "Needs a new fender, taillights, bumper." I groaned. "Probably a trunk." I'd just finished working on the goddamn trunk. "You'll never find replacement parts." As if I didn't know. "It'll cost a bundle to fix this baby."

Clearly, her skills as an appraiser were still intact.

20

AFTER SYLVIA and Lovely had driven off, I moved my car to where I could get a better look. Steaming, I inspected the damage. The rear quarter panel was dented and scraped. The trunk wouldn't close and the rear bumper was hanging off on one side. So much for the last six months of work. I took hold of the bumper and yanked and twisted, cursing and stomping until I managed to break the whole thing loose. Then I stuffed as much of it as I could into the trunk and tied the trunk down with some cord. I slid underneath and flashed a light up at the chassis. Oh, shit. That crimp in the frame wasn't something I'd be able to fix myself.

I drove home, the car shimmying, replaying the accident over and over in my head. The sound of tires screaming, metal against metal, metal against concrete. The overturned wheelchair. Syl's body, shaking with terror, pressed against mine. The little silver handgun. Nurse Lovely's anger and then shock.

Sylvia's overdose, the hit-and-run on the Charles, and now this. There had to be a connection. Or was I being paranoid? Accidents happen in parking lots all the time. But why hadn't he stopped? I closed my eyes and tried to picture the car, the driver. Why did I think a man was driving?

Preoccupied with my thoughts, I wasn't prepared for the scene at my house. Two police cruisers, blue lights flashing, were parked in front. A dark sedan was backed into my driveway. As I bolted out of my double-parked car and tore up the walk, my heart racing, time seemed to slow. Please God, I thought, not again. My mother's front door drew open and she stood silhouetted in its frame. I was flooded with relief, noticing at the same time that there wasn't any yellow scene-of-the-crime tape strung across our front porch.

"What's going on? You all right?" I asked when I got to her and put both hands on her bony shoulders, just to assure myself that she was really there.

"I called the police because *that person*," she said, outraged, pointing a shaking finger at the dark sedan, "was trying to get into your house. And then he got back into his car and sat there, casing the joint."

One of the uniformed cops was shining a light into the face of the driver of the dark sedan. Sergeant MacRae glared back through the open car window. The tips of his ears were scarlet.

I clenched my fists and stalked over to him. "What the hell do you think you're doing? After what we've been through, don't you think you could show a little consideration. Skulking around out here, scaring the living daylights out of an elderly woman? What's she supposed to think?"

"I needed to talk to you," he muttered.

"So you can't call me? Make an appointment, like everyone else in the world?"

My mother had come up behind me. Now she stood beside the car, her Nikes firmly planted about two feet apart, hands on hips, chin out. She rapped her knuckles on the car window. "Listen, Mister," she said, "now you can tell the police why you tried to break into my son's house."

"He *is* the police," I told her.

She looked at me, open-mouthed, then shook her head in disgust.

MacRae got out of the car and tried to draw himself to a dignified stance, but he was withering in my mother's accusing glare. "I'm sorry, Mrs. Zak," he finally said. "I didn't realize you'd be home. I needed to talk to him."

"You needed to talk to my son?"

I could hear alarm bells going off in my mother's head. "It's about this case I'm working on, Mom. Tell her," I urged MacRae. "Tell her it's not about me personally."

He gave me a sideways look that I knew wouldn't be lost on my mother. "It's about a case."

Addressing the uniformed cop, she said, "Shouldn't he be arrested for"—she looked at me for help but I threw up my hands—"loitering?" Her voice cracked. "Trespassing?" She started to weep. "Isn't there anything illegal about frightening a person to death?"

I turned and hugged my mother. She was tight and stiff. I glared at MacRae. "I'm going to go inside now with my mother. If you want to talk to me, you know my number."

21

THE NEXT morning, I went to the Cambridge police station. I was filling out an accident report when MacRae came out from one of the inner offices.

He glanced at the form I had nearly completed. "Another accident."

"Seems like that's all you and I ever talk about. My accidents."

"When?"

"About an hour before I got home last night. You going to tell me you were waiting for me in my driveway all that time?"

He drew himself up. "What's that supposed to mean?"

"Just that I wouldn't be surprised if you already know more about what happened yesterday evening than I do."

He didn't get mad. He got huffy. "I'm a police officer, Dr. Zak, and I've been assigned to the Jackson case." He puffed out his chest, doubled his chin, and strutted up and back on legs that were a little too short for all that torso. "My job is to make sure Sylvia Jackson stays in one piece so that she can walk, roll, or crawl to the witness stand. The hospital staff has standing orders to call if anything unusual happens to her. And I'd say last night was unusual." He stopped in front of me and pressed a palm down on the accident form. "So, as it happens, I do already know about your accident. Though I'm not sure that's what I'd call it." About that, we were in complete agreement. "I'd appreciate it if you'd tell me what happened."

Grudgingly, I told him.

"A sporty red car?" he repeated my description.

"Sylvia Jackson said it reminded her of the one she drives."

"You get a look at the driver?"

"No."

I couldn't tell if he was annoyed at my incompetence, or relieved. He mused, "Accidents happen in parking garages all the time. People drive too damned fast. And they often hit and run because they're not insured, or if they are, they don't want to see their insurance premiums increase. But I think there's a pattern here and I don't like it. If I were you, I'd watch my back." Yeah, right. A brilliant observation. "And I think we'll give Sylvia Jackson a round-the-clock guard, just to be on the safe side."

From the police station, I went to get the damage to my car appraised. The appraiser did not share Sylvia Jackson's enthusiasm for venerable old cars. The figure he came up with was underwhelming—fine if we'd been talking a Chevy Cavalier. But I didn't argue. I'd be doing most of the work myself anyway, and I wasn't up to another confrontation. I just wanted to get back to the hospital and crawl into the comfort of my daily routine.

I was back at the Pearce before noon. Gloria was at the nurses' station writing in a patient's record. I'd just pulled Maria Whitson's file when I felt a tug on the tail of my jacket and a familiar voice hissed in my ear, "What sartorial splendor have we here?"

Kwan turned me around gently. There was mischievous delight in his eyes. "Well, let's see. It appears to be a unique shade of—hmmm—green?"

"Brown," I corrected.

Kwan looked doubtful as he held a bit of the sleeve fabric between his thumb and forefinger. "Wool?"

"Camel," I said hopefully.

Kwan turned me around again. "Lapels a tad wideish, don't you think? And bit low-slung back here?" He was pulling on the back panel. "And the double vent is a nice touch. Goes with those lapels."

"A perfect fit," I insisted. I held out my arms to show how the sleeves just hit my wrist.

"Don't tell me. Filene's Basement." It was infuriating—he was right, of course. I'd bought it last spring and it had hung in my closet waiting for the right moment. Clearly, I'd jumped the gun.

"Are you two quite finished?" Gloria asked. "Because if you're not, I'd appreciate it if you'd take your clever banter elsewhere. I've got work to do."

"Killjoy," I muttered. We moved down the hall and out of earshot. "I suppose you think I should go to *your* tailor at Needless Markups."

"I don't think they'll let you into Neiman's in these clothes."

Before I could come back at him, Kwan peeled off to visit a patient. I went looking for Maria Whitson. It had been ten days since she was admitted. She wasn't in her room. I found her perched on a window bench in the living room, off to one side behind the group of about a half dozen patients who were listening to our music therapist singing over a syncopated piano. In a falsetto voice that rivaled Little Anthony's, he belted, "The joint is jumpin'. . . ."

And it was. A cacophony of tambourines and maracas accompanied the music. Mr. O'Flanagan was there, his foot pumping up and down. Mrs. Blum was singing along in her own inimitable falsetto. Silhouetted against the morning sun, her eyes half-closed, her mouth relaxed, Maria Whitson swayed gently to the music. Her strawberry blond hair was pulled back and she wore blue jeans and a dark, loose-fitting sweater.

The song ended with a piano flourish. Maria raised her hands to clap. The din of maracas and tambourines continued haphazardly after the song's end. She looked expectantly toward the piano.

I walked over to her. "Ms. Whitson? I hate to take you away from this, but would you mind coming with me so we can chat for a few minutes where it's quieter?"

I led the way into the dining room. Maria took the seat she usually occupied during meals. I poured a cup of coffee for me, decaf with milk and two sugars for her, and brought them to the table.

She stirred the coffee, set the plastic spoon on the table, picked up the cup, and took a cautious sip before setting it down again in front of her. I waited. Maria's eyes darted around the room before coming to rest on the bowl of fruit on a side table. She started to get up.

"You seem to be a little better today," I said. "Clearer."

She stopped moving but she didn't stop looking, her hands twisting at the bottom of her sweater. I didn't want to move the food away. Better if she could resist on her own.

"Yes," I said. "I think you definitely do."

She turned to face me and sank back into the chair. "I'm still not myself," she said.

"Remember, you've been on some very powerful medications. Your system is getting rid of their effects. You're probably still feeling odd, less in control than you're used to. But you're definitely looking better." In fact, Maria Whitson looked almost pretty. Cheekbones and a strong chin were emerging from her formerly doughy face. Her blue eyes were clearer, more focused. She must have realized it as well because she was looking past me to where I knew we had a large mirror hanging on the wall.

She picked up the plastic spoon off the table and held it in her lap, staring at it.

"How are you sleeping?"

"Fine," she said quietly.

"I wonder if you could tell me a little about your family. Why don't you start with how you feel about your parents?"

"My parents," she said, her face turning dark and angry. The spoon snapped in her hand. She closed her fist around the pieces. "My parents." Her look softened. "You know, it's like I still love them, but I know I shouldn't."

"That's good," I said.

"What do you mean by that?"

"It's good because you're being honest with yourself. Were there good times?" I asked.

She stopped and thought. "My father always wanted a son, but they got me instead. Not that he didn't love me," she said, looking even more confused and starting now to pick at a thread in her pants. "Or he said he did, anyway. He taught me to throw a mean curve. I was about the only girl in Melrose who could throw overhand. But how could he . . . ?" She wiped a tear from the corner of her eye with the heel of her hand. "You see, that's the whole problem. Just when I start thinking nice things, the flashbacks start. It's like I've got these two channels going in my brain."

Maria folded one arm in front of her and with the other hand, pulled down a piece of hair from above her forehead and tugged on it.

"You have images playing and replaying in your brain?" I asked.

She nodded, now twirling the hair around.

"I wonder if you could just hold that thought for a little bit and tell me about the car accident? I'm curious to know what started all of this, and afterwards, how you came to remember, what made you pull up all of these—uh—images." I was trying to avoid the word "flashback." It implies a faithful replaying of actual events, and one thing I've learned is that the brain can be a very unreliable historian.

Maria took a brief sideways look at the bowl of fruit. She shook her head and gnawed at a cuticle. I set a box of tissues on the table and Maria took one.

"It was two years ago," she said. "Happened practically in my own driveway. I was out running. Sprinting the last mile. My husband got back at the same time."

"You said it was an accident?"

"It was real dark out and my street isn't too well lit," Maria answered, avoiding my eyes. "I'm just coming up the driveway, the idiot pulls in without looking. We collided, only he was bigger." Maria made two fists and bashed them together. "Kaboom."

"And your husband?"

"He does what he always does when something unexpected happens. He gets angry. Furious with me. Always looking for someone to blame. That's what happened later, too."

"Later?"

"When I stopped wanting him to touch me. When I couldn't stand even being near him. He got angry. First he blamed me." She was biting at her cuticle between sentences, and now it was starting to bleed. "Then my parents. Then, when he heard about the sexual abuse, he was ready to kill Uncle Nino."

"Did he ever try to harm you?" I asked.

She stared at the blood oozing from her finger and slowly licked it away. "No, not exactly. It's more like he wanted to control me. To own me."

She glanced at me and shifted her attention to a little hole in her jeans, picking at it with a stubby finger.

"And?" I asked, poking at the unsaid thoughts.

"Oh, nothing." She pulled at a loose thread. I waited. "It's just that sometimes I wonder if I made it happen. The accident. Only I screwed up." Maria directed the words into her lap as she scraped and dug, widening the hole in her jeans leg. "Maybe I've been trying to get it right ever since. Only I keep screwing it up. Because I can't do *anything* right."

Despite three attempts, she hadn't succeeded in killing herself. And now she was starting to ask herself why. Curiosity is a healthy impulse. I wanted to move her away from the depressive affect that hung over her, explore these same issues but focus on the externals of the events.

"I read in your medical file that you hit your head on the windshield."

Maria rubbed her left temple and forehead. "Right here." She sniffed. "Broke my arm, too. They gave me X-rays at the hospital. Supposedly there wasn't any brain damage. But for months, I just couldn't get it together. At first I was dizzy. I couldn't even get out of bed without throwing up. I couldn't focus or remember the simplest things. It was so frustrating. I couldn't work, so I went out on disability. I felt, like, really lardy. Like some big enormous slug. I had nothing to do. And I couldn't run. Just like when I was twelve years old, I started to obsess about food."

Maria stole a quick look at the fruit bowl and looked back at me. "I kept thinking, I'm not going to have enough to eat, like when my mother put me on a diet in junior high and we had tofu and grapefruits for weeks on end. So I kept a stash in the car. My husband wouldn't go near that car after the accident. Even after it got fixed. Like *it* was somehow responsible. Oreos, Mallomars, Cheez Doodles, Doritos. Ring Dings," she said dreamily, chewing again on that cuticle. "I'd eat and eat, and then feel so disgusted that I'd make myself throw up. I couldn't stand to even look in the mirror, I was so fat and repulsive."

Maria was kneading and tugging on her sweater again. "Rehab was a joke. The PT helped my arm. But the rest? Give me a break. They treated me like a retard. They had me doing picture puzzles. Arts and crafts. Connect the dots." Maria opened her mouth, stuck her index finger inside, and made a gagging sound to demonstrate what she thought of their so-called therapy. "It seemed so stupid. And the worst thing? I couldn't do any of it. So finally I just stopped going.

"Then I'm getting more and more depressed. I can't sleep because I keep having these weird dreams. And I'm constantly afraid that something terrible is going to happen." Maria paused and gulped for air, her face convulsing with the memory. "Honest to God," she sobbed, "I couldn't even go to the mall without having a panic attack in the parking lot."

She took another tissue and wiped her eyes, pausing a few moments to collect herself before starting again. "I kept going to my doctor and saying, 'Help me!' And he'd scratch his head and say, 'Give it time.' And my family would say, 'Give it time.'" Her hands were jerking, tearing the tissue into shreds. "I got really desperate. There didn't seem to be any way I was going to get better. I wanted to kill myself."

Maria took a long pause and a deep breath followed by a little hiccup. "That was when I started to see Dr. Baldridge."

"You must have thought you were going crazy," I commented.

Maria nodded, her face now red with emotion and slick with perspiration.

This was the kind of story I heard over and over again from patients who suffer needlessly at the hands of health care providers who act like a bunch of robots, treating symptoms without paying the slightest attention to context. It was textbook medicine at its worst.

I tried to get past my own diatribe on this and say something helpful. "You know, it's very easy for me to armchair quarterback at this late date, but let me tell you about two things that often happen to people who have minor head injuries like yours. First, even though the MRI didn't show any damage, when your head hit the windshield, the sudden force probably stretched your axons—the nerve fibers in your brain. This results in a condition we call post-concussive syndrome and people with PCS get exactly the symptoms you describe: memory loss, concentration difficulties, dizziness. And your doctor was right—left untreated, it disappears in a few months."

As I talked, Maria stared at me and chewed on her thumb. Her breathing slowed as she took in what I was saying.

"But then that second thing I mentioned kicks in. Your own psyche reacts to the fact that your brain isn't functioning. You get upset and anxious," Maria was nodding, "and the tricky part is that it looks like the post-concussive syndrome isn't getting better. But what's really happening is that post-traumatic stress, which is an emotional thing, is taking over. In terms of symptoms, they're the same. You're anxious, depressed, you have trouble remembering, trouble paying attention, you don't sleep well, you have funny dreams. But because the brain really is healed, sometimes doctors think you're malingering. And for someone who's really sick, there's nothing worse than to hear a doctor say, 'There's nothing wrong with you! Why aren't you getting better?'

"Problem is, the doctor treats what is now post-traumatic stress—an emotional condition—as if it were post-concussive syndrome—a physical condition. And as you discovered in rehab, it's exactly the wrong treatment. You're already very anxious and they have you doing these repetitive exercises. Instead of experiencing success after success, relearning things gradually, you experience frustration after frustration, and your anxiety level climbs even higher. You become more dysfunctional, to the point where you can't even do everyday tasks like going to the mall."

Maria's eyes were wide. Her hands were fluttering in her lap.

"The reason I tell you this is because it sounds like you thought you were going crazy. And I want to reassure you that you weren't."

"That's just how it was," Maria said, leaning toward me. "I thought it was my fault. Like I wasn't trying hard enough or something."

"Trying harder can actually make it worse."

For the first time, Maria sat completely still. "Dr. Baldridge understood. I knew the minute I met him that he'd be able to help me." She paused, her eyes shining. "He just radiates so much wisdom and understanding." Dr. Baldridge's brand of medicine encouraged just this kind of hero worship—doctor as savior, prophet, and God, all rolled up in one neat package and brought to you, care of your friendly health insurance provider.

"So you started to see Dr. Baldridge on a regular basis?"

"Yes, and I told him about the dreams I was having. How I couldn't sleep. And then I couldn't stay awake the next day because I wasn't getting enough sleep. He said the only way for me to free myself was to get to the bottom of it. He said the dream was a repressed memory. And it was trying to tell me something. I was gorging and vomiting because I was trying to vomit up the truth. He said if I could remember the truth about my past, then I wouldn't need to purge myself anymore.

"I felt so good during our sessions. Like I was a real person and he understood everything that was going on in my mind. He asked me, had I ever been sexually abused? He told me to open my mind's gateway. Not to be afraid. I felt so safe with him. I let the memories come." There was some sadness in her voice as she continued. "He kept saying, 'The truth will set you free.' He was so pleased when I started to remember."

Now Maria started pulling on the edge of her sweater with one hand and twirling her hair with the other. "There was this dream I kept having. At first it was fuzzy. Dr. Baldridge hypnotized me to help me see it more clearly.

"In the dream, I'm in the basement of our house. We had a big rumpus room down there with a TV and some beanbag chairs. All I could remember at first was that it felt like I was suffocating in one of those beanbag chairs. It was just closing in around me, cutting off the air.

"Dr. Baldridge kept asking me, 'Who else is in the room with you?' At first I couldn't see anyone. I thought it was only me.

Then I realized, Uncle Nino was down there with me. He was standing at the foot of the stairs, staring at me."

The room seemed eerily silent as Maria continued. Her hands came to rest in her lap and bits of tissue fell to the floor. Her eyes were focused in midair in front of her. "Then he came over and sat beside me. He reached inside my shirt and touched my breasts. I was very scared. I remembered hoping that he'd stop and go away. Then he unzipped his pants and made me touch him. Then he took off my shorts and got on top of me. When I struggled, he started to choke me. I can still remember, this bowl of M&Ms somehow ended up wedged into my back—"

Her story was interrupted by a clanging. Maria gave a startled leap. The bell rang again and continued ringing. Maria clapped her hands over her ears and shook her head.

At best, fire drills at the Pearce are the ultimate in bureaucratic nonsense. Because we'd run the risk of losing patients if we actually left the building, we dutifully herd everyone into the common area. Then it's like trying to keep puppies in a basket. And because they never tell us when there's going to be one, the unexpected interruption can come at just this kind of critical juncture, destroying hours of work.

I cursed under my breath. Out loud, I said: "Fire drill. I'm afraid we'll have to take a little unscheduled break. But then we'll pick up where we left off."

I fully expected Maria to be as upset as I was by the interruption. But she wasn't. She followed me out into the hall, her hands still covering her ears.

To anyone who didn't know better, it looked like utter chaos. The alarm bell was still going. Gloria, looking very much like a drill sergeant with an invisible whistle in her mouth, was marching up and down making sure that every patient was attached to a staff member. Kwan was wheeling Mrs. Blum down the hall while coaxing Mr. Kootz along in front. Kootz had an aviator's hat jammed onto his head and the earflaps now flapped along with his sneaker laces. True to form, Mrs. Blum was in ecstasy, wailing, "Cataldo! Cataldo!" in her screechy little voice, as if her ship had finally come in.

Maria and I wound up shoved into a corner. The room quickly turned warm and pungent, body odor competing with the smell of pine cleaner and bleach. Gloria's shouted orders cut through the din. Maria stood silent, her eyes unfocused, arms now loose at her sides, immune to it all.

I checked my watch and fidgeted as stragglers continued to enter the room. The timing couldn't have been worse. I didn't want Maria to slip so far away that we'd be unable to resume our talk.

When the clanging finally died out, twenty-five of us were packed in like sardines, waiting for permission to resume our normal craziness. I checked my watch again. Gloria would be pleased. Although it had seemed like an eternity, our so-called evacuation had been accomplished in record time.

With the all-clear signal, Maria returned to the dining room with me.

"I'm really sorry about the interruption," I said.

Maria shrugged and settled into her chair. "Um, I was telling you about my dream."

"Right," I said, relieved that she seemed to be willing to pick up right where we'd left off. "You dreamed that you were in the basement of your house—"

"And Dr. Baldridge helped me to see my uncle in it . . . raping me." Maria reached for a tissue and pushed her hair out of her face.

She settled back and started to recite in a hollow singsong. "It was in the basement of our house. I was in the beanbag chair. He came over and sat beside me. He reached inside my shirt and touched my breasts. I was very scared. I remember hoping that he'd stop and go away. Then he unzipped his pants and made me touch him. Then he took off my shorts and got on top of me. When I struggled, he started to choke me."

There was no point in my taking notes because the story she told was almost identical to the one she'd told me earlier. I noticed that Maria was dry-eyed as she recited. I was reminded of how Sylvia Jackson described the night she'd been shot. Like Sylvia, Maria had probably already told this horrific story so many times that it had lost its power. After all, that was the point of telling and retelling. Surely it was healthier than the avoidance at which I'd become expert.

But something else was going on here. It was as if a phonograph needle had paused, midair, and then reengaged. Apparently, Maria had only one image of this event, and that image was synchronized to a set script. I scratched my head and stored the thought.

"After I remembered my uncle raping me, Dr. Baldridge helped me recover other memories."

"You saw Dr. Baldridge often?" I asked.

Maria ran her hand down her neck, tugged her sweater hard across one shoulder. "At the beginning, I did. Twice a week. He just blew me away. I'd get to his office and I'd feel closed up— you know, like something all dried up inside a shell. I'd lie down. He'd light candles. It was wonderful. I'd lie there, watching the candles flicker. Then we did relaxation exercises. I could feel the tension leave every part of my body.

"Then he told me, 'Clear your mind and focus on the pain.'" Maria sang the words like an incantation. "'When you're in the circle, it's safe. Look at the pain. Feel the pain. Transform it! Find the images.'

"At first, I didn't see any images. But I kept trying." She giggled. "I felt, like, constipated, know what I mean? Like I had to go to the bathroom. I'd sit there and sit there and nothing happened. But I didn't give up. I kept trying and trying until I saw him—Uncle Nino, standing on the stairs. Then, little by little,

I remembered the dream. And finally I remembered that it wasn't a dream at all. It was real.

"Then it started to get easier. We worked on another image that I had. An image of someone else. And I realized it wasn't just Uncle Nino. It was my father, too. He started it. I was two and a half years old. Still in my crib. He put his fingers up inside me.

"Then, it seemed as if the floodgates opened and I could get at all of these images. I remembered how my father made me shower with him after we played ball. He'd touch me and make me touch him. And one time we went to my grandparents' house and he raped me in their backyard. Once he threatened to rape me with a fishing pole in the garage. I must have been six or seven years old." Maria panted for air as if she'd been running.

"Tell me," I asked, "besides the terrible memories of abuse, what are your other earliest memories?"

Maria squeezed her eyes shut. She opened them. "I remember getting a Wonder Woman lunch box. It was something I really *really* wanted. And my father bought it for me. I remember, he called me his little wonder girl." Maria's brow wrinkled and her eyebrows dipped together. "But he just bought it because he was feeling guilty about what he was doing to me. Later, I lost it in the school cafeteria. I think I must have deliberately left it there."

"So was that in kindergarten?"

Maria shook her head. "First grade."

"Do you have any earlier memories?" I asked. Maria squeezed her eyes shut and strained forward. Uh-oh. Was this the trap she'd fallen into with Dr. Baldridge? "Don't worry if they're not there. Your uncle—have you remained in contact with him?"

Maria Whitson stared into her lap. "For a long time I wasn't. I cut myself off from all of them." She crossed her arms, tilted her head and looked past me, hardened her expression, and then looked directly at me. "But I confronted him before he died."

"And when was that?"

"Earlier this year," she said. A little bell went off in my head. Hadn't Maria Whitson's second suicide attempt been six months ago? "I told him what he'd done to me. Of course, he denied everything. Then he cried and begged me to forgive him. The bastard."

Despite the strong language, her face had little expression and her voice held little emotion. And she continued staring at me. I waited for her to go on, but she seemed to have run out of words.

"I was wondering about something you said at the beginning of our talk—that when you see your parents, some of the images they bring to mind are pleasant. This will be something important for us to understand."

"I guess it is weird," Maria observed, "considering how much I hate them."

"Didn't you call your father when you tried to kill yourself."

Her jaw dropped. "You think I called him for help? I called him because I wanted him to know what he'd done to me."

"But in fact, he did help you. You would have died."

Her voice turned strident. "I *wanted* to die. And I wanted him to know it was his fault."

Not far in the back of my mind I was feeling the pressure of time. With managed care, Maria Whitson's days with us were numbered. Before we released her, we'd have to put in place the support and protection she needed. So I pressed forward with a question I knew she wasn't quite ready to tackle. "Have you thought any more about whether your parents can visit you? We'd like to—"

Maria interrupted with a vehement. *"No!"*

"Ms. Whitson, have you started to consider what you're going to do when you leave here? You'll need money. A place to stay." She didn't answer. "Are there friends you can stay with?"

She shook her head. "I have no friends."

"Relatives?"

She shook her head harder.

"Well, we're thinking about those things, too. Meeting with your parents doesn't mean you forgive them. It doesn't mean you accept their help. But it might turn out that they can help you, even indirectly, after you leave here. Or it might turn out that we need to set up an environment that protects you from them. That's why I want to meet with them here, where it's safe." I pressed, "Perhaps there's someone on the staff you'd like to be with you when you see them?"

Maria seemed to soften. "Maybe I could handle it if Gloria's there. She understands."

"Gloria, then. Absolutely. I'll make the arrangements."

I left Maria Whitson feeling as if we'd made progress, but convinced there was much more ground yet to be broken. Later that afternoon, I found Gloria sipping an afternoon cup of coffee and dragging on an unlit cigarette in the little kitchen behind the nurses' station. I pulled up a chair opposite her.

"Why can't they at least tell us when they've got a fire drill scheduled," I grumbled.

"You know as well as I do that would defeat the whole purpose."

"I know, I know, but it seems designed to destroy exactly the kind of therapeutic environment we're trying to build."

"Having a tough day?" she asked.

"Sorry, I'm not criticizing you. You did a great job, as usual. It went off without a hitch."

"It took five minutes to get everyone herded together. That's the best we've done."

We sat in companionable silence, looking out the window into the dusk that was descending earlier and earlier each afternoon. I cleared my throat. I was nervous about broaching the subject of Maria Whitson's family meeting.

Gloria finessed me. "Maria Whitson asked me to be there with her when she sees her parents."

"And?"

"And what? Of course I will."

I waited. Gloria crossed her arms in front of her, cocked her head, and pursed her lips. I gazed back at her, letting the silence grow. "This one's got you tied up like a pretzel, hasn't it?" I observed.

Gloria stood up, crossed over to the window, and contemplated the twilight. I shuffled through my appointment book, feigning interest. When I looked up again, her reflected image was staring back at me, chin thrust out. I recognized the stance. On the rare occasion when Gloria is convinced that the rest of us are blind to a patient's vulnerability, she turns into this block of granite, challenging one and all to take a poke at her or to back off.

"When it happened to Rachel, there wasn't anyone to protect her," she said. Rachel was Gloria's partner, the woman with whom she shared her life. "She went through this with her family. Her father abused her—sexually, physically, and emotionally. And no one, *no one* was there to get her through it. She's very damaged. And the only way she's been able to heal is by confronting her family, asserting control, and cutting herself off from them completely." She stared out the window. "So it's very hard for me to be objective. Of course I realize Maria Whitson is not Rachel. But their situations are so similar."

I took off my glasses and rubbed the bridge of my nose. "I think your empathy has been very helpful for Maria. It makes her feel safe. But you're right, her situation is not at all clear-cut."

"Believe me, I see that. Forgetting for twenty years what she now remembers as repeated, violent abuse?"

"And each time she tells me about what happened, she uses virtually the same words, like she's reading a movie script," I added. "And Dr. Baldridge bringing it back through hypnosis.

We may never know what did or didn't happen to Maria Whitson when she was a little girl."

Gloria licked her lips. "That's what I keep telling myself. And it's not the point, anyway. She's only here with us for a short time. After that, she hasn't got a whole lot of options."

"She makes all of us feel like protecting her."

"Protect her, yes. But she doesn't need to be infantilized. She deserves to work through her own pain and reach her own decisions. And that's what I'd like to help her do."

Sometimes Gloria made me want to stand up and cheer.

22

I HAD a quiet weekend at home while the Head of the Charles Regatta turned my river into a big frat party. Six thousand rowers clogging the river and two hundred thousand spectators occupying every bit of the riverbank—not my scene.

Monday morning, I didn't even try to get on the river. With everyone trying to get their boat out of the water at once, it would have been like driving on Beacon Street near Boston University on September 1, National Student Moving Day. Unmitigated chaos. With the start of the trial a week away, I went directly from home to Chip's office for a strategy session. I parked on Mass Ave in Central Square, fed the meter six quarters, and headed down the street.

Chip's office was in one of the only office buildings for miles. A cement tower apparently molded by some immense waffle iron, it had stood alone for decades, a harbinger of someone's urban renewal nightmare that fizzled on the drawing board. With the demise of rent control, the surrounding blue-collar neighborhood was rapidly turning white, property values were skyrocketing, and the long-awaited makeover of Central Square was finally beginning to happen. A Starbucks across the street was being picketed by a motley array of local characters carrying signs protesting its takeover of the old Harvard Donut Shop.

Purists aside, change has been good for the area. The best ice cream could now be found down the street at Toscanini's. With each wave of immigrants, new ethnic restaurants have taken their place alongside Irish pubs. Cambodian, Thai, and Indian restaurants rub shoulders with sub shops. The Falafel Palace sits enthroned on one corner in an oversize chess piece, a white-tiled honest-to-God castle complete with turret. In bygone days a White Tower hamburger stand (or hamburg as they say around here), it epitomizes Central Square's transition from a white bread to a pita bread neighborhood. The next wave— yuppie coffee and Gap jeans—would be a whole lot less interesting.

A bank and a downscale Buck a Book occupied the first floor of Chip's building. I pushed through the double doors. The lobby had a slightly dilapidated air to it, but it was clean and someone had actually dusted the plastic plants that flanked the building directory.

I took the elevator to the seventh floor. The preservationists would have been delighted at how little had changed here in two years. As I walked the familiar walk to the end of the hall, I felt anxiety tighten my stomach. Breathe, I told myself, and counted steps.

The door to the law office was open and I could hear phones ringing. I looked through the doorway. The central room was crowded with a squadron of steel desks with an assortment of very young men and women at work there or close by. Around the edges were small offices, separated from the center area by glass partitions. I stepped inside. I spotted Chip through one of the partitions. He was on the phone but he saw me. He waved and held up one finger.

I found a chair and perched on the edge of it, shifting my bulging leather briefcase onto my lap. The office teemed with activity. Voices were raised, phones rang. I felt apart, awkwardly suspended, as if I weren't even in the room but looking at it from the wrong end of a telescope. I opened my briefcase and rummaged through the papers.

The smell of fresh-cut watermelon made me look up. Annie was an alien among the well-dressed young legal types. In her jeans and plaid flannel shirt, her long brown hair curling wildly around her face, Annie felt like a breeze blowing in from an open window.

In spite of myself, I grinned.

"Been awhile since you were here," she said.

I nodded and went back to rummaging.

"Heard about your car," she said. "And after losing the boat . . ." Her voice trailed off. I knew she was watching me but I couldn't meet that look. I could handle loss. It was sympathy that made me want to throw up.

"I talked to Mac." Now her voice was brisk, all business. "Swears he didn't know Sylvia Jackson until after the murder. Admits he knew of her."

Now I looked up. "Meaning?"

"Some of his buddies knew her—well. And you were right. They're not on the official list of early suspects. They were questioned. Discreetly."

"You don't think he's hiding something, do you?" I asked.

"I told you before, I'm not entirely unbiased. If he helped an old lady across the street, I'd suspect ulterior motives."

"He does seem so"—I searched for the word, rejecting "rabid" and "insane"—"overreactive. It's more than bad chemistry between him and me. Maybe he's protecting his buddies. Or maybe he's protecting himself."

"Or maybe he's just an asshole," Annie said.

"Right," I said. "Except that he's put himself in a good position to shape what she remembers. How do we know her memories didn't develop courtesy of his suggestions?"

"We don't," Annie said.

"I found something out, too," I said. "You know the pleated

paper cup that held the meds Syl OD'ed on? They don't use that kind of cup for medication. They use white plastic ones."

"So, the pills Sylvia Jackson found in her bathroom weren't left there by a nurse."

"Or doctor. Or any of the hospital staff. At least not in an official capacity. Speaking of which, would you expect a nurse to carry a handgun around in her purse?"

"Well, it's certainly not your typical nurse gear. But you'd be surprised how many people—women—have guns these days. And nurses aren't so good at doing what you'd expect them to do, either. Ever notice how many of them smoke?" Annie stopped. "Who are we talking about, anyway?"

"The nurse I have to get past every time I go to see Sylvia Jackson. Carolyn Lovely. She was with Syl in the parking garage. A gun fell out of her purse when she jumped to get out of the way. Can you check on something? Find out if she's got a restraining order against an ex-husband."

"That would explain the gun."

"It would. And another thing. Angelo Ruggiero, the nephew Syl refers to as her guardian angel—"

"I think the police interviewed a nephew early on. But the name doesn't sound right. Not Ruggiero. Angelo something-else-Italian. I've got it in my notes somewhere."

"I'd like to know more about him and his name's a good place to start. I wonder if he was involved in any business with his uncle. Stuart mentioned that Tony was waiting for some deal to happen before he'd marry Sylvia Jackson."

"Typical male excuse."

"Yeah. But what if there was some big deal that he was about to close? And what if Angelo and he were doing business together? And what if—?"

Annie held up her hand to ward off my onslaught of what-ifs. "I know he had an alibi. I'll see what I can find out."

Just then, Chip appeared and led me back to his office. Annie disappeared into a similar office along the opposite wall.

I unloaded documents onto a round table, alongside the files Chip already had stacked there. The phone rang and I waited while Chip disposed of the caller. The windows of the corner office were filmed with dirt and the furniture was gunmetal gray—a desk, file cabinets, and chairs. Only the chair behind the desk—a swivel chair with a dark leather seat cushion and padded armrests—looked like it had been picked out by an actual person.

One wall was floor-to-ceiling law books. Hanging on the wall behind the desk was a series of portraits of a girl, starting with a crude crayon drawing and evolving into an accomplished pencil and watercolor sketch. In a series of photographs, a girl's face matured from infant to prom princess.

"Your daughter's growing up," I commented.

"She got rid of her braces and now, look out," Chip said.

A Grateful Dead poster hung on the back of the door—a red, white, and blue skeleton. Fillmore East, 1976. I should have known. That wry sense of humor, the intensity, a social conscience long after it had gone out of fashion. Chip had the soul of a Dead Head.

"New poster?" I asked.

"Got it in on e-Bay. I couldn't resist."

"Were you there?"

"I was," he said wistfully.

"That's amazing. I was there, too."

"If you'd told me then that this is where I'd end up." Chip laughed and shook his head.

I glanced through the glass, into the busy office. "This place hasn't changed. Not a single one of your colleagues has gotten a day older. How do you do that?"

"We send out for replacements every six months."

"But you're still here."

He looked around, as if surprised to find that he was. "It's definitely not inertia that keeps me here. I still buy into the notion that people who can't afford a private attorney need me. And this place is addictive."

I noticed a framed photograph on Chip's desk: Chip and four men, all wearing three-piece suits topped off incongruously with baseball caps, grinned back at me. I could make out the inscription on one of the caps: MURDER SQUAD. As if defending killers were part of some perverse game. "When they come to certify you insane, I'll offer this photograph as evidence," I told him.

"Not a great way to hang on to your family, though. My wife left me last year. I guess she couldn't take the roller-coaster ride and the all-nighters. Never mind the threats in the mail, the nasty phone calls. Can't say that I blame her." He swallowed. "I think Kate's death was a piece of it. It showed how vulnerable this work makes us all."

I stared at the patriotic skeleton. None of us at the Grateful Dead concert had any inkling of the evil in the world. Or of how oblivious we'd be if the devil himself were sitting beside us, sharing a toke.

Annie pushed the door open and slid inside carrying another dozen file folders and some small spiral notebooks.

I spent a few minutes explaining Syl's personality tests. I summed up the results: "Naturally, this thing that's happened to her is a very significant event in her life and it's left her feeling incomplete, broken, small and powerless. The tests tell us that she uses denial and distortion to deal with all of these negatives. She sees something frightening or disturbing and she runs the other way — coming up with happily-ever-after flowers and paper butterflies."

"Paper butterflies?" Annie asked.

I nodded. "For instance, she'll turn an inkblot one way and see severed limbs and hatchets. Then she flips it around, and lo and behold, a paper butterfly. It's called reaction formation. She's using it to deal with the unpleasant images that are originating both inside and outside of her."

"She gave Stuart Jackson paper butterflies the day before the murder. It was his birthday," Annie said.

"One thing's for sure. They represent safety for her now."

"By the way, I checked around," Annie said as she flipped open a small notebook. "Turns out Sylvia Jackson told a friend at work that story about how Tony walked in on her when she and Stuart were in bed together."

"Did Syl mention what Tony was wearing?" I asked.

Annie laughed. "She did. This woman remembered because she thought Syl said Tony was dressed in a gorilla suit—like a monkey. Then when Syl described it, she realized she'd meant the other kind of guerrilla."

Chip said, "I want to bring that earlier incident out at trial without calling Stuart to testify."

"It's just the kind of thing Sylvia Jackson does—mix old memories up with her more recent past," I said.

"So we've got that," Chip said. "We've got the test results. Seems as if they couldn't be more clear. But how to show that to the jury," Chip slowed down, thinking as he spoke, "without turning them off? They're going to want to believe her. She's appealing, sincere, and very vulnerable. And I have to undermine every single word she says without appearing to be an ogre—not an easy line to walk." He continued, eyes narrowing as strategies formed in his head. "If I'm solicitous and gain her trust, then we should find that she's just as suggestible on the witness stand as the police who questioned her found her to be in the hospital."

I shifted in my seat, feeling acutely uncomfortable. I pushed aside a vision of Syl dressed in a hooded red cape and Chip in a sheepskin. I wasn't her protector. I wasn't even her physician. None of the normal doctor-patient responsibilities and restrictions applied. Still, the vision of Red Riding Hood returned, only this time I was the wolf in sheep's clothing.

Chip went on, "And then, after she tells the court what happened, we hit her with the discrepancies between what she's just said and her earlier statements. She's going to get confused and flustered."

"Poor thing," Annie commented, "she's contradicted herself a million times."

"On the other hand," I argued, "don't you think everyone's had that experience? You know, you tell a story and then, over time, the details drift. Ever reminisce with a friend about something you did together and find out that your memories are totally at odds with one another? It doesn't mean the event didn't happen."

"Sure. It happens to everyone," Chip answered. "It's a question of degree. We need to poke so many holes in the foundation of her story that it's clear to the jury that it's built on sand."

Annie offered, "But you'll need to be careful. Badgering can backfire."

Chip agreed. "Right. I don't want to make her seem more of a victim than she already is."

"Sylvia Jackson's not on trial for murder," I said coldly, echoing the words of her ex-husband. Annie and Chip stared at me. I got up and tried to pace, but the office was too small. "It would be a whole lot more satisfying if murder trials were about figuring out who's guilty. About getting at the truth. Instead, they're all about appearance, about manipulating the jurors' perceptions. I know. Let's design a board game. Call it Murder Squad. The goal is to collect as much money as you can and never go to jail."

"Peter," Annie said gently, "we're the good guys. The trial starts next Monday and Stuart Jackson is depending on us."

23

THE TRIAL was into its second week and I was more and more anxious as the day I'd have to testify approached. I was getting up early to work on my car, putting in a full day at the Pearce, rowing at dusk, relying on routine to pull me through.

Chip called me every other night with an update. They'd selected a jury and forensic evidence was being presented. The D.A. was using that evidence to meticulously build a case that pointed to Stuart Jackson as the murderer. But there were holes. No one had seen him in Cambridge on the night of the murder, a night when he claimed to be home with the flu. The gun still hadn't been found. The prosecution speculated that it was the .22-caliber handgun now missing from Syl's bedside table. No one had been able to explain how Tony's hair wound up in Stuart Jackson's camouflage cap. The single thumbprint on the steering wheel of Syl's car, a steering wheel otherwise wiped clean of prints, remained unexplained. It didn't belong to Syl. It wasn't Stuart's or Tony's, either. Find the owner of that thumbprint, Chip had suggested to the jury, and you'll find the real killer. Find the owner of that thumbprint, the D.A. told them, and you'll find the mechanic who last serviced the car.

At the hospital, we had our hands full. Miracle cures are always suspect, and Maria Whitson was having one.

Gloria spotted it first. "Have you noticed the change? She's too bright and it's too all of a sudden. It feels as if she's on something."

"You're worried?"

"Concerned. No question about it, she's made progress. But there's something about her that doesn't add up."

When I found Maria Whitson, she looked nothing like the puffy, doped-up person we'd admitted more than four weeks earlier. Once lifeless little indentations, her eyes were now bright and enormous, with less face around them. Her skin was clear and her hair was clean and artfully arranged to frame her face. If you disregarded the baggy sweats that needed a good washing, she looked like a woman you'd see on Newbury Street having wine at a tapas bar.

"I'm feeling so much better," she told me. The words came out in a rush and seemed a little too loud. "And I've decided to see my parents. I know I'll be ready to leave soon."

As she waited for me to respond, she shifted back and forth from one foot to the other. Though her arms were still, I could sense the effort it took on her part to keep them from flying about.

I hedged. "I'm glad you're feeling better. You're certainly looking brighter. Let's discuss it this afternoon when we meet."

I walked away with a strong sense of unease. When I saw Gloria again, I told her I agreed—something didn't feel right. "I'd be less concerned if this were less sudden and if we had a better idea of what kicked off this most recent suicide attempt."

Gloria pulled out Maria's chart. We went through it, not sure what we were looking for.

"Her weight's down," I commented. "She came in at one-sixty. She's down to one fifty. Not extraordinary since she's stopped bingeing."

"She look like one fifty to you?" Gloria asked. "I'd have

guessed one thirty-five." Gloria pursed her lips and stared off in the direction of Maria's room.

I checked the weekly lab reports. "Her fluid balance is off. The lytes are skewed. Not a lot. But some."

"Shit."

"Gloria, I've got a session scheduled with Maria in an hour. Can you check her weight before then? And while you're doing that, get someone to search the room for drugs—just to be on the safe side."

When Gloria found me later, she was grim-faced. She handed me four blue plastic pouches. They were weights with Velcro fasteners, the kind joggers wrap around their arms or legs to give them an added challenge. "She was wearing these under her sweats when she got on the scale. Something else, too. I checked with housekeeping. Someone's been dropping food under the table at mealtimes. It's either Maria or someone sitting near her."

"Any drugs in her room?"

"Nothing. But in the process, we did find something. A cell phone. Hidden inside an empty pitcher."

"If that isn't the most bizarre. For a woman who keeps insisting that she has no friends, no relatives, nobody in the world who cares about her, who's she so concerned about staying in touch with?"

In my office, I set the weights on my desk and waited for Maria to arrive. The pouches together weighed easily ten pounds. That meant Maria was losing weight faster than was healthy. She couldn't be eating much. And the skew of her fluid balance suggested that she was making herself throw up the rest.

She arrived sullen. She flopped into a chair, slid down on her spine, and hugged her knees to her chest. "I want to go home," she said, addressing the space between her knees, her jaw stiff and set.

"And we want you to go home. Just as soon as you're well enough."

She looked at me through tears. "I am well," she insisted.

When I didn't answer, she screamed it. "*I am well!*"

"Ms. Whitson," I started.

"What good are you, anyway?" she shouted. "You don't understand anything. This place is a snake pit! And you're no Dr. Baldridge! He explained what was going on. You . . . you don't explain anything. Rules for this, rules for that, rules for everything. But you never tell me what the rules are!"

How quickly I'd gone from being the good Dr. Zak to the nasty Dr. Snake Pit. "Ms. Whitson, everyone here is trying to help you. But you have to help yourself, too. And right now, you're not."

Maria stood up and walked over to the window. She ducked her head into the dormer and leaned her head against the glass.

"You're not eating. You're making yourself throw up."

She scowled. "It's Gloria, isn't it? That wasn't my food she found under the table. Someone else threw it there. It's all crap anyway. You make us eat crap!"

"And," I held up the plastic weights, "you're pretending that everything *is* fine."

She started out gently tapping her head on the window, but it quickly escalated to banging as Maria sobbed, "Everything is fine. Everything *is* fine."

I leaped up to grab her but not before her head connected one final time, accompanied by the sound of splintering glass. When I pulled her away, there was a small empty circle in the windowpane with a spiderweb of cracks radiating from it.

"Everything is *not* fine. And I think you know it."

Maria struggled to get back to the window. Then she turned on me, her face white with rage, and shrieked, "You don't know anything, you bastard!" She scraped her stubby fingers harmlessly across my cheek. "You sonofabitch!" She kicked me in the leg.

Pain radiated up and down my shinbone. I backed away.

"Calm down and sit down, Ms. Whitson," I ordered sternly. "If you don't, I'm going to call Security to restrain you."

"What do you know about me?" Maria said, still yelling, taking a step toward me. "You don't understand the first thing about who I am. You think you do, but you don't get it at all."

"Okay. Then help me. Help me to understand. You want to get on with your life. And I want you to. Let's help each other."

Bright red blood oozed down Maria's forehead. She swiped her hand across her face and stared at the scarlet smear on her palm. "Oh God," she sobbed. Maria put her hands onto her temples and sank down onto the floor. Crying and rocking, she whispered, "I'm such a mess. A fat, ugly, useless slug."

I said nothing. The wound was bloody but it didn't look serious. I went back to my desk. I waited until the rocking stopped and she'd subsided into a heap. "This can't happen again, you know," I said then. "I can't allow it. You could hurt yourself or someone else." Maria stared down into her lap. "Let's talk about what you want."

I waited.

Maria sniffed and looked at me defiantly. "I want to get out of this snake pit. That what's I want."

"That makes two of us. Let's talk about the things you need to do to make that happen."

I wouldn't continue until she agreed. Silence wasn't enough.

Finally, Maria muttered, "So?" I waited. "So, what do I have to do?"

"We're going to make a contract. I'm going to write down what you have to do, and you're going to agree. Then we're both going to sign. All right?"

Maria nodded and struggled to stand. Grudgingly, she took the hand I offered.

When she was seated again, I crouched beside her to check her forehead. There didn't appear to be any glass in the wound. I took a tissue from my desk and pressed it over the gash. "Hold this until the bleeding stops." Maria held the tissue in place. "And when you go back downstairs, have one of the nurses check it."

I returned to my chair and started to write. "First, you have to eat, really eat, three meals a day. No more dropping it on the floor. We'll be noticing." Maria snuffled and watched as I wrote. "And second, no more throwing up after you're finished. We'll be checking your electrolytes and your weight every day to be sure you're not cheating. We'll have to put you on a fortified liquid or an IV if your weight doesn't stabilize." Worried that she might retreat to her room after this, I added, "And I want you to participate in activities on the unit."

I turned the paper around to face her and handed her a pen. While she stared at the three items I'd listed, I rubbed my shin where a tender lump was growing. It could as easily have been a knee to the groin. I was grateful for small favors.

As Maria signed her name, I wondered about that cell phone. She could make any calls she wanted. Keeping it hidden didn't make sense. On the other hand, one of the things that institutions like hospitals do is rob patients of their privacy. Maybe keeping the cell phone made Maria feel she still had something that was private, her own. And it seemed harmless enough.

24

THAT NIGHT, I dreamed that my phone was ringing. I picked it up but it kept ringing. I ran downstairs and tried picking up the extension in the living room, then the one in the kitchen. Then, with a logic that makes perfect sense in dreams, I found myself by the phone in the nurses' station on the unit. I picked up the phone there and the ringing stopped. I held the receiver to my ear and heard the muffled sound of a teapot whistling. I tried, but I couldn't pull the receiver away from the side of my face, the whistling growing louder and louder. I screamed, "Stop!" and was awakened by the sound of my own voice.

A moment later, my beeper went off. It was weird. The number flashing at me was the phone on the unit at the Pearce — the phone in the nurses' station.

I called. Kwan answered.

"There's been an accident," he said.

"What happened?"

"Gloria's been hurt. She slipped and fell in Maria Whitson's room. An ambulance is on the way."

"How's Maria?"

"Hysterical. She keeps insisting that it's her fault."

I checked the clock. It was after three. "I'm coming in," I said.

I got up, threw some cold water on my face, and pulled on a pair of jeans and a sweatshirt. I was out on the porch locking my front door when my mother's door cracked open. "You're going out?" she asked. She seemed tinier than usual inside her pink quilted bathrobe.

"They beeped me. What are you doing up? You okay."

"I'm up! That's how my nights are. I sleep a little. I'm up a little."

"Go back to bed. You look very tired. Sure you're okay?"

"You get to be my age, you'll look tired, too."

When I got to the Pearce, an ambulance, lights flashing and back doors flung open, was sitting at the back entrance to the unit. I parked on the access road and sprinted the rest of the way. The EMTs were carrying Gloria out on a stretcher. I trotted alongside. I wouldn't have admitted it but I was completely freaked out. Gloria looked ghastly. Her eyes were shut and her skin was white. Her forehead was loosely bandaged. Her beige cotton shirt was spattered with blood. I took her hand. It felt cool and clammy. Her eyelids fluttered. "Peter . . ." she said.

"You okay?"

She got in a half nod before freezing, grimacing with pain. The terror I felt must have shown because she squeezed my hand and whispered, "I'm okay. Really, Peter. I'm going to be fine. Don't worry."

"How did it happen?" I asked.

"Maria screamed. I went in. Must have slipped." It looked like every word hurt.

"I get the picture," I said.

Gloria closed her eyes and seemed to relax. I watched as they hoisted her into the ambulance and closed the doors. Silently, the ambulance pulled away and wound its way out of the complex.

I hurried inside, past the common area and down the hall to Maria Whitson's room. One of the night nurses was standing just outside the door. Inside, Kwan was crouched alongside Maria. She was on her hands and knees, rubbing at the floor with a wad of towels. What must have been blood had turned into pink smears. I started toward her but I couldn't go there. I gagged and backed away. I caught hold of the doorjamb and managed to keep my knees from buckling. The bloody scene in Kate's studio, a memory which I usually kept far in the recesses of my consciousness, came rushing forward.

I watched from what seemed like miles away. Maria was muttering the same thing, over and over. It sounded like her uncle's name—Nino. Then, "My fault. It's all my fault." Tears were streaming down her face.

"Ms. Whitson," Kwan said, taking hold of her hands gently, "you don't have to do this. We have a staff who can clean this up."

She gave him a wide-eyed stare. Then she looked past him and saw me sagging against the door frame. She seemed to pull herself up. She held her hands up in front of her face and stared at her palms. "I must have had a nightmare. I woke up, scared, on the floor. I screamed. The blood . . ."

She seemed overwrought. In fact, over-overwrought. The strong smell of Lady Macbeth in the air brought me back to the present like a whiff of smelling salts.

"Head wounds can make a mess," Kwan told her. "Gloria didn't lose consciousness, that's what counts."

"I was so angry with her. She said I was faking it. You don't think I'm faking, do you?" She was talking to me.

I swallowed and got my voice. "She meant you were faking your weight. And pretending to eat when you were really throwing away your food. And you were, weren't you?" Maria looked down at the floor.

"Ms. Whitson, being angry with someone doesn't make them get hurt," Kwan said.

I wondered if Maria believed him. For her, the line between feeling and reality was transparent and exceedingly permeable.

An orderly carrying a pail and mop squeezed past me into the room.

Kwan said to Maria, "Why don't you let Andrew here do this job and clean up." He helped her to her feet. "Jane?" he said. The night nurse came over. "Can you help Ms. Whitson?"

I managed to follow Kwan out of the room.

"You okay?" he asked.

I nodded wearily. Of course I wasn't okay. That wasn't new. What was new was that for the first time, not being okay had affected my work. I closed my eyes and opened them again, but not before my mind played back the pool of blood on the floor of Kate's studio, the blood that was all that remained after they'd taken her body to the morgue.

"Go back to bed," Kwan said. "Everything's under control here. Accidents happen."

"You think Gloria's going to be okay?"

"Just a nasty bump. The hospital's a precaution. They'll probably keep her for twenty-four hours and then send her home."

"Where were they taking her? Maybe I'll go—" I looked at my watch.

"Peter, there's not a thing you can do there but get in the way. Go home."

I didn't want to go home. I wanted to stay and hit my morning routine with a vengeance. But it was quarter past four. Such a stupid time. Too early to stay at work. Too late to go back to sleep. And the days were getting shorter so fast that it wouldn't be light enough to row for hours.

I trudged back out to my car and drove home, trying not to let any more pictures replay themselves in my head. At home, I lay down on the couch in the living room. After an hour, I got up and made a pot of coffee.

At six-thirty, I called in. Maria was sound asleep. I made another call and found out that Gloria's condition was "good."

I breathed a sigh of relief. I could manage without my boat. I could fix the car. But the Pearce without Gloria was a prospect I didn't want to contemplate.

25

Two DAYS later, Sylvia Jackson's picture was on the front page of the *Globe*. The prosecution's star witness was on the stand, listening intently, her mouth drooping ever so slightly on one side. In grainy black-and-white, she was an ordinary middle-aged woman. The photograph did nothing to convey her sensuality and quirky appeal.

According to the article, when the D.A. asked her, "And who did this to you?" she hesitated only a moment before pointing to the defendant and pronouncing his name, "Stuart Jackson."

I wondered how the jury imagined that this man, whom Annie so aptly described as "a hundred twenty pounds dripping wet," forced two-hundred-forty-pound Tony Ruggiero to submit as he strapped a pillowcase over his head and then inflicted forty-six bruises and fifteen stab wounds before shooting him. It was a beating so severe that the pathologist speculated it might have been administered by two assailants.

Chip had to be pleased with his cross-examination. He'd questioned Sylvia about the days before the murder. He asked her what she'd done, whom she'd talked to. She could remember very little. She couldn't remember what gift she'd given to

Stuart the day before the killing—those paper butterflies that kept showing up in the inkblots.

Chip hammered at the contradictions between her testimony and her earlier statements. Had she driven to the cemetery or had her assailant? Had she watched the beating from the stairs or from the living room? Hadn't she said at first that Tony was in the trunk of the car? When Chip pressed her to explain why she changed her mind, she'd snapped at him, "I know he wasn't in the trunk." When he asked her how she knew, her reply was all he could have hoped for: "I've read enough articles in the paper to find out what happened to him."

Chip must have let the remark hang there, hoping the point was not lost on the jury. If one memory had been shaped by information she'd picked up from the newspaper, then how many others had been molded the same way?

Chip walked Sylvia Jackson painstakingly through the interviews she'd had with Sergeant MacRae in the weeks after she woke up. He quoted the questions that had become more and more specific, more and more leading each day, tracing the shift from "Who did this to you?" to "Stuart did this to you, didn't he?"

He asked her if it was true that she'd wondered why Stuart didn't visit her in the hospital. Hadn't she confided her concerns to a nurse at the hospital? Chip put the question directly: "Did that nurse suggest a reason why Stuart wasn't coming to visit you at the hospital?"

"She told me why he wasn't coming to visit me at the hospital," she answered. "It was because he was a suspect."

And yet, despite all of the discrepancies that Chip exposed, despite the evidence that Sylvia Jackson had been reading the newspapers and talking to friends, gathering information that could then be incorporated into her memories, she'd been the star witness the prosecution had hoped she'd be. The newspaper described jurors in rapt attention, straining in their seats to catch her words, weeping openly when she described the murder. Could any amount of memory theory and test results offset the emotional power of her testimony?

I was so absorbed in the news of the trial, I nearly forgot we'd scheduled Maria's family meeting for nine that morning. Gloria was still out. I was parking my wounded Beemer in the lot down the hill from the unit when a black Lexus pulled up beside me. I introduced myself to the distinguished-looking couple who got out. "You must be Maria Whitson's parents. I'm Dr. Peter Zak."

"My daughter—how is she?" Mrs. Whitson asked. She was a tall, handsome woman with shoulder-length, white-blond hair. Her face was wrinkle-free and her eyebrows arched in an expression of surprise. Her eyes radiated anxiety.

"She's better," I said cautiously. "Let's go inside and talk."

I led the Whitsons up the hill and into the unit. They hung back, checking out the place like a couple deciding whether to take a room in a fleabag motel.

When we reached the conference room, Mrs. Whitson removed her black cape. Underneath, she wore a skinny black dress that buttoned up the front. When she sat and crossed her legs, the bottom slit rode up to reveal a shapely leg. With her long neck, prominent nose, and full mouth painted a brilliant scarlet, she was like some great exotic bird beside the pale, colorless Mr. Whitson. He sat down stiffly beside her, resting his hands uneasily in his lap. He was tall and lean, with a head of thinning, gray hair. A peacock and Ichabod Crane. They were an odd pair. And Maria seemed nothing like either one of them. She must have grown up feeling like a chick whose mother had left her in a stranger's nest.

Despite his colorless appearance, it was Mr. Whitson who asked the forthright question, "When can we see Maria?"

"I wanted to spend some more time talking to you first. Then, if everything works out, Maria will join us."

Reddening, Maria's father straightened in his seat and said,

"If what works out? We're her parents. We have every right to see her." There was a pause that filled the room. "It's that incest crap again, isn't it?"

Mrs. Whitson had placed her hand on her husband's arm and was whispering, "Shhh."

The hostility didn't surprise me. And after what they'd been through, it seemed entirely appropriate. "I know you're concerned about your daughter. I can tell you how she's doing now. We've gotten her off most of her medications. As you know, she came in here in a state of delirium."

"Delirium? What exactly do you mean?" Mr. Whitson asked.

"That's when a person looks confused, has fluctuating moods. One minute she's elated and the next she's crying. She has trouble remembering." By now Maria's mother and father had exchanged knowing nods. "Often she doesn't know where she is, when she is. Most often, delirium is either drug-induced or caused by some kind of physical condition."

"Drug-induced," Mr. Whitson repeated the words.

"That's right. Your daughter was on a variety of prescription drugs, the combination of which could have caused that kind of altered state."

"I knew that asshole doctor was no good," Maria's father muttered as his wife gently squeezed his arm.

"She's doing much better, now that the drugs are nearly out of her system. She's settling into the routine of the unit. I was hoping to get some background information from you so that we can plan the best course of treatment for Maria." I hurried ahead into the relatively uncharged territory of medical history. "You're both how old?"

Mrs. Whitson answered, "My husband is sixty-eight. I'm fifty." I didn't argue, though I suspected that Mrs. Whitson was in her sixties, too. Her plastic surgeon hadn't touched the backs of her hands where the skin was loose and speckled with age spots.

"And Maria is your only child?"

She nodded

I continued asking the standard questions about birth, development, childhood illnesses. According to Maria's parents, she'd had an idyllic childhood. She'd been a tomboy, very athletic. No bumps in the road until she started school.

"Tantrums," Mr. Whitson explained. "She had tantrums at school. Then she starting having them at home, too. When she didn't get what she wanted, she'd lie on the floor, screaming and crying."

"We tried ignoring her," Mrs. Whitson said, "but how can you ignore a six-year-old banging her head against a hard floor? As you might imagine, we went through a lot of nannies. My little brother Nino was the only one who could control her. She was his pet."

"He was around a lot? Alone with Maria?" I asked.

Mrs. Whitson's eyes widened as she grasped the implication. "We didn't know, Dr. Zak. She was an only child and he was like a brother to her. And having him there seemed to help. She adored him. She'd do whatever"—Mrs. Whitson stared into her lap—"she'd do what he told her to."

Mr. Whitson placed his arm around his wife's shoulder. He glared at me. "You've no right. It wasn't until years later that Maria told us what Nino did to her. She said I abused her, too." He looked me in the eye. "Now you listen to me." He was stony with anger. "Let's get this straight right here and now. I have never, ever touched my daughter in any"—his mouth hung open as he searched for the word—"inappropriate way."

"I hear you, Mr. Whitson, I know it's painful for you both, going over these old accusations. Let me just assure you, what I'm interested in is how we're going to move forward. Maria needs a support system in place when she gets out of here, and right now, I'm just trying to understand what's possible."

Mr. Whitson was still glaring at me but his expression had softened. "Believe me, Doctor, that's why we're here. We want our daughter back. But if we thought that never seeing her again was best for Maria, then that's what we'd do."

"Excellent. Then as far as that goes, we're on the same page. But we're not quite there yet. There's just a couple more questions I need to ask. I was wondering when you became aware of Maria's issues around food?"

Mrs. Whitson shifted uncomfortably. "In junior high. She had trouble keeping her weight down. We tried all kinds of diets." We? I wondered if Mrs. Whitson had always been as stick thin as she was now. "And exercise."

"She ran," Mr. Whitson said tersely.

"Yes," his wife agreed. "In high school, she ran every day."

I noted this down. Typical pattern. Girl who already has an assortment of family issues hits adolescence, becomes acutely aware of her body. Her desire to be perfect translates into a compulsion to be thin. She exercises. And exercises some more. Until she's addicted to exercises. And then, when that doesn't do enough, the dieting and hyper-interest in food begins.

"That's the trouble with her," Mr. Whitson commented. "Never goes at anything half-assed. Couldn't run one mile. It had to be ten. And when she started to sell houses, she had to be the best. Had to sell more, bigger, faster. Ambition and nerve," Mr. Whitson said, brushing away a tear that had leaked from one eye, "that's my little girl."

Ambition and nerve. I wouldn't have associated those words with Maria Whitson. I wondered if the car accident had changed her personality that profoundly. Or was the Maria Whitson I'd gotten to know a temporary aberration?

"Were there any other significant traumas?" I asked.

"You mean other than—?" Mrs. Whitson asked. I nodded. Mrs. Whitson pondered. "Not really," she said slowly. "Though there was the time her friend Marjorie got hurt."

"I'd forgotten about that," Mr. Whitson said.

"Marjorie was Maria's best friend," Mrs. Whitson explained.

"Attached at the hip all through junior high," Mr. Whitson remarked.

"Marjorie had an accident. She slipped and fell down her cellar stairs. She was pretty badly hurt."

"So why was that so traumatic for Maria?" I asked.

"Maria found her lying unconscious," Mrs. Whitson explained. "I'd dropped her off at Marjorie's house on our way back from a dentist appointment. Maria came running out of the house before I even had a chance to pull away."

"Maria was completely thrown by it," Mr. Whitson said. "Wouldn't eat a thing for days after. Kept insisting that it was her fault. If only she'd gotten there earlier, that sort of thing."

"I kept telling her, we couldn't have gotten there any earlier," Mrs. Whitson said.

"And were there any lasting effects?"

"After Marjorie recovered, the girls were never close," Mrs. Whitson recalled. "In fact, months later I asked her about Marjorie and she practically snapped my head off."

"Wasn't that around the time she started refusing to go down into our basement?" Mr. Whitson asked.

"I think you're right. We had a big rumpus room where the kids used to hang out. Then, Maria refuses to go down there. I never connected it, but maybe it was because of the way she found Marjorie at the bottom of her basement stairs."

"I understand Maria confronted you with her accusations. That must have been difficult."

Mr. Whitson stiffened and looked away. Mrs. Whitson shook her head. "We were stunned," she said simply. "As far as I was concerned, it came out of nowhere. Nino and Maria were so close." She stared down into her lap. "If I loved her, she asked me, then how could I love him, too?" Mrs. Whitson choked. "How could I answer such a question?"

Mr. Whitson reached for his wife's hand. "My wife's younger brother was killed earlier this year," he explained.

Killed? If he died suddenly or violently, that certainly could have put an additional strain on Maria's already fragile state. I put a box of tissues on the table between us. Mrs. Whitson took one and blew her nose. "How did—" I started to ask, but Mrs. Whitson had already started down another path. "Everything changed after Maria was hit by the car," she said.

"And that's when she found that manipulative sonofabitch doctor," Mr. Whitson added.

Mrs. Whitson nodded miserably. "I blame myself. For not seeing how desperately she needed help."

"She got help all right," Mr. Whitson muttered.

"Please, tell me about the accident," I said.

Mrs. Whitson frowned. "Of course, we weren't there. It happened in front of her house. Her husband struck her with his car. She went up right over the top. Her head hit the windshield. Knocked her unconscious. Broke her arm. It's a miracle she wasn't killed."

"How did it happen?" I asked.

Mr. Whitson answered carefully, "Doctor, the truth is, we don't really know. At first, even Maria couldn't remember." There was a pause. I waited. Mr. and Mrs. Whitson exchanged looks.

"There was a time when Maria said it was deliberate," Mrs. Whitson said. Meaning what? That her husband deliberately hit her or that she deliberately threw herself in front of the car? "I think it was an accident. Even today, that poor boy is still crazy about her. He was so upset afterwards he refused to get back into that car. Remember, Rob? Nino took care of getting the car fixed. Then he got rid of it for them."

"And after the accident?"

"She was hospitalized," Mrs. Whitson explained. "She seemed to heal quickly and at first we were so relieved. But afterwards, she was different. She had trouble remembering things. She'd miss appointments with clients. Show houses and then leave them unlocked. And she was flighty—you know, couldn't sit still. She told us she wasn't sleeping well. And she complained of dizziness."

"She couldn't run. I think that bothered her a lot," Mr. Whitson put in.

"She started to gain weight." Mrs. Whitson crossed her arms and hugged herself. "And she turned cold. She didn't like to be . . . touched." Mrs. Whitson bit her lip. "I'd try to hug her and she'd push me away."

Mr. Whitson added, "That's when she pulled away from us. She stopped dropping by. Stopped calling. And she told us to stop calling her."

"We didn't hear anything for months," Mrs. Whitson said. She was crying, the unchecked tears making dark tracks down her face. "We didn't know what to do. I called her friends, hoping to find out how she was. But they didn't know either. She'd cut herself off from everyone."

"After she threw him out," Mr. Whitson said, "her husband used to hang around our house for hours at a time. Then he got angry. Blamed us. One time, we had to call the police. He'd been drinking.

"Then, out of the blue, she calls and wants us to come to this doctor's office and meet with her. We were thrilled. Hoping for a breakthrough. But that wasn't it at all."

Flushed and trembling with outrage, Mrs. Whitson sobbed, "It was so humiliating. She accused Nino and Rob of . . ." She stopped, her shoulders shuddering. "She blamed me. Said I'd been a—what was the word she used?"

"An enabler," her husband said softly.

"She didn't call again for months." Mrs. Whitson seemed to grow smaller in her seat. "And when she did, it was to say she'd slit her wrists."

"And that was six months ago?"

"That's right. Just after Nino's funeral, wasn't it, Rob?"

"Just after."

There didn't seem to be anything more to say. Mr. and Mrs. Whitson each sat there staring ahead, immobile. Battle fatigue. Clearly, they cared about their daughter. Why else would they be back, talking with yet another doctor, knowing they risked more abuse, more accusations themselves.

"By any measure, you've been through a very difficult period," I said.

"You have no idea," Mr. Whitson said.

"You're right. No one can know that but you."

"Dr. Zak, we came, hoping that we'd be able to see our daughter. Can we?" Mrs. Whitson asked, her voice prickling with hope. "Please, even for just a few moments. I've missed her so much."

"Yes," I said. "I think it's time."

I called for a nurse to get Maria and then we waited. As the minutes ticked by, I could feel the tension build in the room. Mr. Whitson got up and paced. Mrs. Whitson fastened two buttons at the top of her dress. She removed one of the combs from her hair and then reinserted it. She was rummaging in her handbag when Maria appeared in the doorway.

"Maria, dear," Mrs. Whitson said, half rising from her chair.

Mr. Whitson stopped his pacing and held his arms open to her.

Maria's face was a kaleidoscope of emotions. From pleasure to fear to anger and back again, her expression changed by the moment as she shifted forward and back, finally launching herself into her father's arms before she backed away. Her parents watched as she hovered warily and worked the hem of her sweatshirt with her hands.

"Maria?" her mother said meekly. "Maria, you know how much we both love you, don't you? Whatever it is we've done, we're sorry. We just want what's best."

The submissiveness in her tone seemed to fuel Maria's anger. She folded her arms across her chest and planted her heels. She addressed her words to me. "They say they want what's best for me? That's a switch. Usually, they want what's best for *them*. I wonder why they ever had me. They were so old by the time they got around to it."

Maria's mother, her face twisted in agony, said, "Doctor, we tried for years to have a child. Maria was a gift. A miracle."

"Some miracle. Fat, ugly, and useless. They don't want me now. They've never wanted me."

Maria's father hung his head. "Doctor," he said helplessly. Unresolved pain and anguish hung like a pall in the room.

"Your daughter agreed to this meeting so that she could start thinking about what comes next after her hospitalization." I knew my official-sounding tone might appear insensitive, but I wanted to move us forward, to provide some neutral content that would allow Maria and her parents to coexist in the same space. "It took a lot of courage. It would be better, all around, if we sat down and talked."

Maria eyed me suspiciously. She looked back at her parents. The Whitsons sat in chairs on one side of the table. Then Maria sidled over to the chair I offered her and sank down. I could feel the tension ratchet down a notch. Sitting at the same table with her parents was a first step.

I continued, outlining what I saw as the task ahead for us. I spoke at some length, hoping that Maria would use the time to become accustomed to being with her parents. By the end, Maria and her parents were talking to each other instead of sending all of their thoughts through me as an intermediary. It was a milestone.

"Maria," Mrs. Whitson said cautiously at the end of our meeting, "your father has to go to work, but I was wondering if I could stay awhile." She brought out a book and lay it on the table. "Remember that shoe box full of old photographs we had in the hall closet? Well, I finally got around to sorting through them. I guess you've made me think a lot about the past and what it was really like. I thought maybe we could just look at some of the old pictures . . . and talk."

Maria stared at the photograph album. She picked it up and opened it to a baby picture. Then she looked at me. "Is it all right?"

Were we moving into dangerous territory? Would Gloria have kicked me under the table to keep me from encouraging an unsupervised visit? The Whitsons were pleading silently, asking me to help their daughter take this step toward reconciliation. But the decision wasn't mine to make.

"Maria," I said, "this is up to you. If you'd like for your mother to stay, fine. If you don't, that's fine, too. Think about it. What do *you* want?"

Maria slowly turned the pages of the photograph album. She looked up at her mother. "Okay" was all she said.

26

I LEFT Maria and her mother in the common area sitting side by side on the couch, the photograph album open between them. I stepped into the nurses' station to call Chip. We'd agreed to talk during the court's lunch break.

"It's going fine," Chip said. "So far, according to script."

"From what I read in the paper, Sylvia Jackson's testimony was a disaster. She contradicted herself all over the place."

"Yes, she contradicted herself. And yes, she couldn't remember squat. But I'm not sure it mattered. She's a terrific asset to the prosecution. A very sympathetic victim. They want to believe her."

This was what I'd expected. "How about MacRae?"

"Very professional. Didn't get ruffled when I asked him about her boyfriends on the force. Said they were just several of many suspects eliminated early on."

"Did you ask him how they happened to miss the camouflage hat during the initial search?"

"Said they didn't know they were looking for one. Made perfect sense, unfortunately."

How conveniently MacRae had disposed of that untidiness.

But if the hat didn't belong to Stuart Jackson, then someone had to have put it there for the police to find. Who else but the police had access to that closet, if that was in fact where they found it?

"When do you think you'll be ready for my testimony?" I asked.

"Maybe Thursday. More likely, Friday."

That was three days away. "I'm as ready as I'll ever be," I said. It was a lie. As each day passed, I was becoming increasingly anxious. I wasn't sleeping well. Anything but the blandest food disagreed with me. If I'd been my own therapist, I'd have recommended relaxation tapes, meditation, a long vacation. Instead, I pretended nothing was wrong. I was so preoccupied at work that I'd gone looking for Gloria, completely forgetting that she was still home recuperating. Kwan patted me on the back and muttered something about how we all have our senior moments.

Chip put Annie on the phone. "A few things. You asked me to check up on that nurse? Carolyn Lovely does have an ex. He lives Florida. And she does have a restraining order out against him. According to her complaint, he likes to beat her up. He was at work, tending bar, the day your car got hit."

That tied up one loose end. "And the blood work on Sylvia Jackson?"

Some paper rustled. "There's a lot of words here, but what it boils down to is an overdose of lithium carbonate, barbituric acid, and benzodiazepenes. Mean anything to you?"

"Sounds like a mental health cocktail. Anyone who's in and out of depression could have any of all of those on hand. Sylvia Jackson had access to barbiturates and benzos. But not lithium."

"Interesting. And I've got some information about Sylvia's angel. His name—Angelo di Benedetti. Thirty-five years old. Divorced. Brought in a year ago but no charges were filed. Probably a domestic dispute."

"Did the police consider him a suspect?"

"They'd never heard of him until he showed up at Sylvia Jackson's bedside after she regained consciousness. They checked up on him, of course. Has an alibi. His ex-wife swears he was with her all night. And they were seen together in a restaurant early in the evening."

"All night? Amazing." Like Syl and Stuart, here was another divorced couple who stayed in touch, so to speak. In my experience, a friendly divorce is a rare bird. "Doesn't sound too convincing."

"I agree. Nevertheless, Stuart's the more obvious suspect. And they did find that hat in his closet."

"What does Angelo do when he's not protecting Sylvia Jackson?"

"He's a personal trainer for one of the big health clubs. Works mostly early mornings and evenings."

"Which explains why he's able to hang out all day at the hospital. So what's his relationship to Tony?"

"None, really. He's a nephew by ex-marriage. His ex-wife is Tony's niece."

"Any business connection?"

"None that I'm aware of."

"Angelo di Benedetti," I murmured. "Now I wonder why . . ."

Annie picked up the thought. "So do I. I wonder why Sylvia Jackson still thinks his name is Angelo Ruggiero."

"Actually, it's just her kind of mix-up—grafting Tony's last name onto Angelo's first."

"But why doesn't he bother to correct her?" Annie asked.

"Good question. Maybe he has a reason for not telling her his last name, which she should know anyway. Question is, why would he do that?"

Neither of us could come up with a good answer.

When I got off the phone, I walked past the common area. Maria and her mother were still sitting, heads close together, looking at the open photo album. I came in and stood alongside them. Maria was giggling.

Mrs. Whitson looked up. "Wasn't she adorable?" She pointed to the bald, wide-eyed infant dressed up in a bumblebee costume.

Maria cringed and rolled her eyes. "Come on, Ma. You always do that." She grabbed the book and flipped the pages to another picture. "That's me at five. I was such a tomboy. And you know who that is with me?" Maria asked with such intensity that I leaned in to get a close look.

In the faded photograph, a muscular, bare-chested teenager stood flexing his muscles. A little girl with wispy blond hair stood on his shoulders, grinning boldly at the camera, her arms flexed like his. I looked at Maria. "Your uncle?"

She nodded.

"Remember that day, Maria?" Mrs. Whitson said. "You guys were down in the rumpus room horsing around."

"The rumpus room," Maria repeated, "horsing around." She stared hard at the picture. "I do remember. Something happened," she said.

Mrs. Whitson nodded. "I think that was the day you fell on the stairs and hurt your back."

Maria gave her mother a puzzled look. "My back?"

"Right here," Mrs. Whitson said, touching Maria at kidney level on the right side. Maria flinched. "Dad and I ran down when we heard you screaming your head off. You scared the daylights out of us. You were all crumpled up at the bottom of the stairs, yelling bloody murder. I was so angry at Nino, I could have killed him. But he was with that girlfriend of his . . ." She stopped and stammered, flushing with embarrassment.

Maria ran a finger lightly over the picture, pausing first on her own image and then on a figure in the background—a pretty, blond teenager wearing shorts and a white, short-sleeved shirt—who was doubled over with laughter.

"Yes," Maria said softly. "I think I remember."

27

THAT AFTERNOON, Maria appeared at my office. Her meeting with her parents had left her raw and agitated. She wanted to talk.

She put the photograph album on the edge of my desk and opened it to the picture of herself and her uncle. "I've been thinking about this picture. I'm sure it's the day—the day when it happened."

"Why don't you sit down," I said. Maria perched on the edge of a chair and stared at the picture. "Tell me what you remember."

"This picture was taken that day, but earlier. It was later that the bad thing happened. He raped me."

"This is the rape you told me about?"

Maria nodded, sitting back in the chair and staring off into space. The curiosity I'd sensed earlier seemed to have ripened into an openness, a willingness to inquire and poke into places she hadn't been able to examine before.

"Let's see if we can get at more of that memory. Start with the photograph. I want you to try to remember as much detail as you can about how things looked and felt when the picture was taken. You say that was the same day?"

"I think so."

"Good. Let's go back to that day, to that room. And, just for the moment, I want you to ignore what was happening. For instance, do you remember what time of day it was?"

Maria looked at the picture again and squinted. "Late afternoon. It was just before dinner."

"What makes you so sure?"

"I was hungry. I was looking for the dish of M&M's I'd left down there."

"Maybe dinner was cooking? Could you smell anything?"

Maria shook her head.

"Is there any special smell that you always associate with that room?"

Maria wrinkled her nose. "Mildew."

"Good. Okay, now you're walking down the stairs. You can smell mildew. What do you see?"

Maria closed her eyes. "Orange. The shag carpet is orange."

"Good. What else do you see in the room? Anything on the walls?"

"Photographs. My parents' wedding picture. A picture of Italy—Venice."

"Are the walls painted?"

"No. There's wood paneling on the walls. And a drop ceiling with acoustic tile."

"Now tell me about the furniture in the room."

"There's a television. A brown vinyl beanbag chair. A card table with four chairs. A bar with some stools. And . . . and . . ." Maria stopped and opened her eyes.

"What else?"

Maria opened her mouth but nothing came out.

"Okay. Let's try it this way. I'm going to draw the room and you can tell me where the furniture goes."

I drew a rectangle. "Is that the right shape?"

Maria shook her head. "It's L-shaped. There's an extra piece over here."

I added it.

"Okay. Let's put the stairs in. Where do they go?"

Maria pointed and I drew lines for the stairs. "Like that?"

Maria nodded.

"Okay, now, show me where the TV goes."

I handed Maria the pencil and she drew an X in one corner.

"Now, where's the beanbag chair?" She put an X in front of the TV. "And the card table and chairs?" She drew an X in a second corner. "And the bar? Where is it?" She drew an X in a third corner.

Three sections of the room were furnished. But the section opposite the staircase was empty. "What's over here?" I asked.

Maria shook her head and squeezed her eyes shut. "I can't do this. I feel like I'm in the beanbag chair. He's raping me . . ." She hugged herself and rocked, moaning softly.

"Ms. Whitson, I know it's scary. But it's in the past. It's okay to look at it. You're safe here." I waited until her eyes opened and the whimpering stopped. "I know this is hard. Try to keep going. I want you to imagine that you're walking into the room. You're coming down the stairs. Okay?"

Maria nodded, her eyes glazed over.

"Where are you standing?"

"I'm at the foot of the stairs."

"Now I want you to look across the room. What do you see?"

"Carpet. Orange carpet."

"Is there anything on the carpet?"

There was a silence while, in Maria's mind, she looked from the stairs toward the place where she said she'd been attacked. "Yes. There are. My M&M's. They're all over the rug. They're spilled everywhere!" Maria was indignant.

"Let's imagine that you go over and pick up the M&M's. Can you do that?"

Maria shook her head firmly.

"Why can't you do that?"

"I can't. Mustn't see."

"Mustn't see what? Maria, what is there over in that part of the room that you mustn't see?"

Maria locked her eyes shut and started to croon.

"Where's Uncle Nino?"

Maria shook her head.

"It's okay," I said gently. "You're safe, here in my office. Can you tell me what you see?"

Maria had her arms folded across her chest, her fingernails digging into her forearms. "There's a sofa over there," she whimpered.

"Good. That's good. Tell me about the sofa."

"Can't look. Mustn't look."

"It's okay to look. As long as you're here and it's safe, it's okay to look. Tell me about the sofa. What color is it?"

Maria's eyes opened a crack. "It's blue. Pale blue velvet. And he's on the sofa. On top of . . . on top of . . . I don't understand." Maria's eyes flew open and she cried out, "It wasn't me!"

She put her hands on top of her head and the look on her face changed from surprise to disbelief. "Jesus Christ. He was fucking *her*! I didn't get it. But now, I'm sure that's what was happening."

I waited. And in the silence, the memory seemed to slide into place like a bullet into a well-oiled firing chamber.

"I was standing at the foot of the stairs, watching. And he was screwing her."

"His girlfriend?"

"Jennifer—Jennifer what's-her-name. Oh God," Maria gasped. "And I watched."

"You watched?"

"I couldn't stop. I was stuck. I knew I shouldn't. But I did."

"And then?"

Maria shook her head. "I guess my mother must have called

us to dinner because he started to turn around and I started to scream."

"How did you feel?"

"Betrayed," Maria whispered.

"Betrayed," I repeated, noting down the unexpected word.

"He was my uncle. And there he was. It was disgusting. And yet, I kept watching. Why did I keep watching?" Maria shuddered at the memory. "When my mother called us to dinner, I must have taken off up the stairs. I tripped and fell." She rubbed her right side.

"Do you remember what happened after that?"

"Uh-huh. I hurt my back and had to stay in bed while it healed."

"And your uncle?"

"They were all furious with Uncle Nino. Wouldn't let him come up to my room to see me." Maria's eyes widened. She sank back into her chair and moaned. "Oh God. He wasn't a monster. He was just a . . . a jerk. An oversexed, eighteen-year-old jerk."

"And you were only five years old. How could you begin to understand what was happening?"

"But I accused him. I made everyone think . . . And now . . ."

Maria stared hollow-eyed out into space. I stood up and looked out the window. Outside, the leaves were turning. I thought about the scenes now converging in Maria's head, details reshuffling themselves with a new image coming into focus.

"Do you remember your parents' reaction?" I asked.

"I was angry when they wouldn't let Nino come and see me. They wouldn't even let him into the house for weeks. I was furious. Especially with my father."

"Because?"

"Because I loved Uncle Nino. He was always there for me when there was no one else."

"Was there any other reason why you were so angry with your father?"

Maria nodded. "Because he knew," she mumbled.

"Knew what?"

"He knew what I'd seen." I waited for her to continue. "He got down the stairs first. While Nino was still pulling up his pants. He knew exactly what had happened, and—"

"And?"

"And he knew that I'd been watching. He knew I was dirty. That I'd seen."

"Is that how you felt? Dirty?"

"Well, wasn't I? I'd kept on watching and watching. I was so ashamed of myself." I didn't say anything. "I just don't understand," Maria wailed.

"What don't you understand?"

"The other memory. Where did it come from?"

"Where *did* it come from? That's a good question."

"Dr. Baldridge helped me remember."

"How did he help you?"

"When I first saw him, he said he knew."

"Knew what?"

"That I was an incest survivor."

"And how did he know that?"

"Because I had all the signs. I was depressed. The bingeing and purging. I couldn't sleep. He said it was typical."

"And he helped you remember?"

Maria nodded. "He hypnotized me."

"Had you been seeing him long?"

"A few weeks, I guess. He was amazing. He just knew. And I believed him."

"So what do you think about that now?"

"It was so vivid. And I kept seeing it, over and over again in my head. I can make myself see it now if I wanted to. What I don't understand is, where did it come from?"

I wondered, too. Probably from the cookbook of the good doctor. Take one young woman, add in a brain injury, a sprinkling of insomnia, an eating disorder, and a handful of designer drugs—it's a bad mix when you start with a patient looking desperately for an answer and a doctor who has one ready and waiting.

"What do you think about that other memory?"

Maria was silent for a moment. "Now? I guess it doesn't seem as real . . . as real as . . . But Dr. Baldridge said—"

"No one can tell you what you experienced. You're the expert on that. So I'm sure it must be very confusing, now that you have two memories."

"But Dr. Baldridge—" Maria hung there, her mouth open.

"Dr. Baldridge isn't the expert on you. You are. You have to decide what's real and what's not." Maria gave me a pleading look. I held up my hands. "I wasn't there so I can't tell you, either. But it is something you might want to talk to your parents about. Maybe they can help you sort it out. We can do it together."

Maria stared down into her lap. She looked up and opened her mouth, as if she was going to say something. I could imagine two little creatures, one on each shoulder, arguing vehemently about whether she was going to say whatever it was that was about to come out. Then she came unstuck, but the words came out slowly, cautiously. "You know, when Uncle Nino died, I didn't know what to do with myself. It felt like I was on a trapeze, swinging back and forth. One minute I'd feel light as a feather, as if the huge weight I'd been carrying had finally lifted. I thought, now that he's gone, everything is going to be fine. The way it should have been if he'd never—" Maria paused and held her breath for a moment before continuing. "But the next minute, I'd get these feelings of overwhelming sadness. And guilt." Maria lowered her eyes. "I felt responsible. I'd get into bed and stay there for days. That's when I tried to kill myself."

"Is that when you slit your wrists?"

Maria pushed up a sleeve and held out her arm, palm up. She looked at the white lines of scar tissue. Then she lifted her wrist to her lips and stared into space.

We ended the session with Maria in what seemed like a fugue state. She moved slowly, apparently immersed in inner turmoil, unaware of the world around her. Anger had fueled her for so long. Letting go of it would be hard. And, as I knew from personal experience, forgiving herself would be even harder.

After she left, I picked up the phone and called the nurses' station. "This is Dr. Zak. I want Maria Whitson put on a suicide watch. Let's check her every five minutes for the next twenty-four hours."

For the tenth time that week, I wished Gloria was around. So I called her at home.

"Hi, this is Peter," I said, knowing it wasn't Gloria who answered the phone. "Rachel?"

"Hey, Peter. Calling to check up on the patient?"

"Patient. Not exactly a word I'd associate with Gloria. How is she?"

"She's a royal pain in the butt. She's supposed to be resting and instead she's up and down like a jumping bean."

"Yeah, well, she's so used to taking care of everyone else."

"Absolutely. Doesn't know how to be taken care of herself. Tell her she doesn't have to rush back." There was a pause. "Will you get back in bed?" she shouted. "All right, all right. I'll bring you the phone already."

"How are you feeling?" I asked when Gloria got on.

"Ducky. Just ducky. I'd be a whole lot better if I didn't have to stay cooped up here."

"You know they're just being cautious. Concussions take time."

"Doctors, what do they know? I hate being sick!"

"You got the flowers we sent?" I asked.

"Yeah, very funny."

"What funny?"

"They arrived in a hard hat."

"Appropriate, don't you think. That was Kwan's idea. And how is the—head?"

"The *hard* head, as you were about to say, is just fine. It only hurts when the roses make me sneeze."

"You're welcome. We miss you."

Gloria laughed. "Ouch! Don't make me laugh."

"Maria Whitson's been asking about you. She still thinks your fall was her fault."

"She wasn't anywhere near me. I ran into the room. Then I slipped. I must have caught the corner of the bed going down. It was an accident."

There it was again—the "a" word. In the last few weeks, in fact ever since I'd gotten myself mixed up with the Jackson case, that word seemed to crop up every other day. But how could this accident be connected to the others?

"She met with her parents today," I said.

"I know. I really wanted to be there. How'd it go?"

"I talked with them at some length. Then they saw Maria."

"What are they like?"

"Bottom line? Concerned parents. Screwed up, of course."

"Who isn't?"

"Absolutely. Of course they're confused and angry. But they seem to care deeply about their daughter."

"Wish I'd been there," Gloria said. "Did she feel safe?"

"Yes, I think she did. So much so that when her mother offered to stay, Maria agreed. Her mother had a photograph album."

Gloria was quiet for a moment before asking, "You think Baldridge planted these memories of abuse, don't you?"

"I'm not so sure Dr. Baldridge is as open to other possible explanations as he should be. Today, Maria remembered an entirely new scenario. Says she walked in on her uncle having sex with his girlfriend. And this memory was triggered by a photograph she says was taken on the same day her uncle raped her."

"So why is this memory any more real than the other one?"

"Good question. Maybe a memory of abuse is less terrible for her than the real memory it's screening, a memory she can't deal with. Seeing her uncle having sex with his girlfriend doesn't seem like such a big deal to an adult. But for a five-year-old, it must have been devastating. She adored her uncle. And even though it was inadvertent, he violated her trust. She didn't understand what was happening, but she knew it was naughty and very exciting. It was even more confusing to her because she couldn't stop watching. On one level, she blamed herself. On another level, she blamed her uncle and her parents. And it forever changed their relationship. Her parents didn't realize how much it troubled her, so she never got it out in the open."

"Oh God. Now what? If she's convinced that her uncle didn't abuse her, and she accused him, told everyone what he'd done, with him dead . . . You've got her on suicide watch?"

"Of course."

"Good."

"Gloria, please get well and get back in here."

"I'm working on it."

28

I SLEPT badly the night before I was scheduled to testify. I got to bed early enough but I kept waking up. First, I dreamed that I arrived at the courthouse in pajamas, the navy and green plaid ones I wore when I was a kid. Then I dreamed that I was testifying and Kate was cross-examining me. My mother was sitting in the jury box weeping while I tried to explain, "I was in the kitchen. I didn't know what was happening . . ."

"Why didn't you know? Why didn't you do something to save me?" Kate asked me.

"I didn't realize . . . I didn't hear . . . I didn't know. . . ."

Back and forth we went. Then Kate reached into her pocket and took out a ringing cell phone. She talked into it, flipped it closed, and started all over. "Why didn't you get home earlier? Why didn't you come upstairs?"

Again I tried to answer and again, Kate reached into her pocket for the ringing phone.

She looked at me sadly. "It's about ego, isn't it. Your ego. Even now, you still can't stop yourself."

"Objection, Your Honor," Chip called from the courtroom door.

I turned to the judge and found myself staring up into the calm, smiling baby face of Ralston Bridges. "Objection overruled," he sneered.

I woke up with a jolt, drenched in sweat. I got out of bed, threw open the window, and stood there shivering, looking out on the deserted street. It was four in the morning. Another couple of hours and I'd have to get dressed. Why *was* I doing this again? Was it ego? And why hadn't I known Kate was in danger?

I'd gone through it in my head hundreds of times. How could I have stood in my kitchen, boiling hot water for tea, unaware that Bridges was already in my house? How could I have been oblivious to him creeping around in my bedroom, then upstairs into Kate's studio? Why didn't I go up to see her when I got home? Why didn't I sense something was wrong? I was there. I could have saved her. Or would both of us be dead? Maybe that would have been preferable to the reality of the past two years.

He never admitted to killing her. Insisted, all the way through the trial and sentencing, that I'd been the one. A suspicious, jealous husband, I'd come home to check up on my wife and found her with him.

He was right about one thing. It was very unusual for me to be home in the middle of the day. But the explanation was simple. I'd spent the morning in Boston, and on my way to the Pearce, stopped at home to surprise Kate with a quick lunch. It was dumb luck that at the same moment, Ralston Bridges had decided to end his stakeout and act. The police theorized that he'd spent days watching us, learning our habits. He knew Kate would be in her studio and he expected me to be at work.

I heard the scuffle, Kate's scream, then a thud. I raced upstairs, but by then it was already too late. He was shirtless, his pants halfway down. Kate was on the floor in a pool of blood.

I reached out blindly and grabbed a metal rod from Kate's workbench and swung. I could still feel the sound as the rod cracked against his skull. He went down and lay on his back, whimpering, holding his arms over his face. I went to Kate and held her. She was already gone. There was so much blood. Her throat was slit.

I heard Bridges dragging himself along the floor. He was reaching for the knife. I kicked away his hand and must have kept on kicking—the next thing I remember is "Peter! Stop!" my mother's scream penetrating the rage. She stood in the open doorway, her hands over her mouth. For the first time I realized I was covered in blood. Kate's blood. Bridges's blood. In a few more moments. I'd have killed him.

"Kate?" my mother whispered.

I could only shake my head. She walked over to the body and picked up Kate's hand and pressed it to her lips.

I turned numb. I went down to my bedroom and called the police. Then I leaned against a wall and closed my eyes. I listened to the sound of emptiness, punctuated only by the sound of my own labored breathing and the muffled sound of the teapot screaming from the kitchen.

It was while we were waiting for the police to arrive that I realized Bridges was wearing my clothes. My pants, my shirt, even a pair of my gloves lay discarded in a corner. The knife was from a drawer in our kitchen. He was going to kill my wife and leave behind evidence that I'd done it.

It had happened so fast. One moment I had everything I could have wanted and I didn't know it. The next, it was ripped from me. The loss was like a great, empty hole that I tried to pretend wasn't there. I'd never even had a chance to say goodbye.

Now I ran a shower, as hot as I could stand. I stood under the pulsing water, my eyes closed, trying to clear my head. I shaved. Later, I went to my closet to get out a suit. I still had a few of Kate's things hanging in the back—the smock she wore when she worked, her bathrobe. I reached for the robe and buried my face in it. It still had her smell.

Then I took out clothes for the day, clothes I hadn't worn since the last time I'd testified as an expert witness. I lined up the pieces on my bed. I put on a freshly laundered shirt, feeling its stiff starchiness scratch my skin. I buttoned the sleeves. I pulled on the gray suit pants. They were looser than I'd remembered. I threaded and fastened a black leather belt. Carefully, I adjusted and knotted a dark red silk tie. The vest buttoned easily across my middle. I shrugged on the jacket.

My reflection in the mirror stared calmly back at me. Satisfied, I went downstairs and checked through my briefcase to be sure I had everything I'd need. As I prepared to leave, there was a shave-and-a-haircut rap at my door. I opened the door.

My mother beamed at me, but I knew she was forcing it. "How handsome you look! I just came over to say good luck." I hadn't talked to my mother about the trial, but I knew she'd be anxious about it, glad it was nearly over. "You have a big day ahead of you. You should eat. Here!" She thrust a little bag into my hand.

The bag was warm. I peaked inside. She'd actually driven to Chinatown to get my favorite pork buns, something I know she cannot tolerate even the smell of.

"Oh, Mom," I said, and gave her a hug and a peck on the cheek. Then I stopped, stepped back, and pulled my mother inside into the light. Her eyes were bloodshot and there were dark circles underneath. "Are you all right?"

"What do you mean, am I all right? Of course I'm all right. Why shouldn't I be all right?"

"You look like I feel. Exhausted."

"I'm an old lady. This is how old ladies look."

"Give me a little credit at least. This is not how *this* old lady looks. What's going on?"

She looked at her feet, then at me, tilting her head to one side like some white tufted woodpecker deciding whether to attack an ant. "I didn't want you to worry."

"If you don't tell me what's wrong, I'll really worry."

"I've been having trouble sleeping," she said.

"What kind of trouble?"

"My phone's been ringing at all hours. I pick it up and there's no one there. I don't pick it up and it rings and rings."

"The other night—when I got beeped. Your phone was keeping you up that night, too?"

My mother pursed her lips and peered up at me. "You thought I was up in the middle of the night for my health?"

That explained the telephones in my nightmares. My bedroom shares a wall with my mother's bedroom.

"Why didn't you say something?"

"I didn't want you to"—we finished the sentence in unison—"worry."

"If you had an answering machine, you could set it to pick up your calls."

"Don't be ridiculous." It was ridiculous. My mother had a terrible time with everything electronic—the VCR being a major exception to the rule.

"You should unplug the phone," I said.

"What if someone's trying to reach me?"

"Who could be trying to reach you in the middle of the night?"

"Your brother. Uncle Milt."

"Anyone like that who's trying to reach you will have my number. Anyone else, you don't want to talk to at three in the morning anyway."

My mother gave a little shiver. "So, Dr. Smartypants," she said, pulling her sweater around her shoulders, "go in that courtroom and knock 'em dead. And don't forget to eat something." Then she scuttled out.

A little while later, Kwan pulled up in his Saab and beeped the horn. On the way to the Pearce, he said, "I don't know what it is, but you've got something edible on you."

"Can you believe it, my mother went into Chinatown and picked up some pork buns. She wanted to be sure I ate well before I had to testify."

"So are we going to eat them or just talk about them?"

I opened the bag and handed Kwan one of the little round pastries stuck to a square of wax paper. He sniffed at it, took a bite, and sighed. "Any time you have these, I'll be happy to drive you. When do you think you'll get your car back?"

"Sometime in the middle of next week, or so they say."

"How is your mother these days, anyway?"

"Fine. Usually. Actually, this morning she looked like death warmed over."

Kwan gave me a sidelong look. "Actually, you don't look so great yourself."

I ignored it. "What kind of person gets his kicks making voiceless phone calls to an old woman in the middle of the night?"

"Probably just kids with nothing better to do. She should take her phone off the hook."

"That's what I told her. But she's a person who anticipates disaster around every corner. She might miss one if she didn't get her after-midnight calls. As if she could do anything if she got bad news in the middle of the night instead of in the morning."

"It's not rational, but when life feels out of control, disconnecting the phone can make you feel even more adrift."

It was true enough. And bad news did tend to come at odd times. My father had died an hour before dawn. It was a fact that haunted my mother. Not that he died. But that he died alone.

Then something occurred to me. After my father's death, my mother couldn't stand seeing his name riding in, over and over again, on the incoming mail. It was one more reminder in days filled with reminders of her loss. She made a big deal about changing all their subscriptions, charge cards, and accounts to her own name. That's when she changed their phone listing to P. Zak. My phone number is unlisted, so, occasionally, someone trying to find me ends up calling my mother. It seemed a whole lot more likely that the late-night caller was trying to disrupt *my* sleep, not my mother's. And on the night before I was scheduled to testify in a murder trial.

29

IT TURNED into a crazy morning. Four new patients had been admitted. Two keep us busy. Three is a stretch. My leaving for court that afternoon didn't help. Thank goodness Gloria was back.

Twice that morning, I noticed Maria Whitson. Once, she was pacing the hall. When she saw me, she ducked into her room. A second time, she was standing in front of the nurses' station. I'd meant to ask her why she wasn't participating in any of the morning activities, but Mr. Kootz picked just that moment to start head banging—his own this time—so I got distracted.

Later that day, Kwan dropped me at the subway so I could get to the courthouse. I arrived just after the lunch break. I got myself a large cup of coffee and rode up in the elevator. I wrote off the waves of nausea to insufficient sleep.

I got off the elevator and sank down on a bench in the hall outside the courtroom. My hand shook as I folded back the coffee lid and a squirt of scalding liquid ended up on my pants. I took a sip. It tasted vile.

I peeled my shirt off my back and wiped a slick of sweat from my forehead. I stared at the wood grain of the bench, the stains on the gray-speckled linoleum. One of the double doors to the courtroom opened and Annie slid out into the waiting area. I tried to get up and found that I couldn't.

She looked at me, concerned. "You look pooped."

"I didn't sleep very well."

"You need help getting pumped?"

Pumped. That was what I might have needed in the old days. Now, I needed a whole lot more than pumped. I was afraid that when I tried to walk, I'd lose traction.

"Thanks, no. I'll be fine, once I get going. How long before . . . ?"

"Shouldn't be long now. Fifteen minutes, max." She turned to go and paused. "Can I get you some water?"

It was such a simple question and I didn't know the answer. She looked at me hard. "You're not okay, are you?"

I closed my eyes and opened them. "Not at this very moment. But I will be. There's nothing you can do, Annie. This is something I have to do for myself."

Annie went back, and I set the coffee aside. I took off my jacket and lay it on the bench. I folded my hands loosely in my lap, centered myself, closed my eyes, and focused. I imagined daybreak, the sun rising on the river. I tried to feel the coolness of the air, see the smoothness of the water's surface, feel my feet locked in place, my body pulling, pulling as the boat cut through the water. I imagined gliding by the Esplanade where a parade of willows reach down to touch the water's edge. Slowly, the river faded. Concentrating on a spot between my eyes, I breathed slowly, in through the nose and out through the mouth.

When an officer came out and called my name, I had it together. I stood, put on my jacket, and strode purposefully into the courtroom.

It was much smaller than I'd remembered. The judge was at the far end, his desk on a raised platform. I sat in the witness box to the judge's left and was sworn in. Chip and Annie conferred briefly before Chip stood and approached me.

He took me slowly through my credentials, point by point, encouraging and coaxing me along. He drew out into minutes a procedure that normally takes about thirty seconds. I knew the kid glove treatment was a stalling tactic designed to help me relax. And it worked. Any hesitation there might have been in my voice vanished after the first few questions. I settled back and felt my adrenaline kick in. Each question and answer was like another stroke on the river.

As we went through my areas of expertise, I surveyed the room. The jurors were lined up in two rows along one wall. Facing me, Annie sat at a table. Montrose Sherman and another lawyer sat at a matching table. I was only dimly aware of the spectators sitting in two rows of pews at the back of the room.

I almost didn't notice Stuart Jackson at Annie's side. Long strands of thinning brown hair were combed artfully over the top of his head. The skin hung from his face like a deflated balloon. He sat forward in his seat, listening intently. I hoped I wouldn't let him down.

"Remember," Chip had warned me, "you're talking to people, not shrinks. Keep it simple. Your job is to teach them about memory." So when he asked me to describe the tests I'd administered and how Syl had performed, I stuck to the basics.

As I explained each test, a middle-aged woman with short salt-and-pepper hair in the second row of the jury box sat in rapt attention. I tried to talk to her and ignore the balding older man sitting directly in front of her. He had his arms folded, torso turned away at an angle, one leg crossed over the other. The body language spoke volumes. The more I talked, the more his face solidified into an unpleasant frown. By the time I finished, the lady in the second row was still wide-eyed while the gentleman in the first row was slack-jawed, catching flies.

The judge called for a ten-minute break.

I met Chip and Annie in the hall. Really seeing Annie for the first time that day, I did a double take. She wore a dark blue suit and high heels. Her wild hair was done up in a knot. The short skirt confirmed something I'd suspected. She had great legs. I must have been staring because she shifted uncomfortably under my gaze.

"Sorry," I apologized, "it's just that you look so different."

She flushed and grinned. "You noticed. That's something. You must be feeling better."

"Let's take a stroll," Chip suggested. We walked in silence to the far end of the hall.

Annie's assessment was encouraging. "You did very well," she said. "I thought the jury was with you."

"That's a relief. I honestly wasn't sure what was coming across. It's been awhile. That guy in the front row was driving me nuts. In a minute he'd have been snoring."

"That's our retired plumber," Chip said. "Has two grown daughters. I don't think we're going to win any points with him."

As we turned at the end of the hall and started to walk back, Chip commented, "Now, to face the lion."

"I hope he had a hearty lunch," I said.

"You're it," Annie whispered.

30

MONTROSE SHERMAN was a compact, pale man with sharp gray eyes who held himself as if he had a broomstick up his ass. Everything about him was stiff and straight-arrow, from the razor creases in his dark pin-striped suit to the starch in his button-down collar. If he had any ethnicity, it had long since bleached out. If there were any laugh lines in his forty-year-old face, I couldn't find them.

While I waited on the stand, Sherman took his time. He straightened several thick file folders on the table in front of him, leaned over to whisper a comment to his colleague, took a sip from a glass of water. Then he picked up a densely scrib-bled pad of yellow paper, stood up, and strode to a spot directly between me and the jury. He held up the pad, creating a wall above which I could just see the deep vertical grooves that ran from the inside corner of each bushy eyebrow to his hairline. He peered at me over the top of the pad. I waited, squelching the urge to shift in my chair. He took a silver pen from his pocket and clicked it open.

It started innocuously enough. He said good afternoon. Then he asked me to describe my expertise in head injury.

"At the hospital, we're involved with a lot of head trauma cases. What I'm primarily interested in is the borderline between organic and functional illness. In other words, looking at an individual's illness and teasing apart the organic factors from the emotional factors."

His disembodied voice floated from behind the yellow pad. "And, in this case, what were you asked to do?"

I answered carefully. "I was asked to help guide the defense in evaluating the memory difficulties that this particular individual has manifested and how they might affect the kind of testimony she might give."

Sherman wrote several words on the yellow pad and underlined them.

"Dr. Zak," he said, lowering the pad and crossing his arms, "you're not one of Sylvia Jackson's treating physicians, are you?"

"No, I am not," I answered.

"You were hired by the defense specifically for this case?"

Here we go, I thought. "Yes, I was."

"At that point, when you were hired, you weren't even asked to do an evaluation of Sylvia Jackson, were you? In fact, you were provided with certain limited information about the case and you were asked to guide the defense in certain areas." The phrase "certain areas" took on sinister significance. "That's what you were asked to do, right?"

"That's correct," I said, trying to keep my voice even.

"Evaluating the victim, Sylvia Jackson, putting her through — how many was it, twelve hours of tests — that was your idea, was it not?"

Obviously this still irritated the hell out of him. "Six hours," I said. "Ms. Jackson's memory is a critical issue in this case."

"So you asked Ms. Jackson to tell you what she remembered about how she was shot in order to help prepare the defense for this case. Is that correct?"

I could feel my hairline prickling. "No. I always ask the person I'm evaluating to tell me how they were injured. It's standard operating procedure."

"Standard operating procedure?" Sherman repeated slowly with mock surprise. "I take it you've been asked, for example, your opinion as to whether Sylvia Jackson could *in fact* recall what she told the police she *did* recall."

"No, I haven't been asked that."

"You have not?" He paused. The grooves in his forehead deepened as he stared at me straight on. "Then it's unclear to me what you mean by" — he referred to his yellow pad — " 'guiding the defense in evaluating memory deficits.' Could you explain that for me?"

"Sure," I said agreeably. "I don't know whether she remembers what she purports to remember or not. I can't make that determination. I wasn't there. I don't know what actually happened. What I can do is make informed judgments about what her memory function is like now, following her very significant brain injury."

Sherman looked at me stoically, tolerating my obtuseness. His eyes focused on the top of my head. I stifled the desire to smooth my hair.

"Is there some kind of acid test for whether or not a person can recall what she says she recalls?"

I stroked my chin. "Bottom line, if your question is, can you ever be certain that somebody recalls accurately an event that occurred in the past, then the answer is no. Not unless you have corroboration for that event."

I wasn't expecting the question that followed. "Have you been provided with information about a prior encounter between Stuart Jackson, Sylvia Jackson, and Tony Ruggiero?"

"Yes," I said cautiously.

"Okay. So you know there was a prior incident?"

"I do."

"Is it your opinion that the details she gives about what happened before she was shot are confused with the earlier encounter?"

"All I can say, definitively, is that she certainly has a tendency to do that now."

"To do what now?"

"To mix together details from different events."

"Okay. Do you have any opinion as to whether she's mixing *those* two things?"

"No."

"And is there any way of telling whether or not she's mixing those two events?"

Sherman knew I'd say no before I said it.

He retreated behind his pad, flipped to the next page, and asked, "What have you been told about how Sylvia Jackson's memory returned to her?"

"My understanding is that several weeks after she woke up, she was interviewed by the police. And after some weeks, during the course of those interviews, she said she thought her ex-husband, Stuart Jackson, did it."

"Okay. Based on your testing of Sylvia Jackson, would it surprise you to know that some weeks after she received her injury, she started having nightmares, saying things either in her sleep or immediately afterwards like 'Please, don't leave me here—you can't leave me here like that'? Would that surprise you?"

Sherman was talking faster now and the volume and tone of his voice were rising. It pushed me into reverse. I answered quietly, "No."

"After those first few weeks, instead of talking to the police, she told a nurse that Stuart Jackson shot her. Would that surprise you?"

"Would it surprise me that she'd tell a nurse?"

"Would it surprise you that she went from having nightmares to remembering who shot her?"

"No, it wouldn't surprise me."

"And then a week or so later she was able to give the police a more detailed account of what happened. Would that surprise you?"

"A more detailed account of what she *believed* happened." The course correction broke his rhythm.

"Okay. Would that surprise you?"

"No."

Then he was back on a roll, the volume rising. "And would it surprise you that four months later she couldn't remember a lot of the details she remembered earlier?"

"Is it surprising that she forgot details of what she *told* the police? No."

A twitch beat a tattoo at the corner of his right eye. "Details of what she told the police?"

"Yes. You see, it's at least possible that what she *claims* occurred on the night she received her injury is inaccurate. I remind you, I don't know what happened that night. But it's certainly possible that she's making everything up."

"Possible." Sherman tasted the word. "Is it likely?"

"What do you mean, likely?"

"Is it more likely than not?"

I sighed—the poor man. His orderly mind with its sharp creases and right angles wanted to apply statistical probability. He'd choke on the glorious chaos of real human behavior. "I would say equally likely that what she's talking about happened or didn't happen. How she remembers information from before the injury is something I can't determine one way or another. Keep in mind, my evaluation has to do with her current cognitive status."

By the time I'd finished, Montrose Sherman was looking at a crack in the ceiling, his mouth set in a grim line, his silver pen tapping rhythmically against the yellow pad. I could almost hear his little gray cells muttering, "Yadda, yadda, yadda."

Then Sherman shifted gears. He asked a whole series of questions about the tests I'd administered. The jurors were good sports, but by the time Sherman was satisfied thirty minutes later, even my salt-and-pepper friend's eyes were glazed over.

"And the content of these tests is as you have described them?" He cleared his throat for emphasis, bringing a few jurors to startled attention. "Houses? Cowboys? Bats and butterflies?"

"They're the standard tests," I told him, bristling, "used by experts to evaluate cognitive functioning."

I glanced at Chip. His raised eyebrow was telling me to stay calm.

"I understand that," Sherman said, more to the jury than to me. "So you felt that Ms. Jackson's recollections of what happened to her weren't as important as how she remembered the pictures of houses and cowboys?"

He was baiting me. Once, I'd have been impervious. Now, I felt anger rising like bile in the back of my throat. "I had no way of validating her recollections. The only way a professional can get a sense of how someone deals with memory is by knowing exactly what the stimulus material—the test—is. I have no idea what happened to Ms. Jackson, but I *do* know that there are houses and cowboys in those test pictures."

"I see," Sherman said, leaning toward me. "So your findings did not rely on any information about the crime itself, is that correct?"

A yellow light flashed in my head as I answered, "Yes. That's correct."

"Although you say you were not concerned with the details of this crime, it's true, is it not, that you were provided with some limited information about the crimes the defendant is charged with?"

"Yes."

"You were provided with, for example, Detective MacRae's report containing Sylvia Jackson's statements last spring?"

"Yes, I was."

"You were provided with the police reports describing the scene at Mount Auburn Cemetery?"

"Yes."

"And you were also provided with a report of what Nurse Carolyn Lovely said Sylvia Jackson told her, correct?"

"No, I was not," I answered.

"Were you provided with police reports stating a bloodstained pillowcase and belt were found at the scene?"

"Not that I recall. If it would be helpful to you, most of what I was provided . . ."

"I'll ask the questions if you don't mind." Sherman spat the words out.

Chip rose. "I'll ask that the witness be allowed to explain his answer."

"It wasn't an answer," Sherman cut in.

The judge agreed and let Sherman continue with his litany of evidence to which I had not been privy.

"Were you provided with the police report indicating that a camouflage fatigue hat was recovered from the defendant's apartment?"

He'd made his point abundantly clear. I had not had access to the massive amounts of circumstantial evidence that made up the prosecution's case. I scanned the jurors and wondered how my cowboys and butterflies stacked up against bloodstained pillowcases and camouflage fatigue hats.

Finally, I responded. "As I've already said a number of times, I was doing an evaluation of her current cognitive status. All of this evidence you're referring to wasn't relevant to my testing."

Montrose Sherman gazed at me, suddenly quite pleased. I had a sinking feeling that I'd just violated the cardinal rule of expert testimony: just answer the question, don't volunteer. The light that had been flashing yellow turned to red.

"So, if all you were concerned with was her current cognitive status," Montrose Sherman gave a sharp cough, "then perhaps you can explain to the court why one of the first things you did when you sat down with Sylvia Jackson was to take a statement from her about the events preceding her injury?"

Now red lights were flashing like a pinball machine. It took me a few seconds to gather a response. "I asked her to tell me what happened. Yes—I do that every—"

He cut me off. "And you wrote down everything she said?"

"Yes, that's part of the testing process—"

He cut me off again. "But you didn't write down everything else she said during the tests. Not everything she said during those twelve hours?"

He was determined to double the length of time I'd spent testing Sylvia Jackson. Correcting him again would only be counterproductive. "No, sir."

"But you *did* write down, specifically, verbatim, exactly what she said in response to your question concerning what happened preceding her injury. Correct?"

I swallowed. "That's correct."

I had no time to ponder why this answer sounded suspect. Sherman was already on the move again. "In fact, taking this statement wasn't necessary at all for your evaluation of Sylvia Jackson, was it?" Sherman turned back to me, the lines above his eyebrows deepening into furrows. "Dr. Zak, would you agree that corroboration is the only way to tell whether someone accurately recalls an event?"

"Yes," I said, "if that corroboration comes from someone who saw the same event."

Sherman looked toward the jury, nonchalant. "You mean, if someone had been in the house, for instance, and had walked in on the murder while it was taking place—"

My mouth hung open and I felt color rising from my collar. Of course, he knew all about my wife's murder. He hadn't been personally involved, but his office had prosecuted the case. I started to get up out of my chair. Chip was on his feet. "Objection."

The judge looked surprised. "On what basis?"

Sherman shrugged. "Question withdrawn."

The callous deliberateness with which he was trying to sabotage me took my breath away. I dropped back into my seat.

Sherman put down his legal pad, crossed his arms in front of him. I barely heard the next question. "So the only way for you to corroborate what someone says they saw is if another person was there and tells you they saw the same thing?"

"Correct," I said.

Sherman took a half turn toward the jury as he delivered a final shot. "So if I told you that it rained outside while you were in this courtroom, and you walked outside and saw the sky was clouded over and there were puddles out there and the grass was wet, it wouldn't be enough corroboration for you, I take it?"

I took a deep breath and smothered the urge to vault out of the witness box and wring Monty's neck. He dangled the absurd question in front of me like bait and I rose to it, just as he must have hoped I would. "No. A sprinkler truck might have come by."

My salt-and-pepper friend tittered in an otherwise stone-quiet courtroom.

"A sprinkler truck," Sherman repeated and glanced at the jury.

"Mr. Sherman, do you have any more questions for this witness?" the judge asked.

"I do, Your Honor."

"In that case, since it's already late," the judge banged his gavel, "court is recessed until Monday at nine."

I left the courtroom feeling I'd been sucker-punched.

"We're going to get a drink down the street," Chip said as we were leaving the courthouse. "Join us?"

I got waylaid by a reporter in the lobby. By the time I got to the tavern, Chip was standing alone at the bar. "Where's . . ." I started to ask when Annie emerged from the gloomy inner reaches of the room. Transformed into herself, she'd changed into jeans and her aviator's jacket. Her hair, sprung loose, curled around her face.

"Phew," she sighed, sinking into the stool beside me and draping a zippered garment bag across the bar, "that's much better. That outfit makes my teeth itch."

"I didn't know teeth could itch," Chip said.

"That's what my dad used to say about wearing a tie," she said, wrinkling her nose.

The beer arrived. Chip raised his glass. "To a fair verdict."

"A fair verdict," I said and tapped mine against his.

We all drank. I barely tasted the beer.

"Sorry about that sprinkler truck," I said. "It just slipped out."

"Peter," Chip said, "he took a cheap shot. Any reasonable person would have reacted."

"Look, I told you I wasn't doing this kind of work anymore. Now I've gone and screwed up your case."

"It ain't over till it's over," Annie said. "One sprinkler truck isn't going to wash away the lack of evidence."

Chip and Annie started to discuss the day's proceedings. Annie dissected the jury's response to the defense case, juror by juror. I tuned out and replayed Sherman's words, "You mean, if someone had been in the house—" It was, as Chip said, a cheap shot. Cheap and potentially lethal. Nothing was the way it had been before Kate was killed. I went to work, I treated my patients, I kibitzed with Kwan, I went home—it looked the same. But sameness was an illusion. Like a house Kate and I had once looked at. It seemed sturdy, but when you took a knife to the foundation, the punky wood gave way like balsa. I had a vulnerability that D.A.s could attack with impunity without the jury even suspecting that something was up.

Just then, my pocket buzzed like an angry bumblebee. I'd turned it from beep to buzz—it's not cool to have your pocket beep while you're testifying. I got up to find a phone. Annie offered me her cell phone.

"Something wrong with your beer?" she asked, noticing that I hadn't touched it.

I pushed the beer away. "I guess my stomach's a little queasy."

I dialed the hospital. Kwan picked up.

"It's Peter. What's up?"

"Maria Whitson's split."

"How?"

"She must have followed someone out through an exit. When she didn't show up for dinner, we went looking for her. She's not in the building."

31

I WAS already out on the street, looking up and down, trying to recall where I'd parked my car, when I remembered. It was in the shop. I returned to the bar where Annie and Chip were still nursing their drinks.

"What happened? Decide to finish your beer after all?" Chip asked.

"My damned car is being fixed," I complained. "I'm going to have to call a cab. I need to get to the hospital right away."

"I'll drive you," Annie offered.

"Would you? I'd appreciate that. We don't often lose patients."

"Who'd you lose?"

"A young woman. And now I'm kicking myself because I noticed that she was acting oddly this morning and I didn't take the time to find out what was up. We were managing so many other crises."

"You think she's in danger?"

"She's attempted suicide before. I don't *think* that's what she's up to. But why split? We were releasing her in a few days. Maybe she's still somewhere on the grounds. I feel responsible. She's my patient and I wasn't paying attention."

Annie tossed a five-dollar bill on the counter, grabbed her garment bag, threw her coat over her shoulders, and headed out. Her Jeep was parked in a lot down the street. I held on as we bounced over the potholes that have achieved landmark status in East Cambridge. The rush-hour traffic slowed her down only slightly as she dodged and weaved with the nonchalance of a veteran cabby.

We pulled onto the rolling hospital campus and I showed Annie where to park. "This place always reminds me of a country club," she commented as we hurried up the hill to the unit.

Kwan was on the phone at the nurses' station. "I'll call you back," he said, "keep looking." He hung up and turned to me. His face was tense. Uncharacteristically, his tie was loosened at the neck. "That was hospital security. They're searching the grounds. Nothing yet. But there are so many nooks and crannies in this place, it could take awhile."

"They've alerted the police?" I asked. Kwan nodded.

Gloria came rushing in from the hall. "I checked her room. Her clothes are still there. Her toothbrush. As far as I can tell, everything except her purse and what she was wearing."

"How long has she been gone?" I asked.

Gloria answered, "She was here when the nurse passed out meds at three. Then didn't show up for dinner."

Dinner on the unit was at 5:30 P.M. It was already after six. A lot could happen in three hours.

"This morning she seemed jumpy," I said. "I asked her why she wasn't participating in any of the morning activities. Then I got distracted." Gloria put her hands on her hips and eyed me. "I know, I know. I should have been paying attention. But there was an awful lot going on around here."

Gloria rubbed her forehead and sighed. "At least you talked to her. I didn't even notice what she was up to. All I know is Maria ate lunch and went back to her room. If I'd been doing my job, this never would have happened."

"Often you can tell a lot about someone's state of mind,

where they thought they were going, by what they take with them and what they leave behind," Annie offered. The three of us looked over at her. I started to say something and then stopped myself. It's not ethical to talk about a patient in front of an outsider. On the other hand, Annie was a trained investigator.

I quickly introduced Annie to Kwan and Gloria. "Annie is a private investigator," I explained. "I'm working with her on a case."

"I know sharing information about a patient probably makes you all uncomfortable," Annie said, "but I couldn't help overhearing. Maybe I can help." Annie took the silence as permission to continue. "Someone who's just looking for a hole to crawl into and die probably isn't going to bother to take her purse along. On the other hand . . ."

The phone at the desk rang and Kwan picked it up.

"Why don't you check out her room," Gloria suggested. "You might notice something I missed. I'm going upstairs to check the rest of the building one more time. Maybe she's taking a nap in someone's office."

Annie and I went down to Maria Whitson's room. Her bed was made but rumpled, as if she'd been sitting on it. Her mother's photograph album lay open on the bed. I looked in the closet. Her clothes were there, neatly folded or hung. The morning paper was on the bathroom floor. I picked it up. There was a story on the front page about the Jackson trial—"Assault Victim's Memory to Be Questioned."

"This is your patient?" Annie asked. She'd picked up the open photograph album.

I glanced at the wedding picture. "That's her," I said and crouched down to peer under the bed.

"Peter, look closely and tell me what you see."

I looked at the page Annie held open. Slim and radiant, her hair done up elaborately with tendrils curling about her face, Maria Whitson beamed on the arm of a dark, handsome, muscular young man, a young man she had since ousted from her life. "Holy shit," I whispered, staring at the familiar face, trying to make sense of what I was seeing. The handsome young man who stood beside Maria, uncomfortable in his rented tux, was Sylvia Jackson's guardian angel, Angelo di Benedetti.

"Isn't Angelo's alibi his ex-wife?" Annie asked.

I nodded.

"And Angelo is Tony's nephew by ex-marriage, right?"

I nodded again.

"Then that makes your patient—"

"—Tony Ruggiero's niece. Sylvia's Tony and Maria's Uncle Nino are the same person." I said the words slowly, running them through my brain like a blind person feeling an unfamiliar feature in a familiar face.

"Wait a minute," Annie said. "Let me get this straight. You're treating a patient who's related to our murder victim?"

"But I had no idea . . ."

"Of course you had no idea. You would have disqualified yourself from the start. Once Sherman gets wind of this, he could file for a mistrial."

I tried to digest what was happening. As Annie had instantly realized, the connection meant I had a conflict of interest. My opinions were tainted. But there was more to it than that. Pieces of information were flying around in my head and I was struggling to connect the dots.

Some pieces of paper that must have been tucked into the photograph album fluttered to the floor. I reached down and picked them up. "Would you look at this," I murmured. There was the newspaper clipping from two months earlier: "Jackson Case to Hear Memory Expert." Also, a Xerox of the feature article that had been written about me, whole sections of text highlighted in yellow. And finally, a copy of a newspaper clipping—I winced at the words, "Slasher Kills Cambridge Artist."

Annie said, "It's almost as if she wanted you to find these." It was what I'd been thinking, too.

"I wonder . . ." I started, and picked up the phone and dialed the hospital operator. "Can you connect me with Dr. Baldridge?" I waited. When I got Baldridge's answering service, I said, "I need to talk to him. Right now."

"He's in group," the drone on the other end of the line told me.

"This is urgent. I know there's an emergency code. Please, use it."

"I'm sorry. I have strict instructions . . ."

"If I don't hear back from him in ten minutes, I'm going to come over there and interrupt the group myself. Am I making myself perfectly clear?"

Dr. Baldridge called back two minutes later. "What's the meaning of this?" he demanded.

"Why did you refer Maria Whitson to the Neuropsych Unit?"

"You interrupt me, get me out of group to ask me—"

"Believe me, it's a matter of great urgency."

"Aren't you being a bit melodramatic?"

"Maria Whitson has disappeared. It's very important that I understand exactly the circumstances surrounding her admission."

"Disappeared? Can't you people . . ." Baldridge sputtered. "Let's see, Maria Whitson"—I had the distinct impression he was trying to recall who she was. "I referred her to you because I knew you'd be able to . . ."

"You referred her on your own? It was your idea?"

There was silence. "She did mention that she'd read about you."

"So she asked you to refer her to me, specifically?"

"Well, with you being an expert on head trauma and all, I concurred." There was a pause. "It was the right thing to do, wasn't it? I wasn't able to treat her any further. Well, of course, I might have done so anyway, given the problems she was having, and of course . . ." He blustered on. I hung up and swore under my breath.

"What was that all about?" Annie asked.

"Would have been pretty amazing, I take on a murder case and a week later, the niece of the murdered victim shows up on the unit." I stared at the phone. "It was no coincidence. It was engineered."

I was still staring at the phone when it rang. Annie and I looked at each other. I picked it up. "Hello?"

It was Kwan, calling from down the hall. "One of the security guards saw a blond woman out jogging on the grounds this afternoon. It was still light. Then, he noticed her again later, outside the gate talking to someone in a car. He had the impression they were having a vigorous discussion. Maybe an argument. They went at it for a few minutes. Then she got into the car and it took off. Says he can show us the tire tracks. I guess the guy was in a hurry."

"Did he get a plate number? Make of car? Description of the driver?" I sounded like my friend, Sergeant MacRae.

"No plate number. Couldn't see the man she was talking to."

"But he had the impression that it was a man?"

"Yeah, I guess so."

I hung up the phone and told Annie. "Did he think she went voluntarily?" Annie asked.

"Well, he didn't get out and force her into the car."

A high-pitched ring sounded. It wasn't coming from Maria's bedside phone. The sound came again. The orange plastic pitcher alongside the regular phone was ringing. I opened the top. The sound came again, louder. I lifted a cell phone from its hiding place, flipped it opened, turned it on, and held it to my ear.

"Hello?" I said.

There was no sound. Then a click.

"Anybody there?" Annie asked.

I shook my head. I wondered, once again, why Maria Whitson felt she needed to keep this phone hidden. Then, I remembered something from walk rounds, the first day we admitted her. When I started to pour her a cup of water from this pitcher, she became agitated. Was the cell phone hidden here from day one? It was a disturbing thought. Which led to another disturbing thought. Had she been tormenting my mother with middle-of-the-night phone calls intended to disrupt my sleep, calls that she didn't want showing up in the hospital phone records?

I pressed the redial button and waited. There were seven beeps in quick succession. As I'd expected, a local call. The phone rang once. Twice. Still no answer. Three rings. I waited. Four rings. I kept expecting to hear my mother's voice at the other end. Instead, the phone rang again. And again. Still no one picked up, not even an answering machine. I was about to give up after the seventh ring when there was a click, a pause, the sound of someone exhaling, and a familiar, breathy voice, ". . . Hello?"

I started to say something when I heard a man's voice yelling in the background. I couldn't make out the words. Then the phone went dead. I pressed redial again. Seven beeps. And a rapid busy signal.

32

"SYLVIA JACKSON?" Annie gasped when I told her who I thought had picked up the phone. "Why would your patient be calling her?"

"Maybe she wasn't calling Syl. Maybe she was calling someone else, someone she knew would be at Syl's house."

"Maybe Angelo," Annie said. "She was his ex-wife. His alibi."

I remembered the first time I'd met Angelo, how his powerful hands had circled Syl's neck. In my memory now, the gesture seemed menacing. This was the same man Maria said became enraged when the unexpected happened.

My mind was churning. I checked my watch, barely noticing the position of the minute and hour hands, acutely aware of the second hand sweeping across the dial. If I was lucky, it wasn't too late to prevent whatever terrible thing I knew in my gut was about to happen. Sitting still and waiting, mindlessly following doctor-patient etiquette, wasn't an option. This time, I wasn't going to be too late.

"Do you know where Sylvia Jackson lives? I think we should get over there. She could be in danger. And so could my patient."

Annie pulled out her appointment book, turned to the back, and read off an address. I hurried out of the room and down the hall with Annie close behind. "Maybe we should call the police," she said.

"And tell them what? To come protect me while I go snooping around at a private home?"

We hurried out past Kwan. He was on the phone, looking harried. He raised his eyebrows in a question. "I think I know where she might be," I told him. Before Kwan could reply, Annie and I were gone.

Annie drove while I struggled to see a map in the beam of her little penlight. After a few wrong turns, we found Syl's house on a side street behind Mount Auburn Cemetery in a mazelike neighborhood of one-ways and dead ends.

As we approached, Annie turned off the ignition and the headlights and rolled to a stop just beyond the house. From the car, I could see a white colonial-style house with an attached garage. Tall bushes shrouded a shadowy front porch. Only a sliver of light between drawn drapes suggested anyone was home.

Someone had made an effort to dress up the house for Halloween. On the small lawn, dried cornstalks were teepeed around a lamppost. A pumpkin grinned from the top of a wheelchair ramp. Opposite the pumpkin was a little barrel of chrysanthemums. Beside the front door, barely visible in the shadow, a scarecrow dummy wearing a cowboy hat was slumped in a chair. I exhaled, realizing I'd been holding my breath.

"Okay, we're here," Annie said. "Now what?"

This time, I wasn't going to do nothing. "Let's just check things out quietly first."

Annie got out and eased the car door shut. I did the same.

We moved cautiously, up the side of the house, crouching as we passed under the dark windows. I was conscious of every sound—my own breathing, traffic whooshing up and down the adjacent streets, the far-off pulsing wail of a siren. At every step, the sound of leaves crunching underfoot seemed thunderous.

Annie disappeared around the rear of the house. I glanced back toward the street. The lights of passing cars briefly illuminated the Jeep.

"Peter," came Annie's urgent whisper as she reappeared around the corner. "Come look!"

In the corner of the yard, lit by the dim glow from what I guessed was a curtained kitchen window and looking like the ghost of a small beached whale, sat a small boat. I raised an edge of the tarp that covered it. Just a stinkpot, like every other stinkpot that plagues the river. I lifted a dark hooded sweatshirt from under the wooden seat. I dropped it back into the boat and sniffed my hand—it smelled of mildewed eau de Charles River.

A nearby branch snapped and we both hunkered down beside the boat. A cat darted out from behind some bushes. In the darkness, all I could see were little white paws mincing toward me and the white tip of a tail held aloft. It sauntered up and rubbed its back against my leg.

"Shoo," I whispered, gently pushing the cat away. It skittered off and disappeared. "Let's check out the garage."

We crept around the back of the yard, staying as deep in shadow as we could. We approached the back of the garage and I peered in through a window. "Can't see a blessed thing," I whispered.

Annie shined the penlight through the glass. We couldn't make out much, but there was definitely a car parked inside, and it was definitely red.

"Let's go around front," I said. "I think there's a door."

It wasn't possible to go around the far side of the garage without making a racket, crashing through the branches that grew close to it. So we crept back around the house, skirting the yard, and returned to the front.

The scarecrow dummy still sat, nonchalant in the aluminum chair on the porch. Scarecrow dummies used to terrify me when

I was a kid. I'd skip the trick-or-treats at any house where one sat guard. This one slouched spinelessly, one leg pointing forward and the other one doubled over, angled back awkwardly, as if he might at any moment lurch to his feet and stagger off down the driveway in search of the black cat. Stuffed garden gloves sewn to the sleeves of a torn plaid shirt rested on threadbare jeans. Close up, I could see the childlike drawing of a jack-o'-lantern face on his pillowcase head. I couldn't help thinking of the pillowcase that covered Tony Ruggiero's head while he was beaten and shot.

There was an ordinary door alongside the garage's overhead door. I twisted the knob gently. I pushed. The door gave about half an inch and then stuck. I pushed harder and felt the pile of objects pressed up against it inch back, just enough so that we could squeeze through.

It was pitch black inside. Annie switched on the penlight. Behind the door were stacks of boxes, one overflowing with old clothes, another exploding with miscellaneous plumbing innards. One bay of the garage was empty. In the other was the red Firebird we'd seen through the back window. Annie ran the light along one side. It was covered with scratches, as if someone had driven it heedlessly through underbrush. We squeezed around behind the car and Annie sidled up the far side, toward the front. She ran the light along the front fender. "Do you see what I see?" she asked, indicating a dent and a streak of dark green paint.

I started to answer when Annie put her finger to her lips and doused the light.

The door to the house on the opposite side of the garage opened. I crouched. Footsteps were barely audible, rubber soles crossing the garage's empty bay. As my eyes got accustomed to the dark, I began to make out a pale round shape, floating, suspended in the shadows at about head height.

There was a click and the room sprang to light. I blinked

away the brightness. "Well, if it isn't the expert witness," a voice sneered.

Angelo di Benedetti stood facing me. He wore a black turtleneck and baggy black pants, rolled at the ankle above combat boots. His handsome face was hard and a vein pulsed in his forehead. He had his hands in his pockets. I wondered where Annie was, but I didn't dare look at the spot where I knew she'd been not more than ten seconds earlier. Another instinct told me not to move suddenly.

Angelo's eyes were cold and disdainful. "So nice of you to join us."

Through the open door behind him, I could make out a figure sitting slumped over a kitchen table. It was Sylvia Jackson. She sat in her wheelchair, her back bowed, her chin resting on her chest. Just like the scarecrow dummy. Two half-filled wineglasses were on the table. Where was Maria? Was she here, too, drugged and comatose in one of the bedrooms?

"Why don't you come inside where we can be more comfortable," he said, drawing out the last word so it took on sinister overtones.

He stood aside and I walked past him into the house. I went over to Syl, trying to move deliberately and not betray the panic I felt. I touched her shoulder. No reaction. I pressed two fingers to the side of her neck. The skin was cool, pulse faint. I shook her gently. Her body listed to one side. She was unconscious. Not dead. Not yet.

"She needs a doctor," I said, keeping my voice even.

"Isn't that what you are? A doctor?"

"I'm not that kind of doctor."

"Oh, that's right," he said, chuckling unpleasantly. "You're the memory doctor. You and your stupid tests. Syl really has the hots for you, you know."

I'd already started walking over to the phone on the wall beside the refrigerator. I picked it up, hoping to hear the reassuring buzz of a dial tone. Instead, I heard the echoes of an empty seashell. No wonder I hadn't been able to call Sylvia Jackson back. Then I heard the door from the kitchen to the garage close.

"Is there another phone?" I asked.

"It's not working? Oh, my, I guess we'll have to get that fixed," Angelo said.

"I have a phone in the car," I said, and started toward the front door. But like a ninja, Angelo materialized in front of it. He stood there, feet apart, knees and elbows flexed, a small gun in his hand. Though he held the gun loosely, pointing it toward the ground, I sensed that every tendon in his body was taut. A jack-in-the-box, he was ready to spring at the slightest nudge.

He smiled at me. His eyes glittered with anger. They were nothing like the flat, lifeless eyes of Ralston Bridges. I had no doubt that the gun was real and loaded. And that Angelo wouldn't hesitate to use it. But for some reason, I wasn't afraid. I felt hyperalert. As if I'd been rowing long enough for the endorphins to kick in and create a center of calm, an ability to focus completely on the task at hand. For a brief instant, I even imagined myself neatly kicking the gun from his hand.

"Don't even think about it," Angelo said, reading my thought.

I held his gaze as we stood, face to face. A rustle of movement broke the spell. Then footsteps. A connecting door pushed open and Maria Whitson appeared.

I took a step toward her and stopped. "Thank God you're safe," I said.

"Dr. Zak. What are you . . . ?Why are you . . .?" she stammered. She seemed surprised and something else that could have been afraid. She wore black leggings with turquoise stripes up the sides and a matching windbreaker. A black sweatband held her hair back from her face.

"Come here, doll," Angelo said, stepping over to her and pulling her toward him. Their wedding picture flashed briefly into my mind. Just as in that carefully posed photograph, Angelo wound his arm tightly around Maria. She was the prize, and he her owner. Once again, I wondered if she'd left that album open on her bed so I'd know who'd taken her.

"Everyone is worried sick about you," I told her.

"I'm fine," she said woodenly, each word occupying the same amount of time and space as the next. "Much better, in fact."

"I'm sure they've called the police by now," I added.

"Shit," Angelo hissed.

"I told you, you should have let me call the hospital," she told Angelo.

Then Angelo turned on me, seeming to grow larger. "I knew I should have gotten rid of you a long time ago," he said. "If you'd just stayed out of it, Doctor, our friend Stuart would have been convicted. That would have been the end of it. But no, you couldn't leave well enough alone. Fuck you!" His angry look turned to scorn as the gun rose. "You poor, stupid sonofabitch."

I still felt eerily calm. As if this were all a movie. Breathe evenly, I told myself, and maintain eye contact. "You don't have to do this, Angelo," I said, as if we were sitting in my office having a chat. "I know you thought there was a reason to kill Tony Ruggiero, but . . ."

"What do you know about that?" he snapped.

"I know you thought killing him was justified. Revenge . . ."

"Uncle Nino," Angelo jeered. "There's no more Uncle Nino now, is there? We fixed that, didn't we?"

I wanted to ask, "Who's we?" But I thought better of it. What mattered at that moment was getting Sylvia Jackson safely whisked away to a hospital, getting Maria away from here, and getting Angelo put away so he couldn't hurt either of them.

"But Syl's different, isn't she?" I droned on, keeping one eye on the gun he still held aloft. "You know as well as I do, there's no reason to kill her. She doesn't remember anything. And she never will. You took care of that when you shot her in the head."

"She has to die. Like he had to die." It was Maria Whitson,

not Angelo, who said the words that trickled like ice water down the back of my neck. She stared at me wide-eyed. "She was *his* girlfriend. They both had to die."

Her eyes were bright. Her pupils were pinpoints. I wondered what she'd taken. And suddenly, I understood. I understood the hurt that the young Maria Whitson had felt when she found her uncle, the young man whom she adored, having sex with his girlfriend. It was a betrayal she had never gotten over. Her recovered memories of sexual abuse were only stand-ins for the real nightmare. Take them away and the malevolence she felt toward her uncle and toward his lovers remained intact.

"You loved your uncle very much, didn't you?" I said.

"What are you jabbering about, asshole?" Angelo spat.

"You still don't get it, do you?" Maria said calmly, her look defying me to contradict her. She took a half turn to face Angelo and said in a flat, lifeless tone, "Uncle Nino raped me. He did it over and over again. We killed him because he deserved to die."

Did she really believe this? Was she holding on to this version of her life because she couldn't do otherwise? "But Sylvia Jackson didn't do anything," I said. "Let me call an ambulance while there's still time. She doesn't deserve to die. You don't have anything to worry about, you know. She's not going to remember."

Maria started to say something but Angelo interrupted. "Don't tell him anything. He doesn't know what he's talking about."

"But you were afraid she'd remember," I told Angelo. "You're still afraid. That's it, isn't it? That's why you didn't tell her your real name. As long as she thought your name was Ruggiero, you knew you were safe."

"Wouldn't you like to know," Angelo said.

"Maybe it was something she saw."

The jeering smile on Angelo's face froze.

"She saw what I needed her to see," Maria said.

"*Don't answer him!*" Angelo screamed.

"It doesn't matter now, does it?" Maria said with a little half-smile. "Soon it will all be over."

"What was it that she saw? What was it that you're so worried she's going to remember?"

"Everything," Maria said simply.

Angelo howled, *"No!"*

But it made no difference. Maria stared at me defiantly and continued. "I held a knife to her throat while we watched Angelo take care of Uncle Nino. Didn't we, Angelo? We watched from the stairs." So Syl had watched Tony being beaten. Only not from the stone steps of the tower. From the stairs of her own home. "But I didn't go to the cemetery with you. You went alone. That's what happens when I let you do something without me," Maria fretted, "it doesn't get done right."

"Why the cemetery?" I asked. "Why not finish Sylvia Jackson off right here?"

"Nino and I had unfinished business," Maria said. "Personal business."

"That's when you confronted him. He was still alive, wasn't he?"

"He was bleeding to death right here." Maria pointed to the bare floor in front of the fireplace. "He still wouldn't admit what he'd done to me. He said none of it happened." Angelo was silent, as if hearing this for the first time. "Then he's bargaining with me. He'll admit to anything if only I'll call an ambulance. He didn't want to die. In the end, he was crying, saying he was sorry. He couldn't remember but he was sorry. He was so pale." She looked up at me hollow-eyed. "It's not like in the movies, you know."

"What isn't?"

"Death. It's not like you gasp, say something profound, and then roll your eyes back and shudder a few times. He just lay there for hours, making this sound in the back of his throat. I don't even know if he could hear me, but I kept on talking. I told him what he'd done to me. I kept hoping he'd open his eyes and remember. But the bastard just lay there. When Angelo got back, Nino was still alive. Angelo wanted to shoot him one more time to end it, but I wouldn't let him. I kept watching him. I wanted to see him go from living to dead. But it was Angel who noticed first."

I knew we'd turned a corner and there was no going back. No wonder Maria couldn't allow herself to accept her uncle's innocence. And now, she and Angelo couldn't let me go free, knowing what I knew. One man had already died in this room. Whatever happened, I was not about to go quietly.

"There never was a camouflage hat, was there?" I said, wanting to know and playing for time.

Maria stood and smiled at me slyly. "But Syl *saw* Stuart wearing it. She swears she saw it."

"Angelo planted that memory, didn't he? And then one of you planted the hat."

"It was Tony's hat," Maria said. "Isn't that just perfect? Angelo hides Tony's hat in the back of Stuart's closet and Sylvia Jackson sends the police over to find it."

"And then you made sure it had some of Stuart's hair in it."

Maria smiled and nodded. "Angelo's so clever. Collected some from the shower drain."

"I wondered where the pills came from that almost killed Sylvia Jackson," I continued. "They were yours, weren't they? Courtesy of Dr. Baldridge. And when that didn't work, you needed to make sure I'd never convince a jury that Sylvia Jackson's memory was flawed, constructed. Running me over with the boat doesn't put me out of commission, so you have to try something else. You get yourself admitted to the hospital as my patient. When we discover that you're the victim's niece, my testimony becomes inadmissible. Mistrial. What an incredible coincidence, everyone would say, but these things happen. That was very risky, taking all those pills. But you wanted it to look authentic."

"I'm an expert when it comes to pills," she said. "Just enough and not too many."

"I should have seen through it. Baldridge has never referred a single patient to us."

"He's so"—Maria searched for the word—"suggestible. I've learned to rely on doctors and their egos."

"What about Gloria? Gloria really cares about you, you know."

"Gloria really cares about you, you know," Maria mimicked me in a whiny voice.

"Was Gloria's accident your idea, too? Did you help her slip and fall?"

"Shut up." Maria chewed on a nail and watched me from slitted eyes.

"Didn't you have a friend who had an unfortunate accident? Slipped and fell down the basement stairs?"

"How do you . . . ?" Maria whispered.

"What was it that poor girl did to make you angry?"

"That little cunt," Maria spat out the words. "She deserved it." Maria stared at me and licked her lips. Her eyes flitted around the room, resting briefly on Syl's inert form before returning to me. "She humiliated me. She told everyone that I had a thing for Mr. Jaffy. Like it was some kind of a joke. She made it seem—stupid. Do you know what those assholes did? They told the principal. And he hauled me into his office. They thought we'd done something in-app-ropriate," she said, holding her nose as she whined each syllable. She snorted with disgust. "I prayed for something bad to happen to her. Something really bad. And it did."

"Think about it, Maria. Praying and pushing are two very different things. You didn't push her down those stairs. You weren't even there when it happened."

"I did it. I pushed her."

"You didn't. Your mother told me you couldn't have. You had a dentist appointment."

"Right. My mother has an excuse for everything."

"She dropped you off at your friend's house after a dentist

appointment. That's when you found your friend. You came running out of her house—there wasn't time for you to push her."

Maria put her hand over her mouth. "Braces," she murmured. "I remember. I had my braces tightened."

"You might have thought about it."

"I wanted to hurt her."

"You might have planned every detail. But planning and doing are two different things."

"It was my fault," Maria insisted.

"It wasn't your fault."

There was a long pause and a deep breath before Maria asked, "I didn't hurt her?"

"You might have wanted it very badly. And then, when she really did get hurt, you felt guilty about wanting it so much. But you didn't hurt her. You didn't *do* anything."

Maria whispered, "I didn't hurt her." This time, it was a statement.

"Sometimes, bad things just happen, Maria. Even if you imagine them, wish for them, it's not your fault when they happen. But Uncle Nino. That's a different story. You prayed for it and then you got Angelo to do it for you. And you were afraid of what Sylvia Jackson would remember, so Angelo had to kill her, too. And Gloria? I wonder. What was it? A good strong push? Maybe a squirt of detergent? Is that why you needed to clean up the floor afterwards? To hide the soap slick?" Maria stared at me, her mouth open, her eyes wide. "It must have been hard. All that blood. Just like when Nino died, wasn't it?" Maria's face was without expression but her cheeks were wet with tears. "You can stop, Maria. You don't have to keep going down this path. You'll only self-destruct this way."

Maria rocked gently forward and back, her arms hugging her body. "Self-destruct, self-destruct," she repeated in a quiet singsong.

"Sorry, Doc." It was Angelo. He came up behind Maria and put an arm around her waist. The rocking stopped. With the muzzle of the gun he stroked her cheek. "No way, babe. There's no stopping now. The only way to walk away from this is to complete the circle. He knows. And one day, she'll remember."

Maria rubbed her cheek against the muzzle of the gun, like a cat rubbing against a favorite chair leg. Then she faced me and her eyes hardened. "They're always trying to take what belongs to me," she said. Angelo loosened his grip on her. She walked over to the unconscious Syl, stooped down, and whispered into her ear, "And I won't let them."

Syl was growing paler by the minute. I couldn't afford to let the clock keep ticking. Whatever they'd given her was slowly shutting her down. "I'm not alone," I said. "There's someone waiting outside. And they've already called the police." I hoped it was true. "So if you kill us, the police will know exactly what happened."

Angelo leveled a look at me. "You're lying."

"See for yourself." I gestured toward the living-room window. "There, on the street. In the Jeep."

Angelo sprang, twisted me around, and pinned my right arm behind my back. Pain arced through my shoulder and down my arm. He jammed the barrel of the gun into my ear and shoved me toward the front door. "We'll just see, why don't we? Open it," he ordered. When I didn't react fast enough, he tightened his grip on my arm. I groaned as my arm tried to separate itself from my shoulder. "Open the door," he repeated, enunciating the words distinctly and punctuating each one with extra pressure on the gun.

With my free hand, I strained to reach the doorknob and turn it. The door remained in place. Angelo eased his hold. I tried again. This time the door yielded. He whipped me away and wedged his body between the door and the frame. Then he pulled me through the narrow opening. Halfway down the ramp

I tried to wrench myself free, but Angelo held on tight.

"Pull that again and you'll be sorry, so help me God," he promised.

Angelo propelled me toward the Jeep. I prayed that Annie wasn't inside. He mashed my face up against the driver-side window. The metallic smell of dust filled my nostrils. Annie's leather jacket lay on the driver's seat. Angelo moved me aside and peered in through the window. He took the gun out of my ear long enough to yank the door handle. The door was locked.

Just then the front door of the house cracked open. "Angelo?" Maria cried out. "Angelo, what's happening out there?"

"There's no one here," Angelo called back to her. "I think he's playing for time."

Angelo pushed me back toward the house. Maria met us half-way down the ramp. "You know what we should do now?" she said. "Take them both to the cemetery and put an end to this, once and for all. Finish it the way it should have been finished in the first place. The way we planned it." The cold words belied Maria's quavering tone. Her voice pleaded with him. "Then we can be together, you and me—the way it was meant to be." Maria sobbed and held her arms open. Angelo released me with a shove.

I stumbled and ended up on my knees on the lawn. When I looked up, Angelo was embracing Maria with one arm while the gun still pointed firmly at a spot between my eyes. Where was Annie? I lowered my head and massaged my arm while I tried to decide what to do next.

I staggered to my feet and took a few steps to one side. Maybe I could make a run for it.

"Stay right where you are, Doctor," Angelo growled.

I caught a glimpse of something just around the corner at the base of the house. I edged over as Angelo bent and touched his lips to Maria's neck and crooned, "We belong together, Maria. I need you with me."

I smothered a gasp. What looked like a human body lay

crumpled and broken in the driveway at the side of the porch. I strained to see more clearly. It took me a moment to put it together. If the scarecrow dummy was lying dead in the driveway, then what was sitting in the aluminum lawn chair alongside the front door?

"Come on, my Angel," Maria said softly, "let's finish this."

The gun wobbled as Angelo took his eyes off me. Maria turned and walked toward the front door. With one hand on the storm door, she paused. I held my breath as she looked directly at the slumped-over scarecrow dummy. "What the —?" Maria said, taking a step back. Slowly, the scarecrow raised its head. Maria shrieked in terror as the scarecrow rose to its feet.

Angelo bellowed, "Look out!"

Maria spun around to face him. He took aim at the scarecrow. Maria stared at the barrel of the gun. She took a deliberate step sideways, then another. Angelo racked the slide. There was a click as a round was jacked into the chamber. One more step and she'd have put herself directly in the line of fire.

I didn't think. I didn't hesitate. I ran as fast and as hard as I could, head down, and caught Angelo behind the knees with my good shoulder, barely aware of the pop of protest in my right ankle. The gun exploded, inches from my head, and Angelo went down. I heard a thud as the gun bounced across the porch, discharging again before coming to rest.

Angelo kicked himself free of my grip and struggled to his feet. Annie ripped the scarecrow's pillowcase off her head and dove for the gun. She grabbed it and lay sprawled on the porch, pointing the gun at Angelo. "Don't move or I'll shoot!" she shouted.

But Angelo didn't see or hear her. He knelt beside Maria and screamed, "Maria!" his voice floating away like the sound of someone calling down an empty well. Maria Whitson lay in a spreading pool of dark red blood. "Maria," he cried, resting his head on her chest.

The darkness was filled with Angelo's sobs and the rasping

sound of Maria's ragged breathing. I crept closer, thinking there might be some way to slow the bleeding.

Maria's face was pale, the whites of her eyes seemed to glow. She stroked Angelo's head but she stared at me.

"Dr. Zak," she whispered.

I could hear sirens in the distance. I leaned closer. "Don't move," I told her. She started to speak again. I put my hand on her moist forehead. "Just lie still."

I stared at her, seeing my wife's face staring back at me as the sirens like the scream of a faraway teakettle grew louder, closer, wailing up from the river. Her eyelids fluttered and the light seemed to fade behind them. "Help is on the way. Hang on. Just a bit longer."

"Not this time," she whispered and closed her eyes. "This time I got it right."

33

THE FRONT of the house was lit up like a movie set with police gathering evidence and cameras flashing. Even though the place swarmed around me, I felt alone and apart. The ambulance bearing Sylvia Jackson screamed away into the night. I shifted back into the shadows. I wanted to close my eyes but I didn't want to risk what I might see. I focused on the pain in my shoulder and the throbbing in my ankle to help me stay anchored in the moment. I reminded myself that I was alive. So was Sylvia Jackson. So was Annie. Stuart Jackson would soon be released. This time, I hadn't been making tea.

I sat in the dark and grieved for Maria Whitson, for her family. It all seemed so unnecessary. I watched as the EMTs wasted their efforts trying to revive her. When they declared Maria dead, Angelo tried to wrench a gun from the nearest police officer. They wrestled him to the ground. Handcuffed, he went limp. Maria was gone. The puppeteer had dropped Angelo's strings. His flat, mirrorlike gaze met mine as he disappeared into the back of a cruiser. Just like Angelo, I'd been her pawn. And though the clues were right in front of me, I didn't put them together in time to save her from herself.

Annie took off for the police station, reluctantly leaving me sitting on the lawn, icing my ankle. I wanted to go home—to go home and just be there, doing nothing in particular.

I jumped at the touch on my shoulder. "You okay?" Detective MacRae was standing over me.

I shrugged. "It's just a sprain. Where'd you crawl out from?"

He ignored it. "On my way to dinner when Annie's call came in." He held out his hand. I took it and he pulled me to my feet. The ankle hurt like hell when I put weight on it. "Need a lift?" I must have looked surprised because he added, "It's the least I can do."

Leaning on him, I limped over to his car. He opened the back door and I gingerly lowered myself onto the seat and scooted back, pulling my injured foot in last.

"Ice and elevation," a voice instructed. The face of Nurse Carolyn Lovely peered at me from the front seat. "And stay off it for awhile."

"You and Mac?" I asked.

"None of your business," she said crisply.

MacRae got in and started the engine. I sat back and watched bits of Cambridge go by through the dirty windows.

"I owe you an apology," MacRae said when we were stopped at a light.

"For what?" For which of the many insults, I wondered.

"For getting in your face all the time. I couldn't believe all those accidents were a coincidence."

"You were right about that," I said. "They weren't."

"And you thought I was involved in this, too, didn't you?"

"Well," I hedged. "I guess I was suspicious of you, and Carolyn, too."

"Me?" She turned around.

"Well, you were so hostile. I mean, I've dealt with hostile nurses before, but—"

"Doctors," she spit out the word like it was bad-tasting medicine. "You had no business sniffing around Sylvia Jackson. She needed rest and therapy. She didn't need you."

"Right," I said. "So Stuart Jackson should serve a life sentence so Sylvia Jackson doesn't get inconvenienced? After all, when you find a wife with a bullet wound in her head, and an ex-husband with a camouflage fatigue hat in the closet, why keep looking?" The self-righteousness temporarily numbed my ankle.

"Nine times out of ten," Carolyn Lovely muttered.

"Hey, truce!" MacRae interjected. "You had your job to do. I had mine. Carolyn had hers. If we all just did our jobs, the world would be a better place." A philosopher. "One good thing about all this—I'm glad I was able to start to square things with Annie." He must have caught my baffled expression in the rearview mirror because he went on, "She called me. When you were in the house talking to Angelo, she called from her car. Said she knew I wouldn't give her a hard time. And I didn't. I made sure a bunch of squad cars and a couple of ambulances got over here pronto. Means a lot to me, her trust. Forgive and forget, that's what I say."

Forgive, maybe. "If it's any consolation, she knows she's not being fair. But it's the kind of hurt that takes a long time to heal."

By the time he dropped me off, it was late. I knew Gloria and Kwan would still be at the hospital, waiting for news.

Gloria didn't say anything right away, after I finished telling her what happened. I heard the muffled sound of her blowing her nose.

"You okay?" I asked.

"I can't believe it," she said finally. "It makes me so angry. Why did it have to end this way?"

"I'm right there with you."

"Do you think she deliberately tried to hurt me?"

"That's what it looks like."

"But why?"

"When you said she was faking her weight, she thought you knew she was faking the rest of her symptoms, too."

"Was she? I can't believe it was all a sham."

As usual, Gloria put her finger on the question I'd been asking myself. Maybe Maria had been faking, from the moment she deliberately overdosed. Maybe every one of our interactions were little soap operas of her own invention. But I didn't think so. I prefer the version I gave Gloria. "She faked a suicide attempt in order to get herself admitted. Dosed herself with the drugs—she knew just how much to take. And maybe she faked the delirium. But once we started working with her, she let her guard down. And we might have been able to help her. I think, to some extent, we *did* help her. But when she started to question her memories of abuse, it was too much to reintegrate. If Uncle Nino was innocent, then how could she live with what she'd done? She couldn't level with us. She'd gone past the point of no return."

When I got off the phone with Gloria, I sat in the Morris chair in my living room, put up my foot, and tried to relax. But I couldn't get comfortable. I didn't want to go to bed. I needed to be somewhere else.

I limped into the kitchen and took a couple of aspirin. Then I tucked a bottle of Zinfandel under my arm and dropped a corkscrew in my pocket, took down a glass, a candle, and some matches, and dragged myself up to the top floor.

The night streamed in through the windows of the studio. I could easily make out the silhouettes of Kate's pots against the windows, her workbench, her wheel. I put the candle on a table, struck a match, and lit it. I opened the '96 Turley and poured myself a glass. The liquid looked nearly black.

I sat on the little settee and swirled the wine in the glass, held it under my nose. I closed my eyes and inhaled. The wine had a hint of blackberry. I took a sip and savored the burning down my throat, the explosion of fruit up the back of my nose. I leaned back and stared into the little pool of light cast by the candle, watched the circle of light dancing on the ceiling.

I imagined Kate, standing at the work table. I raised my glass. A toast: To love. I drank. She raised her glass to me. To life, I heard her voice say.

I was still there the next morning, the bottle empty, the candle burnt down to nothingness. I was awakened by the faraway sounds of the doorbell ringing and someone banging at the front door. The minute I moved, I was reminded of my mangled ankle. By the time it was better, the river would be ice. I wouldn't be able to run on it for weeks. The prospect was depressing.

Going down the stairs was more laborious and painful than coming up, and the insistent ringing and rapping at the door didn't help. "I'm coming!" I bellowed.

I pulled the door open to reveal the anxious faces of Annie and my mother. "Why didn't you answer your phone?" they asked in unison. My mother added an accusatory, "And you didn't turn off the porch light last night. I've been worried sick."

"I was upstairs. You can't hear the phone up there."

"You're hurt," my mother said sharply. "You have ice?" she asked, shifting into Florence Nightingale mode.

"Yes, I have plenty of ice."

Then I noticed Annie was holding a bunch of daisies. It made me grin like a little kid.

My mother didn't miss that, either. "Well, next time, don't forget to turn off the light. I'll be home if you need anything."

"Thanks, Mrs. Zak," Annie said. My mother reached up and gave her a little hug and a kiss on the cheek. Annie kissed her back. "You're a peach," she added.

"Call me Pearl." My mother beamed. Then she disappeared into her side of the house, but not before I caught a glimpse of a figure hovering in her doorway, someone shortish and bald. I looked at my watch. It wasn't yet eight in the morning and already my mother had a visitor. I tucked away the thought. It would be something to torment her with at some time in the future.

"Coffee?" I asked Annie.

"Definitely," she said and followed me into the kitchen.

I assembled a pot of coffee and when the smell of the first hot water hitting fresh coffee grounds filled the kitchen, I asked, "Have they released Stuart Jackson?"

"They will. As soon as they've compared Angelo's thumbprint with the one found on the steering wheel of Sylvia Jackson's Firebird. And I'd be willing to bet that the gun Angelo was waving around turns out to be the one that killed Tony Ruggiero."

"Who could have guessed that a car accident would set all of these events in motion in the first place?"

"What car accident?" Annie asked.

"Two years ago. Angelo hit Maria or she threw herself in front of the car—take your pick. If she hadn't been misdiagnosed, she would never have sought Dr. Baldridge's help. If she hadn't seen Baldridge, I doubt very much if she would have had flashbacks of abuse. If she hadn't had those flashbacks, her hostility toward her uncle probably wouldn't have turned murderous. And I'll give you three guesses how Syl met Tony."

"The same accident?"

"Syl was the claims adjuster. Tony, the kind and helpful Uncle Nino, does his niece and her husband a favor by making sure that their car gets taken care of. And in the process, he meets the seductive Sylvia Jackson."

"Binding her fate to his," Annie said. "She really is quite something, don't you think? She exudes—pheromones."

I poured two cups of coffee and we both drank it black. It was strong, aromatic, acidic.

"I've been wondering," I said, "how exactly did you manage to wind up on the porch?"

"I hid in the garage until you went inside. Then I ran out to the car and called Mac. After that, I wanted to be close to the house—in case there was something to hear. So I crept up and hid in the bushes. That's when I realized that the dummy was wearing my uniform. It seemed like a sign." Annie had the same outfit on this morning. A plaid flannel shirt and jeans. But they fit her a whole lot better. "I'm glad it's over," she said.

"For us, it's over. But not for her."

"You mean for Syl?" Annie asked. "I agree. It's got to be hell to get on with your life when you don't know, for sure, what your past is about."

I nodded. When Sylvia Jackson woke up, she'd need to change lenses, switching Angelo from angel to villain and Stuart from villain to fall guy. "On the other hand, she may adjust with a minimum of emotional whiplash. For once, her defective memory is a blessing. And even with all that's happened, I suspect Stuart Jackson will be there for her."

I knew it wasn't over for the Whitsons either. Here was a fresh horror for them to absorb—the pain of losing Maria compounded by the realization that she'd been responsible for her uncle's death. I sighed. "Poor Maria Whitson."

"Poor Maria Whitson was ready to kill you!"

"I'm not so sure," I said. "She saw Angelo take aim at you. Then she moved, right into the line of fire."

"Maybe she didn't realize he'd shoot."

"She knew. She knew Angelo better than she knew herself. She's been trying to kill herself for two years, and maybe it's what she said—she finally got it right. I think that car accident damaged Maria Whitson a lot more seriously than her doctors realized."

"In what way?"

"Before that, she was already perched on the borderline, fuzzy about the difference between her own acts and fantasies. She felt guilty all the time about her thoughts, about things she hadn't done. But that car accident pushed her over. I think it breached the part of the brain that helps us distinguish between external and internal reality. And then the therapy she got didn't help. What she needed was a therapist who could rebuild the wall between fantasy and fact. What she got instead was someone who took a wrecking ball to what was left of it."

Annie nodded. "It's as if she started out being a person who *felt* like she was guilty and turned into a person who *was* guilty."

"Exactly. When the boundary between reality and fantasy went, so did the one between innocence and guilt."

"Boundaries," Annie murmured, fingering the petals on one of the daisies.

"We should put those in something." I limped down the hall to the foot of the stairs and stared up. Two flights up and two flights down.

"Let me go. Just tell me where," Annie said.

"Up two flights, top of the stairs." My voice turned hoarse. No one but me had been up in Kate's studio since she died. For two years, until just a few weeks ago, I hadn't been able to go there myself.

Annie put her hand on my shoulder. I hardened myself against what I expected to see in her eyes. But when I looked, I found amused impatience, not pity. "For goodness sakes, we can put them in a coffee can," she said.

I shifted aside. "Two flights up. There's a bunch to choose from. Take your pick."

Annie came down a few minutes later carrying one of Kate's vases in one hand, two wineglasses in the other, and the empty bottle tucked under her arm. "Thought you'd want these down here eventually," she said.

"Thanks," I said, staring as she set the glasses on the counter. "Where were the glasses?"

"One was on the floor by the couch. The other was on the potter's wheel." She looked at me curiously. "You okay?"

"Here, I'll take them." She handed me the glasses. I sniffed one, then the other. Both smelled of blackberries. I set them on the windowsill. "I'll wash them later," I said to no one in particular.

"Got a scissors?" Annie asked.

I rummaged in a drawer full of odds and ends and unwrapped a garden shears from a tangle of twine. Annie cut the ends off the stems of the daisies and put them into the vase she'd brought down. It was white porcelain with a pale blue and green border, the very last one Kate finished. Annie filled the vase with tap water and set it on the counter.

"It is a lovely thing," she said, stroking the surface with her index finger.

"Yes," I said, standing behind her and inhaling the sweet, slightly fruity scent that was Annie. "It's a very lovely thing."

MATTHEW FARRELL stumped onto the stage of the Medical School amphitheater, folded his six-foot-plus frame, and sat on the chair opposite me. He clutched a near-empty Evian bottle in both hands. His Save the Whales sweatshirt gaped around his thin neck as he glanced quickly at the screen behind us on the raised stage. The electric blue of the slide background reflected off his face, turning the pimples on his forehead purple. He didn't seem to read the canary-yellow words, *Asperger's Syndrome*.

He stared down at the bottle, squeezing it and releasing it in a slow, steady rhythm. He avoided eye contact with me or the second-year students who filled the hall, all squeaky clean in their shirts and ties, sweaters and ponytails.

"Dr. Zak," my colleague, Dr. Kwan Liu, stage-whispered to me from the side of the stage, pointing to his Rolex. I checked my Timex. We'd finished with the lecture portion of our presentation, and it was time to get on with the clinical interview. We had only about fifteen minutes before our audience would summarily abandon us to their various obligations.

I cleared my throat and waited for the whispering in the hall to subside. I introduced Matthew to the audience and thanked him for agreeing to come and help our medical students better understand Asperger's syndrome. The plastic bottle went *pok* as he released it. "I'd like to ask you a few questions," I said.

I could feel the audience of second-year medical students strain forward into the silence.

"You like to ask questions," Matthew said, staring at the bottle. The words were delivered in an automaton voice, each syllable taking up as much space as the next.

There was uneasy laughter in the hall. "Yes, I guess I do like to ask questions. I thought I'd ask you if you are having any problems."

"That's what you thought," he said, and waited patiently, presumably for me to tell him more about my thought processes.

"Are you having any problems in school?" This time, I'd phrased the question so it was harder to misinterpret.

"Yes, I'm having problems." I could understand how teachers who encountered Matthew Farrell found themselves barking, "Look at me when I talk to you!"

"What kind of problems are you having?"

"Kind of problems . . . hard problems."

"Do you have trouble with your schoolwork?"

"I do okay," Matthew said, still addressing the water bottle.

"Do you like hanging out with other students?"

He shrugged. "They laugh, and I don't know why. Maybe they are laughing at me." Matthew concentrated on the bottle as if it were a crystal ball. I waited. Finally he added, "Makes me do things I should not do."

Things-he-should-not-do included throwing a chair through the window of his high school English class. That's why he was spending a few weeks with us in the Neuropsychiatric Unit at the Pearce Psychiatric Institute, getting evaluated and having his medication adjusted. It was fortunate for the students attending the lecture—a live patient makes a much stronger impression than just a psychiatrist and a psychologist lecturing at you.

"Matthew, I'm going to show you some pictures." I clicked the remote control and a photograph of a smiling man was projected onto the screen behind us. "Please, look at his face and tell me what this man is feeling."

Matthew stared at the screen, tilted his head to one side, and stared some more.

"How does this man feel?" I repeated.

"His glasses are crooked," Matthew said at last.

The second photograph was of another man, his face twisted with rage. "And how does this man feel?"

"He needs a shave," Matthew offered.

And so it went, through a half-dozen pictures. No matter what the facial expression—from surprise to sadness to disgust—Matthew commented on some physical detail.

"Matthew, now I want you to repeat this: People who live in glass houses shouldn't throw stones."

There was a pause. Matthew repeated the phrase.

"Good. Now tell me, what does that mean?"

"What that means . . . Throw a stone and you'll break the glass house."

"Anything else?"

"People will get angry at you. Say you should not do that."

After some more questions, I thanked Matthew and the aide escorted him from the lecture hall. We still had a few minutes before the hour was up.

I called on a young Asian woman with a close-cropped cap of glossy black hair, her hand raised tentatively. "His speech sounds almost like deaf speech. Is he deaf?"

It was a good question. "The simple answer is no," I responded. "But he takes what he hears literally. He's deaf to nuance, to inflection, to the emotional content of speech. And forget about humor, sarcasm, even anger—goes right by him. And in a sense, he *is* deaf to emotion. As you saw from his responses to the photographs, he can't interpret emotions in the faces of others. He can't express emotions either. The monotone voice, the flat demeanor—they don't give us a clue about his inner state."

A young man who could have doubled for Tom Cruise asked, "He seems withdrawn, depressed. Would you treat him for depression?"

"You're raising a very important point. It might appear that Matthew has an emotional disorder. But Matthew's problem isn't primarily psychiatric. It's likely caused by a brain dysfunction involving the right hemisphere. In his case, it's developmental, though you can get similar symptoms in stroke patients."

I glanced at Kwan. He picked up without missing a beat, "If we only pay attention to the psychiatric presentation, we might prescribe Prozac or another SSRI." When it worked, Kwan and I were like a team of relay runners, passing the baton back and forth, our narrative flowing like a single stream of consciousness. "But in this case, an antidepressant is contraindicated. It could end up making him more distant from his own emotional states, feeling more out of control, possibly suicidal."

"What's the prognosis?" The question was called out from the back corner, an area usually occupied by faculty who drop in when one of our weekly lectures piques their interest. "Are there treatments, drugs? How do they do out in the real world?"

Surprise turned to pleasure as I recognized the voice, saw the face. It was Channing Temple. She still wore her straight blond hair pulled back from her face. She'd never been exactly pretty, but she had the kind of looks that made an impression, made you listen when she spoke. We'd been friends for years. Back in college, I'd been in love with her.

She delivered her question standing up, canted forward with a finger raised. It was a stance she'd used to good effect when I'd first laid eyes on her. She was twenty years old, grilling the university provost about institutional investments in tobacco stocks. Today, her tone had none of the in-your-face brashness that irritated the provost to the point where he found himself, much to the students' delight, red-faced and screaming back at her.

There was a hesitancy to her voice that made me pause before answering, take a few extra seconds to edit the usual blunt way I allow myself to talk to doctors about mental illness. Asperger's syndrome is a difficult diagnosis, and I wondered if her question was personal.

Before I could phrase a response, Kwan answered. He always likes to get in the first word—and the last. "There is no cure, per se." The unvarnished words made me cringe. "There are medications to help control the anger that arises out of their frustration with the world." At least that sounded a bit more encouraging.

I added, "In terms of treatment, we might try cognitive behavioral therapy to help the individual use his intellect to adapt. We can work with them, teach them to notice what they *don't* notice—facial expression, for example—and get them to take a step back and ask questions whenever they're perplexed. The good news is, there's potential for living a satisfying life."

Channing mouthed, "Thanks, Peter," and sat.

I nodded back. I tried to remember the last time Channing and I had gotten together socially. It might have been a catered dinner at her and Drew's Back Bay town house—could that be right, two years ago? It might even have been the last party I went to before my wife Kate was killed.

Since Kate's death, I'd avoided parties—and old friends, too, for that matter. I was working long hours, keeping busy, and generally keeping to myself. I'd seen Channing from a distance, run into her at meetings. She'd left a message on my voice mail some weeks earlier, but it had been business—she'd called to recommend a resident for a rotation on my unit. Fortunately or not, the Pearce Psychiatric Institute is so big that it's easy to avoid anyone you don't work with directly.

If I'd been my own therapist, I'd have explained that grief has to be felt in order to be worked through. You can dull the ache for only so long with busyness. Remove the anesthetic, and the pain returns double. But I was lousy at taking my own advice.

Kwan thanked the students for coming and reminded them of the agenda for next week's lecture. Channing stood at her seat. She waved at me, pointed out to the lobby, and held up one finger. Even from a distance, her face seemed strained with anxiety. I nodded and smiled back.

• • •

I waded into the lobby and poured myself a cup of coffee from a large metal urn. Kwan was already there, helping himself to a cookie. He glanced up at me and tsk-tsked. "How many cups is that for you today?"

I took a sip and grimaced. The coffee tasted boiled. "One too many."

Channing emerged into the lobby. When she saw me, her expression morphed from pleasure to hesitancy. *No*, I wanted to whisper, *it's not your fault that we've become strangers.*

She came over. We did a little awkward dance where she went left and I went right, and we ended up air-kissing nose to nose instead of cheek to cheek. She laughed. "Peter, it's so good to see you." She put her arms around me and hugged hard. She still smelled of citrus. "We've missed you."

I held up an empty coffee cup.

"No thanks. They never have any tea at these things," she said, "and when they do, the water's usually tepid."

"Ah, another tea aficionado," Kwan said. "So few of these Philistines understand."

I knew it was killing him to know what kind of relationship I had with Channing Temple. Friends, just friends, I would have told him. But he'd have guessed we were once much more.

"Hi there, Kwan," Channing said. "Long time no see." They executed a flawless, cheek-brushing-without-colliding air-kiss. She let her hand linger on his arm. "Mmm, nice fabric. Nice suit. Armani?"

"No, but close. Some of us try," he said, eyeing the Harris tweed jacket I'd bought in England a decade ago.

"At least mine still fits."

Kwan sniffed. "Oh, so now I know why you never wear a hat—can't find one big enough to cover that swelled head of yours."

Before I could come up with a snappy retort, he tugged at his vest, gathered his dignity, and turned to talk to a group of medical students.

"What brings you to a lecture about Asperger's syndrome?" I asked Channing.

"Actually, you were on my mind," Channing said. Her hair was wound around and anchored to the back of her head with ivory chopsticks. It was a severe look that emphasized her strong chin and prominent cheekbones. There were lines now, etched around her eyes and along the upper edge of her thin lips. "The other day, Drew brought me a beautiful spray of orchids, and I was putting them in a vase, the one that Olivia made with Kate." She put her hand on my arm. "You know how terrible we feel about what happened."

I nodded and blinked. Sympathy still threw me. I hate being out of control.

"That vase, it's really quite lovely," Channing went on.

"Kate thought Olivia had talent," I told her. I remembered the night of Channing's party, Kate had offered to teach potting to her quiet, gawky preteen daughter, who seemed to evaporate into the corners of the home. Kate had enjoyed the "lesson," and she'd been looking forward to another one.

"Then it seems like the very next day," Channing went on, "I see your name on a bulletin board in the cafeteria announcing this lecture. Asperger's syndrome. I've been seeing articles about it in the popular press."

"It's actually an old syndrome with a new diagnosis—wasn't in DSM-III," I said.

"Something like dyslexia for interpersonal nuance," Channing said.

"Exactly."

Channing lowered her voice and took a step closer. "Peter, I had an *aha* in there, listening to you." For a plain, severe-looking woman, she could become quite beautiful when she turned on, lit from within. "Know how you can be an expert in something, but when it's someone you love, someone in your own family, you turn stone-blind? Well, as you were talking, I realized—that's Olivia. She's been seeing a therapist, tried antidepressants."

I led Channing over to the window, away from the crowd. "Are you concerned about anything in particular?" I asked, the clinician kicking in.

"It's everything in particular. You wouldn't recognize her. You could say that she's using her appearance to make a statement. And her behavior—she's turned moody and dark. She comes home, goes upstairs. Wham, shuts herself into her room. Spends hours alone."

At sixteen, how I'd longed to have a room to close myself in and the world out. But in a one-bedroom apartment—my brother and I slept in the bedroom; my parents slept on a foldout sofa in the living room—there's only so long you can lock yourself in the bathroom before someone threatens to kill you.

"I know what you're thinking," Channing said. "What do I expect from a seventeen-year-old? You don't have to tell me this is normal. And God knows, it would probably help if I'd experienced good mothering when I was her age."

I remembered. Channing's mother had killed herself when Channing was still in grammar school. Shot herself in the head. But there was no bitterness or self-pity in Channing's voice. It was just a fact, something she'd learned to live with. Once we'd stayed up most of the night, looking through Channing's family photo albums and comparing childhoods. I'd been struck by the change she'd undergone, before and after her mother's suicide. As an eight-year-old, she'd flirted with the camera, sturdy and buoyant, her blond hair short and soft around chubby cheeks and mischievous eyes. A year later, she looked away, morose and brooding. Her hair had grown long, stringy bangs creating a veil over her eyes.

"But Livvy's turning more and more inward," Channing went on. "Blows hot and cold like that." Channing snapped her fingers. "She says nothing she does is good enough for me—but the truth is, she's the one who's so ashamed of her own work that sometimes she refuses to even try. When she has to do something that seems hard, she has an anxiety attack.

"When she's in her room, she's on her computer. Hard to believe she's my daughter." Channing gave a wry laugh. "It's all I can do to answer my e-mail. What do they do in chat rooms, anyway?"

"You probably don't want to know," I said.

"Probably not. What I do know is that she's in another world, all the time, one I don't understand at all"—her voice broke—"one I can't reach into."

I squeezed her arm. "She has friends?" I asked.

"I really don't know," Channing said wearily. "She doesn't bring kids home. But she goes out. I think she's got computer friends. If you can call that friendship. Who knows who they are. I worry. She's so young and inexperienced."

Channing was the one person who'd always had everything under control. Figures—it would take a teenage daughter to throw her off-center.

"Peter, I'll bet if you spent even fifteen minutes with her, you'd be able to give us a better sense of what's going on."

I knew what was coming. I should have stopped her right there, invoked the unwritten rule: Thou shalt not treat friends or their relatives. That's if she'd been a casual friend or a colleague. But Channing was much more than that.

"Please. See her informally," she begged.

I knew what Kate would say: "If you can't help your friends, then what's the point of the fancy degree?" And I remembered a picture in our photo album of Kate playing with six-year-old Olivia at a picnic in the Berkshires, one of the few times we'd seen Olivia when she was very young. The two of them sat beside a puddle, making mud pies. A pair of kindred spirits. On the ride home, Kate had talked about the daughter we'd have one day, and how she hoped our little girl would be as open to life's possibilities as Olivia. Kate and I never did have that little girl—or little boy, for that matter. There was always a reason why *now* wasn't the right time.

"You say she's seeing a therapist?" I asked.

"Daphne."

"Daphne?" I was surprised, yet not surprised. Daphne Smythe-Gooding was Channing's longtime mentor.

"I know, I know. But she analyzed me more than fifteen years ago, and she'd never spent much time with Olivia. Besides, she's a brilliant clinician. . . ." Channing's voice trailed off.

"But?"

"Let's just say the chemistry doesn't seem to be working. Lately, seems like I have to drag Livvy, kicking and screaming, to her sessions with Daphne," Channing said, avoiding my eyes. "Besides, Daphne's a psychiatrist, like me. We come at this from a different point of view than you would as a psychologist. Maybe ours is the wrong point of view, in this case. If you spent even five minutes with her, I think you'd see things both of us miss." She looked at me, her eyes pleading. "Nothing formal. Just a casual meeting, and then you tell me I'm being an overanxious parent."

I chuckled lightly, but I knew better. Whatever it was that Channing was sensing in Olivia, it was probably real. Perhaps not Asperger's syndrome, but something with a name, and hopefully a treatment.

"I'd be happy to see her. Informally," I said.

"How about this weekend?" Channing rushed on, as if she was afraid I'd change my mind if I thought about it for ten seconds more. "Saturday night. It's my birthday, and we're having some people over to celebrate. Olivia will be there."

"A party? Doesn't seem like the ideal place to talk to her," I said. The last party I'd been to at their house was a suit-and-tie affair, the kind a teenager would rather clean her room than attend.

"I want you to get a fresh impression. If she knows you're evaluating her, she'll clam up. Say you'll come."

Saturday I had plans for a quiet dinner with Annie Squires. Annie was a private investigator. For years I'd worked with her and attorney Chip Ferguson evaluating defendants, until I helped them defend Ralston Bridges, a sociopathic killer who violently objected to my diagnosis. Turned out, no one ever called him crazy and got away with it. After a jury pronounced him not guilty, he took his revenge by stalking and killing my wife.

After that, I retired from forensic work. Permanently—I thought. But then I let Chip and Annie talk me into defending a man accused of murder. The prosecution's entire case rested on the memory of his ex-wife, who'd survived a gunshot wound to the head. In the end, I wasn't sorry I'd taken the case. It helped me a put a few of my own demons to rest.

"Are you free?" Channing asked.

She glanced at my left hand. I fingered my wedding ring. "Actually, I have a date," I said.

"You're seeing someone?"

The question gave me pause. I wasn't ready to think of myself as *seeing* anyone. Over the last six months, Annie and I had had a couple of dates and a bunch of near dates. A few times, she'd had to cancel because of her work. I'd had to cancel because of my work.

Our last date had been by accident—we'd run into each other at Wordsworth's in Harvard Square and gone out for drinks, which turned into dinner, which might have turned into something more except Annie had plans to see her sister that night. Since then, Annie's time had been occupied working and moving her office and Chip's to a renovated building near the Cambridge Courthouse. They were going into private practice.

I'd been busy. She'd been busy. I knew if I didn't get off the dime, she'd soon be getting busy with somebody else. But I wasn't sure I was ready yet for a serious relationship.

"That's wonderful! Bring your friend," Channing said.

Visions faded of juicy grilled steaks and that bottle of Turley zin I'd been saving. Not to mention the rest of a long, empty evening waiting to be filled.

"Please, come," Channing said.

"Sure, can do," I said finally. At least I'd still be seeing Annie.

Relief flooded Channing's face. She took a business card from her jacket pocket, wrote quickly on the back, and handed it to me. "Here's where we are." I recognized that precise, backward-slanted handwriting, more printing than script. "It's right near our old house. Saturday night. Seven o'clock."

I walked Channing out. We plowed through the clouds of smoke that hung under the Corinthian columns at the front of the building. Nurses and doctors who knew better were huddled there, getting their nicotine fix. We crossed the pristine grass quadrangle, flanked by five, perfectly proportioned Greek Revival buildings, holding their own in the shadow of towering modern medical buildings that crowded in from behind.

As we headed down the path toward the parking lot, Channing had her head down. She was holding her coat together under her chin, her shoulders hunched against the cold. March in New England can be so discouraging. More cold nasty weather when we're all good and sick of it.

- Channing gaze a furtive look behind her before she spoke again. "You saw the note in *JAMA*?"

"What note?" There was a pile of unread journals on my desk, including the last four issues of the *Journal of the American Medical Association.*

"I'm amazed no one's shown it to you. A team from Hopkins dismissed my research as"—with two fingers, she drew quotation marks in the air—" 'too flawed to be meaningful.' "

In polite scholarly circles, the phrase was the ultimate insult. Her detractors—and there were many, since Channing minced few words when it came to exposing the questionable practices of others—were probably rubbing their hands together with glee.

A pair of doctors passed us going in the opposite direction. One of them nodded and then resumed his conversation with his colleague. "They're all talking about it," Channing said, lowering her voice. "They're treating me like a car wreck they don't want to get involved in. It makes me so goddamn mad. And it's complete bullshit. When I got a call from the team that reviewed my research, they told me their results appeared to be confirming mine. A month later, it's like 'Never mind, her research is corrupt.' I want to know what happened to change their minds."

I smiled. Here was the old Channing, the maverick who followed her own compass—which probably explained why she'd run the Drug and Alcohol Rehabilitation Unit for years but had never officially been named director.

"What's the study about?" I asked.

"I was reporting the preliminary results of a pilot project— about twenty subjects. A treatment for addiction. We got patients fresh out of detox programs—they take care of the easy part, the physical addiction. Then we focus on the psychological craving." Channing's voice was animated and enthusiastic. "Keep them for two weeks. Treat them with a compound called Kutril."

"What is it?"

"You're going to laugh. It's actually a highly concentrated extract of kudzu, combined with Trilafon."

"Kudzu? Isn't that the vine that's devouring the state of Florida?" I envisioned a viscous green potion.

"That's it. Actually it's the root that's medicinal. The Chinese used it at least as far back as the first century A.D. to inhibit the desire for alcohol."

"You're serious, aren't you?"

"Completely. There had been trials with rats that showed promise. Imagine if it works for humans? Kudzu isn't even a prescription drug! And Trilafon has been on the market for nearly thirty years. It's cheap. We've got a company in New Jersey making up batches of the compound in pill form."

Trilafon was one of the first antipsychotics developed. It tranquilized without sedating. "What about side effects?" I asked. I recalled that was one of the reasons doctors had stopped prescribing it.

"From long-term use, yes. This treatment is short and intensive — patients take a dose every four hours the first day. Every eight hours for a week. Twice a day for a week. Then we discharge them with a dose a day for two weeks. Then nothing. Kills the craving right from the beginning, and it doesn't seem to return, even after the treatment is discontinued."

"What's the success rate?"

"We just finished analyzing the results of the full-blown study. It confirms the findings of our pilot. Eighty percent after six months. Sixty-five percent after twelve months."

I whistled. That was impressive.

"The only serious adverse events we had were two patients who had seizures, which were then well controlled with Neurontin."

"Can it be administered outpatient?"

"Perhaps. Eventually." Channing glowed with satisfaction. "Sounds like a magic bullet, doesn't it? Talk to the drug companies, you'd think it was a subversive plot to put them out of business. Acu-Med went ballistic when they heard. And oh, big surprise, one of the guys who submitted that note to *JAMA* used to work for them." She gave a disgusted sniff. "Wouldn't surprise me if he's still on retainer."

"They're probably trying to develop a prescription drug to do exactly the same thing."

Channing's eyebrows rose in surprise. "Peter, you're starting to think like me. Actually, they are. Liam Jensen is running the clinical trials." Jensen was a doctor who worked with Channing in the Drug and Alcohol Rehabilitation Unit. Channing slowed down until a middle-aged couple walked past. "I've got most of my final report drafted. The final stats are being reviewed now."

"Sounds like you think they're out to get you."

"You think I'm being paranoid?"

"It's not paranoia when you're surrounded by assassins," I said. "After all, you're the one who's still fighting greed, injustice, and the American way. I think you've got it written into your job description."

Channing didn't smile. "How much longer, I wonder? You've heard the other allegations against me?"

"I haven't." I tried to keep my head out of the noxious cloud of gossip that floats around the Pearce.

"You're probably the only one, then. They're questioning my clinical judgment."

Clinical judgment—a euphemism vague enough to cover just about anything. That and *not a team player* were the terms used to brand those who didn't go along or get along.

"They're saying that I behaved inappropriately. Got too close. Violated the boundaries."

I paused, mid-step. "You?"

Channing laughed. "Oh, come on, Peter. I'm not that much of a prig." She gave me a sideways glance. "Well, maybe I am." She took my arm and pulled me forward. "Anyway, some people find it credible. The worst part is that these allegations are being